Manhattan Noir

Manhattan Noir

EDITED BY LAWRENCE BLOCK

AKASHIC BOOKS
NEW YORK

This collection is comprised of works of fiction. All names, characters, places, and incidents are the product of the authors' imaginations. Any resemblance to real events or persons, living or dead, is entirely coincidental.

Series concept by Tim McLoughlin and Johnny Temple

Published by Akashic Books
©2006 Akashic Books

Manhattan map by Sohrab Habibion

ISBN-13: 978-1-888451-95-5
ISBN-10: 1-888451-95-5
Library of Congress Control Number: 2005934818

First printing
Printed in Canada

Akashic Books
PO Box 1456
New York, NY 10009
Akashic7@aol.com
www.akashicbooks.com

Inwood

George
Washington
Bridge

NEW JERSEY

Washington
Heights

Harlem

Upper West Side

BRONX

HUDSON RIVER

Central
Park

Yorkville

MANHATTAN

Hell's
Kitchen

Clinton

Midtown

QUEENSBORO BRIDGE

QUEENS

Times
Square

Garment
District

QUEENS MIDTOWN TUNNEL

Chelsea

Greenwich
Village

EAST RIVER

Lower
East Side

BROOKLYN

Battery
Park

WILLIAMSBURG
BRIDGE

BROOKLYN BRIDGE

MANHATTAN BRIDGE

TABLE OF CONTENTS

INTRODUCTION
WELCOME TO A DARK CITY

The City.

See, that's what we call it. The rest of the world calls it the Apple, or, more formally, the Big Apple, and we don't object to the term. We just don't use it very often. We call it the City and let it go at that.

And, while the official city of New York is composed of five boroughs, the City means Manhattan. "I'm going into the City tonight," says a resident of Brooklyn or the Bronx, Queens or Staten Island. Everybody knows what he means. Nobody asks him which city, or points out that he's already *in* the city. Because he's not. He's in one of the Outer Boroughs. Manhattan is the City.

A few years ago I was in San Francisco on a book tour. In conversation with a local I said that I lived in the City. "Oh, you call it that?" he said. "That's what we call San Francisco. The City."

I reported the conversation later to my friend Donald Westlake, whose house is around the corner from mine. "That's cute," he said. "Of course they're wrong, but it's cute."

The City. It's emblematic, I suppose, of a Manhattan arrogance, of which there's a fair amount going around. Yet it's a curious sort of arrogance, because for the most part it's not the pride of the native. Most of us, you see, are originally from Somewhere Else.

All of New York—all five boroughs—is very much a city of immigrants. Close to half its inhabitants were born in another country—and the percentage would be higher if you could count the illegals. The flood of new arrivals has always kept the city well supplied with energy and edge.

Manhattan's rents are such that few of its neighborhoods are available these days to most immigrants (though it remains the first choice of those fortunate enough to arrive with abundant funds). But it too is a city of newcomers, not so much from other countries as from other parts of the United States, and even from the city's own suburbs and the outer boroughs as well. For a century or more, this is where those young people most supplied with brains and talent and energy and ambition have come to find their place in the world. Manhattan holds out the promise of opportunity—to succeed, certainly, and, at least as important, to be oneself.

I was born upstate, in Buffalo. In December of 1948, when I was ten-and-a-half years old, my father and I spent a weekend here. We got off the train at Grand Central and checked in next door at the Hotel Commodore, and in the next three or four days we went everywhere—to Liberty Island (Bedloes Island then) to see the statue, to the top of the Empire State Building, to a Broadway show (*Where's Charlie?*), a live telecast (*The Toast of the Town*), and just about everywhere the subway and elevated railway could take us. I remember riding downtown on the Third Avenue El on Sunday morning, and even as my father was pointing out the skid row saloons on the Bowery, a man tore out of one of them, let out a bloodcurdling scream, turned around, and raced back inside again.

I think I became a New Yorker that weekend. As soon as I could, I moved here.

"Why would I want to go anywhere?" my friend Dave Van Ronk used to say. "I'm already here."

Manhattan Noir.

While I might argue Manhattan's primacy (assuming I could find someone to take the other side), I wouldn't dream of holding that everything worthwhile originates here. Even as so many Manhattanites hail from somewhere else, so do many of our best ideas. And the idea for this book originated on the other side of the world's most beautiful bridge, with a splendid story collection called *Brooklyn Noir.*

It was that book's considerable success, both critical and commercial, that led Akashic's Johnny Temple to seek to extend the *Noir* franchise, and it was Tim McLoughlin's out-standing example as its editor that moved me to take the reins for the Manhattan volume.

I sat down and wrote out a wish list of writers I'd love to have for the book, then e-mailed invitations to participate. The short story, I should point out, is perforce a labor of love in today's literary world; there's precious little economic incentive to write one, and the one I was in a position to offer was meager indeed. Even so, almost everyone I invited was quick to accept. That gladdened my heart, and they glad-dened it again by delivering on time . . . and delivering what I think you'll agree is material of a rare quality.

My initial request wasn't all that specific. I asked for dark stories with a Manhattan setting, and that's what I got. Readers of *Brooklyn Noir* will recall that its contents were labeled by neighborhood—Bay Ridge, Canarsie, Greenpoint, etc. We have chosen the same principle here, and the book's contents do a good job of covering the island, from C.J. Sullivan's Inwood and John Lutz's Upper West Side, to Justin

Scott's Chelsea and Carol Lea Benjamin's Greenwich Village. The range in mood and literary style is at least as great; noir can be funny, it can stretch to include magic realism, it can be ample or stark, told in the past or present tense, and in the first or third person. I wouldn't presume to define noir—if we could define it, we wouldn't need to use a French word for it—but it seems to me that it's more a way of looking at the world than what one sees.

Noir doesn't necessarily embody crime and violence, though that's what we tend to think of when we hear the word. Most but not all of these stories are crime stories, even as most but not all are the work of writers of crime fiction, but the exceptions take place in a world where crime and violence are always hanging around, if not on center stage.

Noir is very contemporary, but there's nothing necessarily new about it. In cinema, when we hear the word we think of the Warner Brothers B-movies of the '30s and '40s, but the noir sensibility goes back much further than that. When I was sending out invitations, one of the first went to Annette and Martin Meyers, who (as Maan Meyers) write a series of period novels set in old New York. Could Maan perhaps contribute a dark story from the city's past? They accepted, and in due course the same day's mail brought Maan's "The Organ Grinder" and a present-day story from Marty.

Every anthologist should have such problems. Both stories are here, both show the dark side of the same city, and both are far too fine to miss.

Most of our contributors live in New York, though not necessarily in Manhattan. (It's hard to afford the place, and it gets harder every year. New York is *about* real estate, and Justin Scott's "The Most Beautiful Apartment in New York" illustrates this fact brilliantly.) Jeffery Deaver lives in Virginia and John Lutz in St. Louis, yet I thought of both early on; they both set work in Manhattan, and reveal in that work a deep knowledge of the city, and, perhaps more important, a New Yorker's sensibility.

It seems to me that I've nattered on too long already, so I'll bring this to a close. You're here for the stories, and I trust you'll like them. I know I do.

Lawrence Block
Greenwich Village
January 2006

THE GOOD SAMARITAN

BY CHARLES ARDAI

Midtown

R ain battered the sidewalk and the storefronts. The wind played games with people's umbrellas, teasing in under the ribs and then whipping them inside out and back again. One umbrella handle and shaft, discarded by its owner, skittered along the curb in an overflow from the gutter.

There were hardly any people on the street. Those there walked quickly, heads bent, shoulders hunched forward, buckling umbrellas held before them like shields. A few sought refuge under awnings and in doorways. One stood bravely in the street, a hand held high in a desperate attempt to hail a taxi.

Harold Sladek sat where he always sat this time of night: in the shadow of the service entrance to Body Beautiful. The doorway offered little protection from the rain since it was less than a foot deep, but it was better than sitting out on the sidewalk itself. At least he wasn't completely surrounded by the elements; at least Harold could feel concrete behind and beneath him. Solidity—that was something.

It was also a matter of habit: He always slept in the doorway at Body Beautiful, even though it was no better than any of the other service entrances up and down the avenue. It was part of his routine, forged over the course of many years, many rainstorms. Solidity of a different sort, but no less important.

Harold held a copy of *Cosmopolitan,* spread open at the center, over his head. He felt water trickle down between his fingers. After a few minutes, the glossy paper become water-logged and slick, and eventually the magazine pulled apart in his hands. When this happened, Harold threw it into the street and pulled another issue out of the plastic bag next to him. He had found the stack of magazines tied with string next to a trash can on the corner of Lexington and 79th. His original thought had been to sell the magazines for a quarter apiece further uptown, on Broadway where all the booksellers were. But if the magazines could keep him dry, or even just a little bit drier, that was worth giving up a quarter or two.

The second issue started dripping ink-stained water onto his forehead. Harold threw it away, wiped his hands on his drenched pants, and started on a third.

He didn't notice immediately when someone approached the doorway and stopped next to his bags. The magazine cut off much of his line of sight, and the rain, spraying him in the face with every fresh gust of wind, cut off the rest. But at one point, between gusts, he glanced beside him and saw a pair of legs in ash-gray trousers and, next to them, a dripping, folded umbrella.

Harold put the magazine down behind him. It wasn't quite soaked through yet, so it was too valuable to throw away. But he wasn't going to sit with a magazine over his head while another man stood next to him with an umbrella he wasn't even using.

He looked up, squinting against the rain. The other man was bending forward, sheltering his head under the overhang. The rest of him was exposed. The rain blew on the man's suit and he just stood and took it, one hand in his pants pocket, the other on the handle of his umbrella.

"Mister," Harold said, "don't you mind the rain?"

The man shook his head. "Just water," he said. "A little water never hurt anyone."

Harold had shouted; the other man had spoken at a normal level, or maybe even a little quieter. So even though Harold had leaned into it, he hadn't caught the words. "What?" he said.

The man bent at the knees. He stuck the umbrella straight out in front of them and pressed the release. It opened up enormously, suddenly cutting them off from the storm. "I said, a little water never hurt anyone."

He still spoke quietly but now the storm was muted behind the umbrella, and Harold heard him. "I don't know," Harold said. "But I'm not going to argue with a guy's got an umbrella."

The man smiled. He took his hand out of his pocket and brought with it a slightly battered pack of cigarettes. "Smoke?" The man thumbed the pack open and extended it.

It was suddenly dry and quiet—relatively dry and relatively quiet—and a man Harold had never seen before was offering him a cigarette. Why? Harold tried to read the answer in the man's eyes. They didn't reveal a lot. They were ordinary eyes in an ordinary face. They had wrinkles at the corners and were overhung by untrimmed gray eyebrows. They were not cruel, or cloudy, or cold, or anything else in particular. Just eyes. Just a face. Just a man doing his fellow man a good turn.

Harold plucked a cigarette out of the pack and stuck it between his lips. Then he looked up again, to get another read on those eyes. Whatever he thought he might see, he didn't.

You're on the street, you can't be too careful, Harold told

himself. Careful keeps you alive. But there are limits. When a guy comes by and offers you a cigarette, you take it and say thank you. It doesn't happen every day.

Harold reached back to take another, for later, or maybe two or even three as long as the guy was offering. But the pack of cigarettes was gone now, replaced with a brass lighter. At least it looked like brass—hard to tell in a dark doorway.

Harold leaned into the flame. It took three tries for him to catch it on the tip of the cigarette. He dragged deep when it caught, let the warmth rush into his throat and lungs. First cigarette in . . . how long? Hard to say. You lost track of exact time living on the street. But it had to have been at least a month.

"Thanks," Harold said.

"Don't mention it." The man straightened up, lifting the umbrella and stepping around so that he was standing in front of Harold. "Make the night a little easier to get through."

"You're a mensch," Harold said. "You know what that is, a mensch?"

The man nodded. "What's your name?"

Harold coughed, a wet, rattling sound he brought up from deep in his chest. "Harry."

"You take care, Harry," the man said.

"Don't you worry about me. I been through storms would make this look like pissing in a can. You take care—you got the nice suit." Harold made himself smile up at the man. He thought, Maybe the guy will leave me the umbrella. Then he thought, What, and walk out in the rain without it? Next he thought, I could probably take it away from him. But finally he thought, The guy gave you a cigarette, talked to you, passed his time with you, kept you dry for a while, and you mug him for his umbrella? Schmuck.

He thought all this in the time it took him to take two more drags on the cigarette.

"I hate to ask," Harold said, not quite able to get the umbrella fantasy out of his mind, "but would you mind standing there while I finish this? A little easier without the rain in my face . . ." He let his words trail off. The man was shaking his head.

"Sorry. I have to be somewhere."

"Nah, that's okay, I understand." Harold raised the cigarette. "Thanks for the smoke."

"My pleasure," the man said.

"Sladek, Harold R. R for Robert." The detective flipped through the creased wallet he'd retrieved from Harold's pocket. There was a long-expired driver's license from New Jersey; a photograph of Harold, when his hair had been brown; another photograph of Harold and a woman standing next to a white-iced, pink-flowered cake; a stained dollar bill with one corner missing; and an ancient business card, smudged and bent, listing Harold Robert Sladek as Assistant Manager for J.C. Penney, New York.

The detective nudged his partner with his elbow. "Check the bags."

The younger man bent to look through the plastic bags, still standing in a puddle of water.

At the curb, a uniformed officer, the one who had found Sladek's body, was coordinating getting the covered corpse into the EMS van. He had radioed for EMS instead of the morgue because he had thought Sladek was still alive.

". . . four, five, six magazines, a pullover, a comb, half a . . . a . . . I don't know, I guess it's a baguette," the partner said. "A French bread. Whatever." The detective took notes.

"A couple napkins. Bag of Doritos. A WKXW-FM baseball cap."

"He must have got that at the Turtle Bay street fair," the detective said. "They were giving them away on Saturday. I got one."

The partner looked up.

"Never mind," the detective said. "Go on."

"One sneaker, no laces. One copy of *The Dark Half* by Stephen King, paperback, no cover. One plastic cup. A roll of toilet paper. A disposable razor. Three, four, five soda cans, empty. One pocket Bible." He stopped, glanced around. "That's it." The partner noticed the issue of *Cosmopolitan* that was lying in the corner. He picked it up, shook off a cigarette butt, and held it out to the detective. "One more magazine."

The detective added it to the list, then flipped his notebook closed and dropped the wet magazine back where it had been lying. He slipped the photos and the business card back into the wallet. "Poor bastard. Guy had a good job once. Had a place to live. Had a family."

"Once upon a time. What he had now was a baseball cap and six copies of *Cosmopolitan* magazine. Seven, excuse me."

"What the hell's wrong with this city? An old man like this lying dead in a doorway, nobody even calls it in."

"It's New York, what do you want?"

"The man's lying there, dead. An old man, dead on the street, and people just walk past him."

"This is news to you?"

The detective walked back to the prowl car waiting at the curb. "You know, my father's name was Harold."

"Lots of people's name is Harold, man. Snap out of it.

This guy's not your father. It's a homeless man was out in the rain too long. Sad story. Unhappy ending. Life goes on."

"Not for him," the detective said.

Angela's finger hovered over the cigarettes, lined up in three neat rows. Finally, her hand darted out and came back with one clamped between thumb and forefinger.

The man closed the pack, returned it to his pocket, and took out his lighter. Angela cupped her hand around the flame and carefully lit the cigarette. "Thanks," she said. "Man, what a night."

The rain had started again. But behind the huge umbrella they were both dry.

"Hey," she said, "you want to have a little fun . . . ?" She picked up the hem of her dress, pulled it above her knees. She had a purple mark on the inside of one thigh. For the first time, the man stopped smiling. Angela said, "It's just a bruise."

"Thank you, no," the man said.

Angela shrugged. She drew on the cigarette. Pushed her dress down over her legs again.

"It's been a pleasure to meet you, Angela," the man said, standing up. "Take care of yourself."

"Yeah." She watched him back away. "Thanks for the smoke. Come back if you change your mind."

The man nodded.

"I don't have any diseases. If that's what you're worried about."

"No," the man said. "I'm not worried about your having diseases."

Something in his voice put her off. "What do you mean by that?"

"I mean it in the best way. You're a young woman,

Angela. You look very healthy. I'm sure you have no diseases."

Angela smiled, a fixed, frozen smile that was part arrogance, part fear, and no part happiness. "That's right. I'm so
clean you could eat off me."

"I'm sure," the man said. "Good night, Angela."

The headline the story carried in the *Daily News* was only
slightly inaccurate: "*Runaway Poisoned Behind Penn Station.*"
Angela Nicholas had not run away. She had been thrown out
of her home. Her mother emphasized that point, stabbing it
into her husband's shoulder with her index finger while the
man looked down at his hands in his lap and mumbled apolo-
gies to her, to himself, to God.

The detective took notes. There had been a fight.
There had been many fights. A boy had been the subject of
one of the fights. Other boys had been the subject of other
fights, or maybe the same boy had. It wasn't clear. What was
clear was that the father had delivered an ultimatum: That
boy doesn't enter this house again or you don't enter it
again.

Angela had brought the boy back. The next day, her
clothes were on the sidewalk. She had beaten on the door,
crying, and the mother had wanted to let her back in. But her
husband had held her back. When they finally opened the
door, Angela was gone. When they phoned around to all her
friends—even, finally, to the boy, who hung up on them—
they couldn't find her.

Three years later, they found her. No, that wasn't quite
accurate, either: The police had found her. The point was,
she had been found. But she had been dead.

Did the police have any idea who had done it? The
detective shook his head. He could have told the mother

that it had probably been one of Angela's tricks, but contrary to popular belief in the precinct house, he actually did have a heart. "We currently have no information, Mrs. Nicholas." Which wasn't entirely true, since that man, Sladek, had turned out to have been poisoned, too, and with the same poison, so that was—maybe—a starting point. But it was close enough to true. Anyway, he said it.

"How did it happen? How could this happen?"

"We aren't certain. Our lab is working on it."

The father finally stirred to life, raising his head, his eyes burning. "You find the man who did this and I'll kill him."

"Haven't you done enough?" Mrs. Nicholas said.

"Do you have a daughter, sergeant?"

"A son," the detective said.

"Well, if somebody did to your son what somebody did to my daughter," Mr. Nicholas said, "what would you do?"

I'd kill the son of a bitch, the detective said. To himself. "I'd let the proper authorities handle it."

Mr. Nicholas shook his head. "With a daughter it's different."

For the first night in a week, it wasn't raining. The detective looked at the map he'd made, showing the streets from 32nd to 45th on the West Side. The locations where the bodies had been found were marked with red circles. They were spread around enough so that it didn't look like there was a pattern. But five homeless people dead in the course of seven weeks? All poisoned? It wasn't obvious that this was the work of just one person, but that the deaths were connected the detective had no doubt.

He started at the uptown end, the theater district. As you left the streets dominated by Disney marquees, you found the remnants of the old Times Square: novelty shops, import/export storefronts, peep shows, *For Rent* signs. Plenty of homeless people to talk to.

The detective took his time, walking slowly, keeping his eyes open—for what, he wasn't sure. He stopped whenever he saw someone sitting on the sidewalk, leaning against a street lamp, lying under a filthy quilt in a cardboard box. He introduced himself, asked whether the person had seen anything unusual lately.

Mostly they said no.

One man said, "You not going to get anyone to tell you anything. They too scared."

"You scared?" the detective asked.

"Bet your ass I'm scared."

"Why's that?"

"I don't want to end up dead."

"We all end up dead," the detective said.

"Not me, man. I'm not ready yet."

"So why don't you tell me, who is it that people are scared of?"

The man just shook his head emphatically.

"Why? Why won't you tell me?"

"Maybe it's you."

"For god's sake, I'm a cop. I'm not going to hurt you."

"You're a cop don't mean nothing. You know that, I know that, everybody know that."

The detective moved on. Could it be a cop? He thought about it. A frustrated beat cop, maybe, out to clean up the neighborhood in his off time? An old PD hack, about to hit retirement, sick of seeing bums lining the sidewalk? It was possible. He didn't want to think about it.

Below Port Authority, the number of homeless people

dropped to only one or two per block. The detective walked down Eighth Avenue, came back on Broadway, walked down again on Sixth.

At 42nd and Sixth, at the entrance to Bryant Park, a blind man was leaning on a propped-up piece of cardboard lettered with the words, "God Bless You If You Help Me." He was smoking a long, filter-tipped cigarette. The smoke formed a gray wreath around his face.

"Evening," the detective said.

"God bless," the man said. He groped for his cup and then raised it, shaking the coins inside.

"I'm with the police." The detective squatted next to the man, pulled out his wallet, and put the man's hand onto his badge. The man's eyebrows rose and his mouth crinkled into a smile. He put the cup down.

"How are you doing, officer?"

"Could be worse. You?"

"Good night for me," the man said, hugging himself against the chill. "Most nights nobody talks to me. Tonight you're the second."

"Really? Who was the other?"

He thought for a moment. "Man about your age, I'd say. Little older maybe. Pleasant fellow. Talked to me a while, just a minute ago." He lifted his cigarette. "Gave me a smoke."

"Nice of him," the detective said. "Listen, you notice anything out of the ordinary around here lately?"

"No. Why do you ask?"

"We're conducting an investigation."

"Well, I haven't seen a thing," the man said. He laughed softly to himself.

The detective dropped a handful of change into the man's cup before walking away.

"My lucky day," the man said, hugging himself tighter. "God bless you."

"His name was Michael Casey. He lived off his monthly federal disability check, plus what he picked up panhandling."

"Damn it!"

"Calm down."

"I was talking to him last night," the detective said. "He was sitting next to me, smoking a goddamn cigarette, telling me what a wonderful night it was."

"You couldn't have known," his partner said.

"Sure I could have. I could have figured it out then instead of now. I could have saved his life."

"We don't know that." The partner stopped the car outside Body Beautiful.

The detective got out and walked to the service entrance. The issue of *Cosmopolitan* was still lying where he had dropped it, crumpled in a dark corner of the doorway. It had dried and hardened and was now stuck to the ground. The detective used a scraper to get it up. Underneath it there was a cigarette butt.

"Bingo." The detective picked the butt up with a pair of tweezers and dropped it in an evidence baggie. He returned to the car. "I told you there was a cigarette."

"There are cigarettes on every sidewalk in the city."

"That's true, and maybe this one has nothing to do with our case. But I don't think so. I think that Harold Sladek smoked it. Why? Because the first time we saw it, it was lying on top of that magazine, and the magazine was lying behind his body. Do you think someone came along, smoking, finished his cigarette, and then tossed it over Sladek's dead body so that it landed on his magazine? I don't think so."

"Okay."

"So: Sladek smoked it. That still doesn't mean it has something to do with our case. But since we didn't find any cigarettes in his bags, or even an empty cigarette *pack*, we can assume that someone else gave the cigarette to him. And we know that someone gave a cigarette to Michael Casey just before he died. And it was the same brand as this one." He waved the bag in front of his partner's face.

"Lots of people smoke Chrome Golds."

"Sure. And lots of homeless people die on the streets. But how many do one right after doing the other? I'll bet that if we analyze this butt, we'll find traces of the same poison they found in Sladek's body."

"Let's say you're right. What would that tell us? We already know Sladek was poisoned."

"It tells us how it happened."

"And . . . ?"

"And now we can get the bastard who did it."

"What do you want to do, arrest everyone who buys a pack of Chrome Golds?"

The detective didn't have an answer to that.

"Then what? All we can do is keep cleaning up after the guy and hope that one of these days he'll try his stunt on the wrong person and get himself shot."

"No one's going to shoot a nice old guy who's offering them a cigarette."

"You don't know that," the partner said. "This is New York."

He sat with a blue knit hat pulled down over his forehead, his hands crammed under his armpits, shivering. Even with two shirts on, he was cold. He had a thin blanket, which he had wrapped and rewrapped around himself, trying to make it hold in as much heat as possible. Under the blanket he had a thermos filled with coffee. Every few minutes he took a swallow.

People passed, hurrying from store to store, from home to theater, from street to taxi. He only saw their legs, their hands swinging by their sides, their packages. Sometimes children passed at his eye level and then he saw adult hands snatch the curious faces away from him. He saw car tires and bicycle wheels. As it got later, he saw less and less. By midnight, he saw nothing but a neon sign across the street and patches of sidewalk, dimly lit in the glow of street lamps.

The doorway he sat in, the entrance to a Burger King that was closed for renovation, was relatively roomy: He was able to stretch his legs almost to their full length. Each night for the previous ten he had sat in a different doorway, on a different street. Unlike Harold Sladek, he was not driven by years of habit. But this doorway was more comfortable than the others had been, and that really did make a difference. He started thinking about staying here, at least for the next few nights.

A pair of high-heeled shoes clicked past, speeding up as they passed him. Sometime later, a taxi braked to a halt a few feet away. The driver got out, unzipped his pants, relieved himself against a tree, got back into his car, and drove away. Then nothing, for several hours.

Closer to dawn than midnight, footsteps approached again. They came at a casual pace, and he waited for them to pass, but they didn't.

"Hello there," a voice said.

The detective didn't say anything. But under the blanket, he put the thermos down and picked up his gun.

"Cold night."

"Sure is," the detective said.

The feet moved a few steps to one side, then the knees bent, and then a man was sitting next to him. "What's your name?"

"What's yours?" the detective asked.

"Arthur," the man said. "You can call me Art."

The detective looked at him. He had a friendly face with great unruly eyebrows, a small mouth, good teeth. Good dentures, more likely. He looked like someone's grandfather. Was this their killer, this harmless-looking man? The detective stared at him and tried to see in him a serial murderer, a cold-blooded exterminator of the homeless. He couldn't.

Arthur reached into his coat pocket and pulled out a pack of cigarettes. "Do you smoke?"

In wide gold letters, the pack said *Chrome Gold*.

The detective felt his fingers tense under the blanket, felt the weight of the gun in his hand. What would he do if I said no? Would he find some other way to do it? Or would he just go off and pick someone else to kill?

"Sure," the detective said. "I smoke."

Arthur flipped open the top of the pack. There were twenty cigarettes inside, lined up in their perfect rows. Which should have been a tip-off that something was wrong, the detective realized: The pack was already unwrapped, but none of the cigarettes were missing. Why would someone have opened a pack of cigarettes but not have smoked even one of them?

He reached out from under the blanket with his free hand, gripped the pack of cigarettes firmly, and pulled it out of Arthur's hand.

"Now hold on," Arthur said, not losing his smile. "Leave

some for me. I was just offering you one." He reached for the pack.

"Oh, I won't smoke them all," the detective said. "Don't worry about that." He turned the pack over and shook the cigarettes out. Arthur caught a few; the rest fell on the pavement. He started scooping them up.

"Don't bother, Art. You've got bigger worries."

Arthur kept snatching up the loose cigarettes until he heard the gun cock. He looked up and the smile finally disappeared.

The detective moved the gun closer to the other man's face. "I'm not going to shoot you, Arthur," he said, "unless you make me."

Arthur's face was trembling. His hands shook. A few cigarettes slipped back onto the sidewalk. He looked left and right, but the street was deserted.

"Nervous?" the detective said. He picked two cigarettes off the sidewalk, wiped them roughly on the blanket. He leaned forward and put one between Arthur's lips. It slipped out as Arthur opened his mouth to talk. "I don't want—"

"Oh, you want," the detective said. He leaned forward and put another cigarette in Arthur's mouth. He pressed the gun against Arthur's forehead, Arthur's head against the wall. "Don't spit it out."

Arthur shifted the cigarette nervously to one corner of his mouth, but he didn't spit it out.

"Good." The detective groped through Arthur's coat pockets until he found the lighter. He opened it. A flame leapt up. He brought it close to the end of the cigarette in Arthur's mouth.

"Please, don't—"

"Why not?"

Arthur shook his head.

"Why not?" Arthur looked at him miserably, but said nothing. "You're going to tell me why not, Arthur, or you're going to smoke that cigarette."

"I don't want to . . ."

The detective passed the flame over the end of the cigarette. The paper and tobacco were singed. A drop of sweat rolled down Arthur's upper lip and onto the cigarette.

"Want me to guess why you don't want to smoke this cigarette?" the detective said. "Okay. How about, because you poisoned it? Could that be it?"

Arthur nodded uneasily.

"Talk to me, Arthur."

"Yes," he said in a small voice. "That's it."

"And why are you going around offering homeless people poisoned cigarettes, Arthur? Do you dislike homeless people? Do you not want to see them around? Or do you just get off on killing people?"

"No," Arthur whispered, "that's not it at all."

"Why don't you tell me what it is, then?"

"They're so miserable," Arthur said. There were tears in his eyes. "Out here on the street, in the cold, on drugs, selling their bodies . . . No one should have to live like that."

"So you kill them?"

"I give them a cigarette. They feel no pain. They never know what happened. They're out of their misery."

"In other words, you kill them."

"They go to sleep and don't wake up."

"You *kill* them, goddamn it," the detective said, pressing the gun harder into the man's skull. "Say it."

"I kill them," Arthur said. "But they're better off for it."

Arthur and the detective sat silently, staring at each

other. The detective saw no sign of understanding or of self-awareness. He saw terror, but no remorse.

He thought of the digital recorder in his pocket, quietly capturing a record of their words, and pictured this grandfatherly man standing in front of a jury, earnestly insisting on his innocence. He looked at Arthur's well-cut suit and polished loafers, at the watch on his wrist, and pictured the caliber of lawyer he would hire to defend himself. He pictured a trial with no witnesses to the crimes, a case where the victims were on the margins of society and the defendant looked like a pillar of the community. He pictured the defense lawyer asking the jury if they could trust a policeman who had held a gun to this nice old man's head. *Of course he admitted the crime, ladies and gentlemen—wouldn't you? With a gun to your head?*

He pictured Harold Sladek, cold and wet, taking a cigarette from this well-dressed benefactor. He pictured Michael Casey passing time with his killer, thanking him for his kindness, whispering *God bless*.

He pictured all this in the time it took for Arthur to swallow, nervously, twice.

The detective passed the flame over the cigarette once more. This time he held it there. "Inhale."

"You can't—"

"Inhale!"

Arthur sucked in, as briefly as he could. The tip of the cigarette glowed red. The detective closed the lighter and pocketed it.

"Again."

"Don't—"

"Again."

"Please—"

"This is the way it has to be," the detective said. "You said the stuff you put in the cigarettes is painless. I hope it is, because I guarantee you, bullets are not." The detective pulled the gun away from Arthur's head and aimed it at his gut. "Not the way I'll use them. Take your pick."

"You're a monster," Arthur said, the cigarette gripped tightly between his lips.

"I can live with that," the detective said. "Now decide."

Arthur looked at the gun, looked into the detective's eyes, and inhaled.

"Again," the detective said.

When Arthur was dead, the detective packed all the loose cigarettes into one of his bags and then stripped the corpse down to an undershirt and briefs. A press of a button erased the memory of the digital recorder, but just to be safe, he'd record over it when he got home.

He bundled everything up under one arm, pulled his hat further down on his brow, and walked east on 38th Street. It was still dark. No one saw him.

The body was found shortly after 9 in the morning.

The papers reported that an unidentified homeless man had died during the night, presumably of exposure. In the *Daily News* it was mentioned that he'd had a thin blanket over him, apparently donated by a good samaritan.

But, the *News* reported, it hadn't been enough to keep him alive.

THE LAST SUPPER

BY CAROL LEA BENJAMIN

Greenwich Village

Harry was late. No problem. Esther knew just what to do while she waited, lifting her hand and finally catching the waiter's eye. He was new, she thought, just a kid, his face eager, as if it really mattered to him what Esther wanted, as if he really cared. Was it a waiter thing, that faux interest? Or just a guy thing, appearing to be listening, to be interested, when they're not. Harry used to be like that. Harry used to be a lot of things. But no more. She'd see him tonight, give him what he asked for, then never see him again.

Esther pushed her empty glass toward the kid, a relative of Howdy Doody perchance, tapping the table the way you'd tap the bar, let the bartender know you were ready for another, let him know to keep them coming.

"Another Manhattan?" the kid asked, picking up the empty glass. Definitely not Mensa material. Esther nodded. He said he'd be right back.

Yeah, Esther thought. It had taken seventeen minutes to get the first one, the kid everywhere but at her table. She had to remind him, too, then listen politely while he pretended he hadn't forgotten, while he told her there was a backup at the bar, the place half empty. Maybe she'd insist on paying just so she could stiff him on the tip. No way was Esther going to be here again, no matter what she tipped the kid.

She looked over toward the door to see if Harry had come in. Maybe he was there already, looking around for her, not seeing her sitting in the far corner. But there was no Harry standing at the door, and anyway, the maître d' would have brought him over. They wouldn't leave him there on his own. Not Harry. Not at his favorite restaurant.

Esther checked her watch and then adjusted her scarf, the silk one he'd gotten her ten years ago when they were in England, the same kind the queen wore. That was when she was still running the office, still doing Harry's books. That was before Cheryl.

Peering out into the dark, as dark as New York City ever gets, which is not very, Esther caught her own reflection in the pane, her droopy eyelids, the soft jaw line, her thinning hair, the crosshatching of wrinkles over her pale, thin lips, all the little tricks Mother Nature plays on you as you age, followed by the little tricks your husband plays on you when he notices.

Esther took the little pot of lip gloss out of her purse, dipping one finger in, absentmindedly refreshing the color of her mouth, feeling hungry as soon as she did, checking the door again. Where the fuck was Harry?

Dropping the lip gloss into the inside zippered pocket so that it wouldn't get lost, Esther took out her pen, then snapped the purse closed. She put the pen on her napkin, where Harry would be sure to see it. She wanted him to know the arguing was over. She wanted him to feel at ease. Enough was enough, Esther thought, turning back once more to look at her reflection. He wanted her to sign the papers, she'd sign the papers. What difference did it make now anyway? Sign them or not, Harry didn't want her anymore and nothing was going to change that. Anyway, she'd made her decision, and once Esther made up her mind, there was no going back.

When another fifteen minutes had passed and there was still no Harry and still no second Manhattan, Esther began to daydream. Ever since Harry left her, she had been concocting ways to bump him off. In the beginning, it was the only way she could fall asleep, and later on, Esther found it elevated her mood any time of day. Looking out into the night through the oversize windows, Esther thought that might be a pleasant way to spend the time while she waited for the pimply waiter and her bald, overweight, philandering, estranged husband to show up.

When Harry first told her about Cheryl, Cheryl who worked for Harry as she herself had done until recently, Cheryl his bimbo, his chippy, his fiancée and about to be his next wife as soon as Esther signed the papers Harry was bringing along, she would write a new story every night. Lying in bed in the apartment she once shared with Harry, the apartment where she now lived alone, staring at the ceiling unable to sleep, Esther began killing Harry. She stood behind him, unseen, and pushed him in front of the Ninth Avenue bus, off the balcony of their penthouse apartment after he'd come crawling back to her, begging her to forgive him, even off the High Line, the old tram tracks the city kept promising to turn into a public space one day. She watched him die slowly at the hospital of some terrible, painful, incurable, slow-acting disease, and she gained access to the penthouse he shared with Cheryl, that tramp—who names a kid Cheryl, anyway?—and killed him there, tossing Cheryl's hair dryer into the bathtub, holding a pillow over his face, even shooting him the moment he came home from work, alone, for once, Cheryl doing some retail therapy or getting the liposuction she, Esther, had refused when Harry suggested it.

She'd killed him in Washington Square Park, right near the famous arch that all the Japanese tourists came by the busload to see. She'd killed him on the refurbished Christopher Street pier, once a gay sunbathing and pickup site, now a park where you can walk with your aged mother or bring your kids; Esther finding a time when the place was deserted, a time when she could be there alone with Harry and end his life. That's the thing about stories, Esther thought, unlike real life, you can make them turn out just the way you want them to. Fiction, she'd come to see, was preferable to fact, at least the facts of life as Esther knew them.

Struggling for the peace of mind that would let her sleep, Esther had killed Harry at The Strand, the world's biggest bookstore, at The White Horse Tavern, one of many places where Dylan Thomas supposedly drank himself to death, at Pastis, the popular restaurant in the meat market where young people talked on their cell phones instead of to each other, and even at one of the few remaining wholesale markets where Harry ended up hanging on one of those nasty-looking meat hooks alongside some hapless cow. There probably wasn't a place left in the Village that Esther hadn't used as a venue for killing Harry—not a seedy bar, an after-hours club, a back cottage, a pocket park; not a street, an avenue, a lane, an alley, a square, a mews.

In her desire for sleep, Esther had devised more ways to kill Harry than you could shake a scimitar at, a new one every night for the first three months. But then she saw that it was even more delicious to repeat a favorite story—there were so many of them, all so scrumptiously detailed and satisfying. That's when she began to name them, then tweak the names, amusing herself with each title change. God knows, she needed a few laughs in her life. A while after that—she had been a bookkeeper, after all—Esther gave them each a number. That's when "Am I Blue?"—formerly "Tampered"—in which Harry accidentally buys a bottle of Viagra that has been tampered with by a vindictive crazy person and falls down dead just as he's about to join the voluptuous slut Cheryl under the sheets, that story became "One." After that, on nights when Esther had done her yoga, taken a hot bath, and washed down an Ambien or two with some of that nice citron vodka she kept in the freezer, on those nights sometimes she could just slip under the comforter, close her eyes, and think "One," and just like that she'd be off to dreamland. Esther, it seemed, had finally found something she was good at. In her stories she didn't just murder Harry, she did it with grace, style, and wit, except perhaps for the one where she'd pulled up a loose cobblestone on Jane Street, one of the most charming of Greenwich Village's many charming blocks, and bashed Harry's stupid head in. That, of course, was the night he'd told her that he and Cheryl wanted to get married. That, Esther thought, had been the beginning of the end.

What used to work, worked no more. Even Esther's favorite plots now left her wide awake. For the last month or so, long nights of sleeplessness had turned into longer days of exhaustion, the tiredness pulling on Esther like a double dose of gravity, her heavy legs feeling like tree trunks, her dry skin sallow now, her eyes dull, making Esther plod through her own life without energy and without hope. Friends told her things would get better, that time heals all wounds, or that time wounds all heels, but either way things only got worse, and in the end Esther could see only one way out, only one way to stop her pain.

That very afternoon, Esther had tossed the perishables

and taken out the trash for the last time. And on the way to meet Harry, to do this one last thing, she'd packed Louie into his carrier and taken him over to that nice Mrs. Kwan at the deli a block from her apartment, a Korean deli a block or two from everyone's apartment in Manhattan, and told her that if she kept Louie in the basement, she'd never have a problem with the Department of Health again. Mrs. Kwan had looked inside the bag, startled at first, then laughing, covering her mouth with one hand, nodding yes, thank you, a cat, good idea. Outside the deli, Esther had dropped her keys down a sewer grating, something else she wouldn't need after her last supper with Harry.

She straightened the pen on her napkin—Esther liked things neat. And when she looked up, as ready as she'd ever be, there was Harry heading toward her. And there was the waiter with her drink as well.

"I ordered you a Manhattan," she told Harry, pointing to his place setting, letting the waiter know the drink was for him, not her, flapping her hand when he tried to put down the little wooden dish of nuts, motioning him to take it away as Harry pulled out the chair and slipped off his scarf, not the one Esther had given him two years ago, this one from Cheryl. "I think I'll have one, too," she told the kid. "A man shouldn't have to drink alone, should he?"

"Still taking care of me, Esther?" Harry said.

"Old habits die hard."

Harry nodded without looking at her, snapping his fingers for the waiter to come back, handing him his coat and scarf instead of hanging it on the rack himself the way everyone else did.

"You're looking good, Esther." Still not looking at her. "New hairdo?"

Esther smiled. "You noticed," she said, smoothing the same hair style she'd worn for the last seven years.

"So, my girl said I should bring the papers, Esther. I was quite surprised. Have you changed your mind? Have you decided . . . ?"

The kid brought Esther's Manhattan and gave them each a menu. Esther lifted her glass. "To your future, Harry," she said, waiting for him to lift his glass, listening to the sound of the glasses as they touched, remembering the champagne she always shared with Harry on their anniversaries, the little robin's-egg-blue box with the white satin bow he'd slip out of his pocket, at least until the last few anniversaries, the one when he was away, the one he just forgot, and the last one, the one he spent with Cheryl.

Harry picked up his menu, and the moment he put it down, the damn kid appeared, that shit-eating grin on his face.

"I'll start with the risotto," Harry told him, more interested in what he was going to eat for dinner than he was in Esther. "And then the steak, medium rare."

He didn't even ask Esther what she was going to have. But the kid was looking at her, waiting. That was as good as it was going to get around here, Esther thought, waving her hand back and forth. "Nothing for me."

"Esther," Harry said. "Come on. Have a bite."

"I'm on that diet you kept talking about, Harry."

"The liquid diet?"

Esther picked up her drink. "Yes, Harry, that one."

Why was it always Esther who was supposed to go on a diet? Didn't Harry ever look at himself in the mirror? But Cheryl didn't mind. She loved Harry just the way he was, old enough to be her father, fat enough to play Santa without padding, and with an income in the neighborhood of two million a year, give or take. Esther figured Harry was doing the giving, Cheryl the taking, as much of it as she could.

If Esther thought Harry would have trouble eating in front of her, she would have been sorely mistaken. But then again, she'd been mistaken about so many things, hadn't she? And what did it matter now anyway?

After a third Manhattan, the second that Harry knew about, she decided to let Harry pay the bill. The kid didn't seem so bad anymore. Let Harry leave him a big tip. Esther no longer cared. She excused herself to go to the ladies' room while Harry looked at the dessert menu. When she got back, no sooner had she sat down when Harry took the agreement out of his pocket and handed it across the table.

"Cheryl and I . . ." he began, then changed his mind. "I really appreciate this, Esther. And I'm sure you'll agree I've been generous. There's more than enough—"

He stopped again when she held up a hand. "Water under the bridge, Harry." She picked up the pen, signed and initialed wherever it was indicated to do so, then folded the document and handed it back to her husband.

"Ready?" he asked, anxious to go now, anxious to get home to Cheryl and show her the signed papers, open a bottle of champagne, toast to their future. Esther nodded. She'd given him what he wanted. That was what this dinner had been about and she'd done it. Esther dabbed on some lip gloss and stood, picking up her coat from the back of her chair, slipping it on without Harry's assistance, as the kid helped Harry into his coat, a new one, Esther noted, perhaps another gift from Cheryl, a gift paid for with Harry's money.

Still, she took his arm as they left the restaurant, the way she always used to. It felt good. It felt right, and besides, the streets were slippery and she didn't want to fall. She'd left her boots back at the apartment. She'd wanted to look nice tonight, her last night with Harry. They walked a block north, to Jane Street, and Esther looked down at the cobblestones showing in patches where the traffic had melted the snow. *Twenty-two*, she thought as they crossed the street, the one where she'd killed Harry with a loose cobblestone. Why had she been so foolish, living on fantasies of revenge instead of moving on with her life?

"I'd like to go on alone," she said when they arrived at the next corner.

Harry patted his coat where the signed papers would be in the inside pocket of his jacket. "Thank you, Esther. You always were a good sport."

"Kiss me goodbye, Harry. Kiss me as if it were the last time."

Harry bent. Esther got up on her toes. Harry was surprised at the force of her kiss, how tightly she held him, and then at the sight of the tears in her eyes when she finally stepped back.

He headed east, toward the bus stop on Greenwich Street. Esther shook her head. She knew him so well. There probably wasn't a thing about Harry she didn't know, including where he'd be generous and exactly where he'd scrimp. As if you could take it with you, she thought, lifting her arm to hail a cab.

Actually, it would be Esther taking it with her, all the money she'd embezzled from him all those years as his bookkeeper, a thousand here, a thousand there. It had added up to quite a sum in the twenty-eight years she'd run her husband's office and done his books.

Esther checked her watch. Feeling a bit lightheaded, she

regretted for the moment that she hadn't eaten, the food on the plane would be so bad. But then she remembered that her ticket was first class. The food might not be so bad after all, and they'd be pouring champagne even before takeoff. She saw a cab a few blocks away and reached into her purse for the little pot of lip gloss and dropped it, along with the syringe of epinephrine she'd taken from Harry's pocket when she'd hugged him, between the grates of the sewer, two more things she wouldn't need again.

The cab pulled up and Esther settled herself in the backseat, telling the driver to take her to JFK. Everything was right on schedule. She had plenty of time to catch her flight, the bus wouldn't be at the corner of Greenwich and Horatio Streets for another five or six minutes, and by that time Harry would be dead.

Nine, Esther said to herself, eyes closed, smiling, the one first called "Nut Allergy" and then "Nuts to You," the one in which Esther adds peanut oil to her lip gloss and kills Harry with a kiss. It had always been her very favorite.

IF YOU CAN'T STAND THE HEAT

BY LAWRENCE BLOCK

Clinton

She felt his eyes on her just about the time the bartender placed a Beck's coaster on the bar and set her dry Rob Roy on top of it. She wanted to turn and see who was eyeing her, but remained as she was, trying to analyze just what it was she felt. She couldn't pin it down physically, couldn't detect a specific prickling of the nerves in the back of her neck. She simply knew she was being watched, and that the watcher was a male.

It was, to be sure, a familiar sensation. Men had always looked at her. Since adolescence, since her body had begun the transformation from girl to woman? No, longer than that. Even in childhood, some men had looked at her, gazing with admiration and, often, with something beyond admiration.

In Hawley, Minnesota, thirty miles east of the North Dakota line, they'd looked at her like that. The glances followed her to Red Cloud and Minneapolis, and now she was in New York, and, no surprise, men still looked at her.

She lifted her glass, sipped, and a male voice said, "Excuse me, but is that a Rob Roy?"

He was standing to her left, a tall man, slender, well turned out in a navy blazer and gray trousers. His shirt was a button-down, his tie diagonally striped. His face, attractive but not handsome, was youthful at first glance, but she could see he'd lived some lines into it. And his dark hair was lightly infiltrated with gray.

"A dry Rob Roy," she said. "Why?"

"In a world where everyone orders Cosmopolitans," he said, "there's something very pleasingly old-fashioned about a girl who drinks a Rob Roy. A woman, I should say."

She lowered her eyes to see what he was drinking.

"I haven't ordered yet," he said. "Just got here. I'd have one of those, but old habits die hard." And when the barman moved in front of him, he ordered Jameson on the rocks. "Irish whiskey," he told her. "Of course, this neighborhood used to be mostly Irish. And tough. It was a pretty dangerous place a few years ago. A young woman like yourself wouldn't feel comfortable walking into a bar unaccompanied, not in this part of town. Even accompanied, it was no place for a lady."

"I guess it's changed a lot," she said.

"It's even changed its name," he said. His drink arrived, and he picked up his glass and held it to the light, admiring the amber color. "They call it Clinton now. That's for DeWitt Clinton, not Bill. DeWitt was the governor awhile back, he dug the Erie Canal. Not personally, but he got it done. And there was George Clinton, he was the governor, too, for seven terms starting before the adoption of the Constitution. And then he had a term as vice president. But all that was before your time."

"By a few years," she allowed.

"It was even before mine," he said. "But I grew up here, just a few blocks away, and I can tell you nobody called it Clinton then. You probably know what they called it."

"Hell's Kitchen," she said. "They still call it that, when they're not calling it Clinton."

"Well, it's more colorful. It was the real estate interests

who plumped for Clinton, because they figured nobody would want to move to something called Hell's Kitchen. And that may have been true then, when people remembered what a bad neighborhood this was, but now it's spruced up and gentrified and yuppified to within an inch of its life, and the old name gives it a little added cachet. A touch of gangster chic, if you know what I mean."

"If you can't stand the heat—"

"Stay out of the Kitchen," he supplied. "When I was growing up here, the Westies pretty much ran the place. They weren't terribly efficient like the Italian mob, but they were colorful and bloodthirsty enough to make up for it. There was a man two doors down the street from me who disappeared, and they never did find the body. Except one of his hands turned up in somebody's freezer on 53rd Street and Eleventh Avenue. They wanted to be able to put his fingerprints on things long after he was dead and gone."

"Would that work?"

"With luck," he said, "we'll never know. The Westies are mostly gone now, and the tenement apartments they lived in are all tarted up, with stockbrokers and lawyers renting them. Which are you?"

"Me?"

"A stockbroker or a lawyer?"

She grinned. "Neither one, I'm afraid. I'm an actress."

"Even better."

"Which means I take a class twice a week," she said, "and run around to open casting calls and auditions."

"And wait tables?"

"I did some of that in the Cities. I suppose I'll have to do it again here, when I start to run out of money."

"The Cities?"

"The Twin Cities. Minneapolis and St. Paul."

They talked about where she was from, and along the way he told her his name was Jim. She was Jennifer, she told him. He related another story about the neighborhood—he was really a pretty good storyteller—and by then her Rob Roy was gone and so was his Jameson. "Let me get us another round," he said, "and then why don't we take our drinks to a table? We'll be more comfortable, and it'll be quieter."

He was talking about the neighborhood.

"Irish, of course," he said, "but that was only part of it. You had blocks that were pretty much solid Italian, and there were Poles and other Eastern Europeans. A lot of French, too, working at the restaurants in the theater district. You had everything, really. The UN's across town on the East River, but you had your own General Assembly here in the Kitchen. Fifty-seventh Street was a dividing line; north of that was San Juan Hill, and you had a lot of blacks living there. It was an interesting place to grow up, if you got to grow up, but no sweet young thing from Minnesota would want to move here."

She raised her eyebrows at *sweet young thing*, and he grinned at her. Then his eyes turned serious and he said, "I have a confession to make."

"Oh?"

"I followed you in here."

"You mean you noticed me even before I ordered a Rob Roy?"

"I saw you on the street. And for a moment I thought . . ."

"What?"

"Well, that you were on the street."

"I guess I was, if that's where you saw me. I don't . . . Oh, you thought—"

"That you were a working girl. I wasn't going to mention this, and I don't want you to take it the wrong way . . ."

What, she wondered, was the right way?

". . . because it's not as though you looked the part, or were dressed like the girls you see out there. See, the neighborhood may be tarted up, but that doesn't mean the tarts have disappeared."

"I've noticed."

"It was more the way you were walking," he went on. "Not swinging your hips, not your walk, per se, but a feeling I got that you weren't in a hurry to get anywhere, or even all that sure where you were going."

"I was thinking about stopping for a drink," she said, "and not sure if I wanted to, or if I should go straight home."

"That would fit."

"And I've never been in here before, and wondered if it was decent."

"Well, it's decent enough now. A few years ago it wouldn't have been. And even now, a woman alone—"

"I see." She sipped her drink. "So you thought I might be a hooker, and that's what brought you in here. Well, I hate to disappoint you—"

"What brought me in here," he said, "was the thought that you might be, and the hope that you weren't."

"I'm not."

"I know."

"I'm an actress."

"And a good one, I'll bet."

"I guess time will tell."

"It generally does," he said. "Can I get you another one of those?"

She shook her head. "Oh, I don't think so," she said. "I

was only going to come in for one drink, and I wasn't even sure I wanted to do that. And I've had two, and that's really plenty."

"Are you sure?"

"I'm afraid so. It's not just the alcohol, it's the time. I have to get home."

"I'll walk you."

"Oh, that's not necessary."

"Yes, it is. Whether it's Hell's Kitchen or Clinton, it's still necessary."

"Well . . ."

"I insist. It's safer around here than it used to be, but it's a long way from Minnesota. And I suppose you get some unsavory characters in Minnesota, as far as that goes."

"Well, you're right about that." At the door she added, "I just don't want you to think you have to walk me home because I'm a lady."

"I'm not walking you home because you're a lady," he said. "I'm walking you home because I'm a gentleman."

The walk to her door was interesting. He had stories to tell about half the buildings they passed. There'd been a murder in this one, a notorious drunk in the next. And though some of the stories were unsettling, she felt completely secure walking at his side.

At her door he said, "Any chance I could come up for a cup of coffee?"

"I wish," she said.

"I see."

"I've got this roommate," she said. "It's impossible, it really is. My idea of success isn't starring on Broadway, it's making enough money to have a place of my own. There's just no privacy when she's home, and the damn girl is always home."

"That's a shame."

She drew a breath. "Jim? Do you have a roommate?"

He didn't, and if he had, the place would still have been spacious enough to afford privacy. A large living room, a big bedroom, a good-sized kitchen. Rent-controlled, he told her, or he could never have afforded it. He showed her all through the apartment before he took her in his arms and kissed her.

"Maybe," she said, when the embrace ended, "maybe we should have one more drink after all."

She was dreaming, something confused and confusing, and then her eyes snapped open. For a moment she did not know where she was, and then she realized she was in New York, and realized the dream had been a recollection or reinvention of her childhood in Hawley.

In New York, and in Jim's apartment.

And in his bed. She turned, saw him lying motionless beside her, and slipped out of bed, moving with instinctive caution. She walked quietly out of the bedroom, found the bathroom. She used the toilet, peeked behind the shower curtain. The tub was surprisingly clean for a bachelor's apartment and looked inviting. She didn't feel soiled, not exactly that, but something close. Stale, she decided. Stale, and very much in need of freshening.

She ran the shower, adjusted the temperature, stepped under the spray.

She hadn't intended to stay over, had fallen asleep in spite of her intentions. Rohypnol, she thought. Roofies, the date-rape drug. Puts you to sleep, or the closest thing to it, and leaves you with no memory of what happened to you.

Maybe that was it. Maybe she'd gotten a contact high.

She stepped out of the tub, toweled herself dry, and returned to the bedroom for her clothes. He hadn't moved in her absence and lay on his back beneath the covers.

She got dressed, checked herself in the mirror, found her purse, put on lipstick but no other makeup, and was satisfied with the results. Then, after another reflexive glance at the bed, she began searching the apartment.

His wallet, in the gray slacks he'd tossed over the back of a chair, held almost three hundred dollars in cash. She took that but left the credit cards and everything else. She found just over a thousand dollars in his sock drawer, and took it, but left the mayonnaise jar full of loose change. She checked the refrigerator, and the set of brushed-aluminum containers on the kitchen counter, but the fridge held only food and drink, and one container held tea bags while the other two were empty.

That was probably it, she decided. She could search more thoroughly, but she'd only be wasting her time.

And she really ought to get out of here.

But first she had to go back to the bedroom. Had to stand at the side of the bed and look down at him. Jim, he'd called himself. James John O'Rourke, according to the cards in his wallet. Forty-seven years old. Old enough to be her father, in point of fact, although the man in Hawley who'd sired her was his senior by eight or nine years.

He hadn't moved.

Rohypnol, she thought. The love pill.

"Maybe," she had said, "we should have one more drink after all."

I'll have what you're having, she'd told him, and it was child's play to add the drug to her own drink, then switch glasses with him. Her only concern after that had been that he might pass out before he got his clothes off, but no, they kissed and petted and found their way to his bed, and got out of their clothes and into each other's arms, and it was all very nice, actually, until he yawned and his muscles went slack and he lay limp in her arms.

She arranged him on his back and watched him sleep. Then she touched and stroked him, eliciting a response without waking the sleeping giant. Rohypnol, the wonder drug, facilitating date rape for either sex. She took him in her mouth, she mounted him, she rode him. Her orgasm was intense, and it was hers alone. He didn't share it, and when she dismounted his penis softened and lay upon his thigh.

In Hawley her father took to coming into her room at night. "Jenny? Are you sleeping?" If she answered, he'd kiss her on the forehead and tell her to go back to sleep.

Then half an hour later he'd come back. If she was asleep, if she didn't hear him call her name, he'd slip into the bed with her. And touch her, and kiss her, and not on her forehead this time.

She would wake up when this happened, but somehow knew to feign sleep. And he would do what he did.

Before long she pretended to be asleep whenever he came into the room. She'd hear him ask if she was asleep, and she'd lie there silent and still, and he'd come into her bed. She liked it, she didn't like it. She loved him, she hated him.

Eventually they dropped the pretense. Eventually he taught her how to touch him, and how to use her mouth on him. Eventually, eventually, there was very little they didn't do.

* * *

It took some work, but she got Jim hard again and made him come. He moaned audibly at the very end, then subsided into deep sleep almost immediately. She was exhausted, she felt as if she'd taken a drug herself, but she forced herself to go to the bathroom and look for some Listerine. She couldn't find any, and wound up gargling with a mouthful of his Irish whiskey.

She stopped in the kitchen, then returned to the bedroom. When she'd done what she needed to do, she decided it wouldn't hurt to lie down beside him and close her eyes. Just for a minute . . .

And now it was morning, time for her to get out of there. She stood looking down at him, and for an instant she seemed to see his chest rise and fall with his slow even breathing, but that was just her mind playing a trick, because his chest was in fact quite motionless, and he wasn't breathing at all. His breathing had stopped forever when she slid the kitchen knife between two of his ribs and into his heart.

He'd died without a sound. *La petite mort*, the French called an orgasm. The little death. Well, the little death had drawn a moan from him, but the real thing turned out to be soundless. His breathing stopped, and never resumed.

She laid a hand on his upper arm, and the coolness of his flesh struck her as a sign that he was at peace now. She thought, almost wistfully, how very serene he had become.

In a sense, there'd been no need to kill the man. She could have robbed him just as effectively while he slept, and the drug would ensure that he wouldn't wake up before she was out the door. She'd used the knife in response to an inner need, and the need had been an urgent one; satisfying it had shuttled her right off to sleep.

She had never used a knife, or anything else, in Hawley. She'd considered it, and more than once. But in the end all she did was leave. No final scene, no note, nothing. Out the door and on the first Trailways bus out of there, and that was that.

Maybe everything else would have been different if she'd left her father as peaceful as she was leaving James John O'Rourke. But had that ever been an option? Could she have done it, really?

Probably not.

She let herself out of the apartment, drew the door shut, and made sure it locked behind her. The building was a walk-up, four apartments to the floor, and she walked down three flights and out the door without encountering anyone.

Time to think about moving.

Not that she'd established a pattern. The man last week, in the posh loft near the Javits Center, she had smothered to death. He'd been huge, and built like a wrestler, but the drug rendered him helpless, and all she'd had to do was hold the pillow over his face. He didn't come close enough to consciousness to struggle. And the man before that, the advertising executive, had shown her why he'd feel safe in any neighborhood, gentrification or no. He kept a loaded handgun in the drawer of the bedside table, and if any burglar was unlucky enough to drop into his place, well—

When she was through with him, she'd retrieved the gun, wrapped his hand around it, put the barrel in his mouth, and squeezed off a shot. They could call it a suicide, just as they could call the wrestler a heart attack, if they didn't look too closely. Or they could call all three of them murders, without ever suspecting they were all the work of the same person.

Still, it wouldn't hurt her to move. Find another place to live before people started to notice her on the streets and in the bars. She liked it here, in Clinton, or Hell's Kitchen, whatever you wanted to call it. It was a nice place to live, whatever it may have been in years past. But, as she and Jim had agreed, the whole of Manhattan was a nice place to live. There weren't any bad neighborhoods left, not really.

Wherever she went, she was pretty sure she'd feel safe.

RAIN

BY THOMAS H. COOK

Battery Park

A burst of light releases the million eyes of the rain, glimpsing the Gothic towers in dark mist, falling in glittering streams of briefly reflected light, moving inland, toward the blunt point of the island, an outbound ferry as it loads for the midnight run.

So like I said before, it ain't like she has long, you know?

Yeah, mon. She just hangin' on now.

Rain streaks down the ferry's windows where the night riders sit in yellow haze—Toby McBride only one among them, single, forty-two, the bowling alley in trouble, thinking of his invalid mother on Staten Island, money leaching away, watching her Jamaican nurse, such big black hands, how easy it would be.

I figure you could use twenty grand, right?

Twenty, huh?

The rain falls on intrigue and conspiracy, trap doors, underground escape routes, the crude implements of quick getaways. It collects the daily grime from the face of the Custom House and sends it swirling into the vast underground drains that empty into the sea. Along the sweep of Battery Park it smashes against crumpled cigarette packets, soaks a broken shoelace, flows into a half-used tube of lipstick, drives a young woman beneath a tattered awning, blond hair, shoulder-length, with a stuck umbrella, struggling to open it, a man behind her, sunk in the shadows, his voice a tremble in the air.

You live in this building?

Long, dark fingers still the umbrella, curl around its mahogany handle.

Name's Rebecca, right?

The rain sees the fickle web of chance meetings, the grid of untimely intersections, lethal fortuities from which there will be no escape. A million tiny flashing screens reflect stilettos and box cutters, switchblades and ice picks, the snub-nosed barrel that stares out from its nest of long dark fingers.

Don't say a word.

Off West Street the rain falls on the deserted pit of the ghostly towers, and moves on, cascading down the skeletal girders of the new construction, then further north, to Duane Street, thudding against the roof of an old green van.

So, when you get here, Sammy?

Don't worry. I'll be there.

Eddie squeezes the cell phone, glances back toward the rear of the van, speakers, four DVD players, two car radios, a cashmere overcoat, a shoebox of CDs, some jewelry that might be real, the bleak fruit of the hustle.

I need you here now, man.

You that hyped?

Now, man.

In the gutters, the rushing rain washes cigarette butts and candy wrappers, a note with the number 484 in watery ink, a hat shop receipt, a prescription label for Demerol. It washes down grimy windshields and as it washes, sees the pop-eyed and the drowsy, the hazy and the alert, Eddie scratching his skinny arms, Detective Boyle in the unmarked car a block away, playing back the tape, grinning at his partner as he listens to the voices on the ferry.

We got McBride dead to rights, Frank.

A laugh.

That fucking Jamaican. Jeez, does he know how to work a wire.

At Police Plaza, the wind shifts, driving eastward, battering the building's small square windows, a thudding rumble that briefly draws Max Feldman from the photographs on his desk, Lynn Abercrombie sprawled across the floor of her Tribeca apartment, shot once with a snub-nosed .38, no real clues, save the fact that she lay on her back, with a strand of long blond hair over the right eye, maybe by a fan of Veronica Lake, some sick aficionado of the noir.

The rain falls upon the tangle of steel and concrete, predator and prey. It slaps the baseball cap of Jerry Brice, as he waits for Hattie Jones, knowing it was payday at the all-night laundry, her purse full of cash. It mars Sammy Kaminsky's view of Dolly Baron's bedroom window, and foils the late-night entertainment of a thousand midnight peepers.

On Houston Street, it falls on people drawn together by the midnight storm, huddled beneath shelters, Herman Devane crowded into a bus refuge, drunk college girls all around him, that little brunette in the red beret, her body naked beneath her clothes, so naked and so close, the touch so quick, so easy, to brush against her then step back, blame it on the rain.

Lightning, then thunder rolling northward, over Bleecker Street, past clubs and taverns, faces bathed in neon light, nodding to the beat of piano, bass, drums, the late-night riff of jazz trios.

Ernie Gorsh taps his foot lightly beneath the table.

Not a bad piano.

Jack Plato, fidgeting, toying with the napkin beneath his drink, a lot on his mind, time like a blade swinging over his head.

Fuck the piano. You hear me, Ern? 484 Duane. A little jewelry store. Easy. I cased it this afternoon.

Ernie Gosch listens to the piano.

Jack Plato, slick black hair, sipping whiskey, cocksure about the plans, the schedule, where the cameras are.

Paulie Cerrello's backing the operation. A safe man is all we need. Christ, it's a sure thing, Ern.

Ernie Gorsh, gray hair peeping from beneath his gray felt hat, just out of the slammer, not ready to go back.

Nothing's ever sure, Jack.

It is if you got the balls.

It is if you don't got the brains.

Plato, offended, squirming, a deal going south, Paulie will be pissed. No choice now but play the bluff.

Take it or leave it, old man.

Ernie, thinking of his garden, the seeds he's already bought for spring, seeds in packets, nestled in his jacket pocket, thinking of the slammer, too, how weird it is now, gangs, Aryans, Muslims, fag cons raping kids in the shower, deciding not to go back.

Sorry, Jack. Rising. *I got a bus to catch.*

The eyes of the rain see the value of experience, the final stop of crooked roads. It falls on weariness and dread, the iron bars of circumstance, the way out that looks easy, comes with folded money, glassine bags of weed, tinfoil cylinders stuffed with white powder, floor plans of small jewelry stores, with *x*'s where the cameras are.

At 8th Street and Sixth Avenue, Tracey Olson leaves a cardboard box on the steps of Jefferson Market. Angelo and Luis watch her rush away from inside a red BMW boosted on Avenue A, the rain thudding hard on its roof.

You see that?

Wha?

That fucking girl.

What about her?

She left a box on the steps there.

What about it?

That all you can say, whataboutitwhataboutit?

Luis steps out into the rain, toward the box, the tiny cries he hears now.

Jesus. Jesus Christ.

On 23rd, the rain slams against the windows of pizza parlors and Mexican restaurants, Chinese joints open all night.

Sal and Frankie. Sweet and sour pork. Moo goo gai pan.

So, the guy, what'd he do?

What they always do.

He ask how old?

I told him eighteen.

Sal and Frankie giggling about the suits from the suburbs, straight guys who dole out cash for their sweet asses then take the PATH home to their pretty little wives.

Where was he from?

Who cares? He's a dead man now.

That plum sauce, you eatin' that?

* * *

At Broadway and 34th, the million eyes of the rain smash against the dusty windows of the rag trade, Lennie Mack at his desk, ledgers open, refiguring the numbers, wiping his moist brow with the rolled sleeves of his shirt, wondering how Old Man Siegelman got suspicious, threatening to call in outside auditors, what he has to do before that call is made . . . do for Rachel, and the two kids in college, do because it was just a little at the beginning. Jesus, two-hundred fifty thousand now. Too much to hide. He closes the ledger, sits back in his squeaky chair, thinks it through again . . . what he has to do.

From Times Square, the gusts drive northward, slanting lines of rain falling like bullets, exploding against the black pavement, the cars and buses still on Midtown streets, Jaime Rourke on the uptown 104, worrying about Tracy, what she might do with the baby, seated next to an old guy in a gray felt hat fingering packets of garden seed.

So I guess you got a garden.

My building has little plots. A smile. *My daughter thinks I should plant a garden.*

Eddie Gorsh sits back, relaxed, content in his decision, grateful to his daughter, how, because of her, there'll be no more sure things.

Daughters are like that, you know. They make you have a little sense.

Near 59th and Fifth, a gust lifts the awning of the San Domenico. Dim light in the bar. Bartender in a black bolero jacket.

Amanda Graham. Martini, very dry, four olives. Black

dress, sleeveless, Mikimoto pearls. Deidre across the small marble table. Manhattan. Straight up.

Paulie's going to find out, Mandy.

Amanda sips her drink. *How?*

He has ways.

A dismissive wave. *He's not Nostradamus.*

Close enough. And for what? Some nobody.

He's not a nobody. He plays piano. A nice gig. On Bleecker Street.

My point exactly.

Amanda nibbles the first olive. *What do you really think Paulie would do?*

Deidre sips her drink.

Kill you.

Amanda's olive drops into the crystal glass, ripples the vodka and vermouth. The smooth riffs of Bleecker Street grow dissonant and fearful.

You really think he would?

Over the nightbound city, the rain falls upon uncertainty and fear, the nervous tick of unsettled outcomes, things in the air, motions not yet completed. At 72nd and Broadway, it sweeps along windows coiled in neon, decorated with bottles of ale and pasted with green shamrocks.

Captain Beals. Single malt scotch. Glenfiddich. Detective Burke with Johnny Walker Black. A stack of photographs on the bar between them. Fat man. Bald. 3849382092.

This the last one?

Yeah. Feldman thinks it's a long shot, but the guy lives in Tribeca, and it seems pretty clear the killer lives there too.

A quick nod.

His name is Harry Devane. Lives in Windsor Apartments.

*Just a couple buildings down from Lynn Abercrombie. Four blocks
from Tiana Matthews. Been out four years.*

    What's his story?

    *He works his way up to it by flashing, or maybe just rubbing
against a girl. You know, in the subway, elevator, crap like that.*

    Then what?

    Then he . . . gets violent.

    How violent?

    *So far, assault. But pretty bad ones. The last time, the girl
nearly died. He got seven years.*

    Ever used a gun?

    No.

    A sip of Glenfiddich.

    Then he's not our man.

At 93rd and Amsterdam, the rain sweeps in waves down the
tavern window, Paulie Cerrello watching Jack Plato step out
of the cab, taking a sip from his glass as Plato comes through
the door, slapping water from his leather jacket.

    Fucking storm. Jesus.

    So? Gorsh?

    I showed him everything. The whole deal.

    And?

    He ain't in, Paulie. He's scared of the slammer.

    Paulie knocks back the drink, unhappy with the scheme
of things, some old geezer scared of the slammer, the whole
deal a bust.

    So what now, Paulie? You want I should get another guy?

    A shake of the head.

    No, I got another problem.

    He nods for one more shot.

    You know my wife, right?

* * *

The rain sees no way out, no right decision, nothing that can slow the encroaching vise. It falls on bad judgment and poor choice and the clenched fist of things half thought through. At Park and 104th, it slaps against a closing window, water on the ledge dripping down onto the bare floor.

Shit.

Charlie Landrew tosses his soggy hat onto the small wooden table that is his office and dining room. Misses. The hat now on the frayed rug beneath the table.

Shit.

Leaves it.

Phone.

Yeah?

Charlie, it's me. Lennie.

This fucking storm flooded my goddamn apartment. Water all over the fucking floor.

Listen, Charlie. I need to borrow some cash. You know, from the guy you . . . from him.

A hard laugh.

You barely got away with your thumbs last time, Lennie.

But I made good, that's all that matters, right?

How much?

Twenty-five.

Charlie thinks. Old accounts. Too many of them. Past due. Lots of heavy leaning ahead. And if the leaning doesn't work, and somebody skips? His neck in a noose already.

So what about it, Charlie?

Not a hard decision.

No.

The rain sees last options, called bluffs, final scores, silenced bells, snuffed candles, books abruptly closed. At Broadway and 110th, the windshield wipers screech as they toss it from the glass.

Listen to that, will ya?

Yeah, what a piece of shit.

A fucking BMW, and shit wipers like that.

Might as well be a goddamn Saturn.

The box shifts slightly on Luis's lap.

I think it's taking a crap, Angelo.

So?

So? What if it craps through the box?

It won't crap through the box.

Okay, so it don't. What we gonna do?

I'm thinking.

You been thinking since we left the Village.

So what's your idea, Luis? And don't say cops, because we ain't showing up at no cop-house with a fucking stolen car and a baby we don't know whose it is.

A leftward glance, toward a looming spire.

A church. Maybe a church.

The rain falls on quick solutions, available means, a way out that relieves the burden. It falls on homeless shelters and SROs and into the creaky, precariously hanging drains of old cathedrals.

At 112th and Broadway, a blast of wind hits as the bus' hydraulic doors open.

Eddie Gorsh rises.

Good luck with the garden.

A smile back at the kid.

Thanks.

I got a daughter, too.

Then take care of her, and maybe she'll take care of you.

Out onto the rain-pelted sidewalk, head down, toward the building, Edna waiting for him there, relieved to have him back, the years they have left, a road he's determined to keep straight. This, he knows, will make Rebecca happy, and that is all he's after now.

The rain moves on, northward, toward the Bronx, leaving behind new beginnings, things learned, lessons applied. At 116th and Broadway, Jamie Rourke steps out into the million, million drops, thinking of Tracey and his daughter, how he shouldn't have said what he said, made her mad, determined to call her now, tell her how everything is going to be okay, how it's going to be the three of them against the world, a family.

The rain falls on lost hopes and futile resolutions, redemptions grasped too late, fanciful solutions. At 116th and Broadway, it falls on Barney Siegelman as he steps out of a taxi, convinced now that his son-in-law is a crook, news he has to break to his wife, his daughter, the whole sorry scheme of things unmasked. He rushes toward the front of his building, feels his feet slosh through an unexpected stream of water. He stops beneath the awning of his building and follows the rushing tide up the side-walk to Our Lady of Silence, where a cardboard box lays beneath a ruptured drain, a torrent gushing from its cracked mouth, filling the box with water, then over its sodden sides and down the concrete stairs, flooding the sidewalk with the stream that splashes around Siegelman's newly polished shoes. He shakes his head. Tomorrow he'll have to have them shined all over again. He peers toward the church, the stairs, the shat-tered drain pipe, the overflowing box beneath it. Disgusting, he thinks, the way people leave their trash.

A NICE PLACE TO VISIT

BY JEFFERY DEAVER

Hell's Kitchen

When you're a natural-born grifter, an operator, a player, you get this sixth sense for sniffing out opportunities, and that's what Ricky Kelleher was doing now, watching two guys in the front of the smoky bar, near a greasy window that still had a five-year-old bullet hole in it.

Whatever was going down, neither of them looked real happy.

Ricky kept watching. He'd seen one guy here in Hanny's a couple of times. He was wearing a suit and tie—it really made him stand out in this dive, the sore thumb thing. The other one, leather jacket and tight jeans, razor-cut bridge-and-tunnel hair, was some kind of Gambino wannabe, Ricky pegged him. Or Sopranos, more likely—yeah, he was the sort of prick who'd hock his wife for a big-screen TV. He was way pissed off, shaking his head at everything Mr. Suit was telling him. At one point he slammed his fist on the bar so hard glasses bounced. But nobody noticed. That was the kind of place Hanny's was.

Ricky was in the rear, at the short L of the bar, his regular throne. The bartender, a dusty old guy, maybe black, maybe white, you couldn't tell, kept an uneasy eye on the guys arguing. "It's cool," Ricky reassured him. "I'm on it."

Mr. Suit had a briefcase open. A bunch of papers were

inside. Most of the business in this pungent, dark Hell's Kitchen bar involved trading bags of chopped-up plants and cases of Johnny Walker that'd fallen off the truck; the transactions were conducted in either the men's room or alley out back. This was something different. Skinny, five-foot-four Ricky couldn't tip to exactly what was going down, but that magic sense, his player's eye, told him to pay attention.

"Well, fuck that," Wannabe said to Mr. Suit.

"Sorry." A shrug.

"Yeah, you said that before." Wannabe slid off the stool. "But you don't really *sound* that fucking sorry. And you know why? Because *I'm* the one out all the money."

"Bullshit. *I'm* losing my whole fucking business."

But Ricky'd learned that other people losing money doesn't take the sting out of *you* losing money. Way of the world.

Wannabe was getting more and more agitated. "Listen careful here, my friend. I'll make some phone calls. I got people I know down there. You don't want to fuck with these guys."

Mr. Suit tapped what looked like a newspaper article in the briefcase. "And what're they gonna do?" His voice lowered and he whispered something that made Wannabe's face screw up in disgust. "Now just go on home, keep your head down, and watch your back. And pray they can't—" Again, the lowered voice. Ricky couldn't hear what "they" might do.

Wannabe slammed his hand down on the bar again. "This isn't gonna fly, asshole. Now—"

"Hey, gentlemen," Ricky called. "Volume down, okay?"

"The fuck're you, little man?" Wannabe snapped. Mr. Suit touched his arm to quiet him, but he pulled away and kept glaring.

Ricky slicked back his greasy, dark blond hair. Easing off the stool, he walked to the front of the bar, the heels of his boots tapping loudly on the scuffed floor. The guy had six inches and thirty pounds on him but Ricky had learned a long time ago that craziness scares people a fuck of a lot more than height or weight or muscle. And so he did what he always did when he was going one on one—threw a weird look into his eyes and got right up in the man's face. He screamed, "Who I am is guy's gonna drag your ass into the alley and fuck you over a dozen different ways, you don't get the fuck out of here now!"

The punk reared back and blinked. He fired off an automatic "Fuck you, asshole."

Ricky stayed right where he was, kind of grinning, kind of not, and let this poor bastard imagine what was going to happen now that he'd accidentally shot a little spit onto Ricky's forehead.

A few seconds passed.

Finally, Wannabe drank down what was left of his beer with a shaking hand and, trying to hold on to a little dignity, he strolled out the door, laughing and muttering, "Prick." Like it was Ricky backing down.

"Sorry about that," Mr. Suit said, standing up, pulling out money for the drinks.

"No, you stay," Ricky ordered.

"Me?"

"Yeah, you."

The man hesitated and sat back down.

Ricky glanced into the briefcase, saw some pictures of nice-looking boats. "Just gotta keep things calm round here, you know. Keep the peace."

Mr. Suit slowly closed the case, looked around at the

faded beer promotion cut-outs, the stained sports posters, the cobwebs. "This your place?"

The bartender was out of earshot. Ricky said, "More or less."

"Jersey." Mr. Suit nodded at the door that Wannabe had just walked out of. Like that explained it all.

Ricky's sister lived in Jersey and he wondered if maybe he should be pissed at the insult. He was a loyal guy. But then he decided loyalty didn't have anything to do with states or cities and shit like that. "So. He lost some money?"

"Business deal went bad."

"Uh-huh. How much?"

"I don't know."

"Buy him another beer," Ricky called to the bartender, then turned back. "You're in business with him and you don't know how much money he lost?"

"What I don't know," the guy said, his dark eyes looking right into Ricky's, "is why I should fucking tell you."

This was the time when it could get ugly. There was a tough moment of silence. Then Ricky laughed. "No worries."

The beers arrived.

"Ricky Kelleher." He clinked glasses.

"Bob Gardino."

"I seen you before. You live around here?"

"Florida mostly. I come up here for business some. Delaware too. Baltimore, Jersey shore, Maryland."

"Yeah? I got a summer place I go to a lot."

"Where?"

"Ocean City. Four bedrooms, on the water." Ricky didn't mention that it was T.G.'s, not his.

"Sweet." The man nodded, impressed.

"It's okay. I'm looking at some other places too."

"Man can never have too much real estate. Better than the stock market."

"I do okay on Wall Street," Ricky said. "You gotta know what to look for. You just can't buy some stock 'cause it's, you know, sexy." He'd heard this on some TV show.

"Truer words." Now Gardino tapped his glass into Ricky's.

"Those were some nice fucking boats." A nod toward the briefcase. "That your line?"

"Among other things. Whatta *you* do, Ricky?"

"I got my hand in a lot of stuff. Lot of businesses. All over the neighborhood here. Well, and other places too. Maryland, like I was saying. Good money to be made. For a man with a sharp eye."

"And you have a sharp eye?"

"I think I do. Wanta know what it's seeing right now?"

"What, your eye?"

"Yeah."

"What's it seeing?"

"A grifter."

"A—?"

"A scam artist."

"I know what a grifter is," Gardino said. "I meant, why do you think that's what I am?"

"Well, for instance, you don't come into Hanny's—"

"Hanny's?"

"Here. Hanrahan's."

"Oh."

"—to sell some loser asshole a boat. So what really happened?"

Gardino chuckled but said nothing.

"Look," Ricky whispered, "I'm cool. Ask anybody on the street."

"There's nothing to tell. A deal went south is all. Happens."

"I'm not a cop, that's what you're thinking." Ricky looked around, reached into his pocket, and flashed a bag of hash he'd been carrying around for T.G. "I was, you think I'd have this on me?"

"Naw, I don't think you're a cop. And you seem like an okay guy. But I don't need to spill my guts to every okay guy I meet."

"I hear that. Only . . . I'm just wondering there's a chance we can do business together."

Gardino drank some more beer. "Again, why?"

"Tell me how your con works."

"It's not a con. I was going to sell him a boat. It didn't work out. End of story."

"But . . . see, here's what I'm thinking," Ricky said in his best player's voice. "I seen people pissed off 'cause they don't get a car they wanted, or a house, or some pussy. But that asshole, he wasn't pissed off about not getting a boat. He was pissed off about not getting his down payment back. So, how come he didn't?"

Gardino shrugged.

Ricky tried again. "How's about we play a game, you and me? I'll ask you something and you tell me if I'm right or if I'm full of shit. How's that?"

"Twenty questions."

"Whatever. Okay, try this on: You *borrow*—" He held up his fingers and made quotation marks—"a boat, sell it to some poor asshole, but then on the way here it *sinks*." Again the quotation marks. "And there's nothing he can do about it. He loses his down payment. He's fucked. Too bad, but who's he going to complain to? It's stolen merch."

Gardino studied his beer. Son of a bitch still wasn't giving away squat.

Ricky added, "Only there never was any boat. You never steal a fucking thing. You just show him pictures you took on the dock and a fake police report or something."

The guy finally laughed. But nothing else.

"Your only risk is some asshole whaling on you when he loses the money. Not a bad grift."

"I sell boats," Gardino said. "That's it."

"Okay, you sell boats." Ricky eyed him carefully. He'd try a different approach. "So that means you're looking for buyers. How 'bout I find one for you?"

"You know somebody who's interested in boats?"

"There's a guy I know. He might be."

Gardino thought for a minute. "This a friend of yours we're talking?"

"I wouldn'ta brought him up, he was a friend."

The sunlight came through some clouds over Eighth Avenue and hit Gardino's beer. It cast a tint on the counter, the yellow of a sick man's eye. Finally, he said to Ricky, "Pull your shirt up."

"My—?"

"Your shirt. Pull it up and turn around."

"You think I'm wired?"

"Or we just have our beers and bullshit about the Knicks and we go our separate ways. Up to you."

Self-conscious of his skinny build, Ricky hesitated. But then he slipped off the stool, pulled up his leather jacket, and lifted his dirty T-shirt. He turned around.

"Okay. You do the same."

Gardino laughed. Ricky thought he was laughing at him more than he was laughing at the situation but he held on to his temper.

The con man pulled up his jacket and shirt. The bartender glanced at them but he was looking like nothing was weird. This was, after all, Hanny's.

The men sat down and Ricky called for more brews.

Gardino whispered, "Okay, I'll tell you what I'm up to. But listen. You get some idea that you're in the mood to snitch, I got two things to say: One, what I'm doing is not exactly legal, but it's not like I'm clipping anybody or selling crack to kids, got it? So even if you go to the cops, the best they can get me for is some bullshit misrepresentation claim. They'll laugh you out of the station."

"No, man, seriously—"

Gardino held up a finger. "And number two, you dime me out, I've got associates in Florida'll find you and make you bleed for days." He grinned. "We copacetic?"

Whatever the fuck that meant. Ricky said, "No worries, mister. All I wanta do is make some money."

"Okay, here's how it works: Fuck down payments. The buyers pay everything right up front. A hundred, hundred fifty thousand."

"No shit."

"What I tell the buyer is my connections know where there're these confiscated boats. This really happens. They're towed off by the DEA for drugs or Coast Guard or State Police when the owner's busted for sailing 'em while drunk. They go up for auction. But see, what happens is, in Florida, there's so many boats that it takes time to log 'em all in. I tell the buyers my partners break into the pound at 3 in the morning and tow a boat away before there's a record of it. We ship it to Delaware or Jersey, slap a new number on it, and bang, for a hundred thousand you get a half-million-dollar boat.

"Then, after I get the money, I break the bad news. Like

I just did with our friend from Jersey." He opened up his brief-case and pulled out a newspaper article. The headline was: "*Three arrested in Coast Guard Impound Thefts.*"

The article was about a series of thefts of confiscated boats from a federal government impound dock. It went on to add that security had been stepped up and the FBI and Florida police were looking into who might've bought the half-dozen missing boats. They'd arrested the principals and recovered nearly a million dollars in cash from buyers on the East Coast.

Ricky looked over the article. "You, what? Printed it up yourself?"

"Word processor. Tore the edges to make it look like I ripped it out of the paper and then Xeroxed it."

"So you keep 'em scared shitless some cop's going to find their name or trace the money to them. *Now, just go on home, keep your head down, and watch your back.* Some of 'em make a stink for a day or two, but mostly they just disappear."

This warranted another clink of beer glasses. "Fucking brilliant."

"Thanks."

"So if I *was* to hook you up with a buyer? What's in it for me?"

Gardino debated. "Twenty-five percent."

"You give me fifty." Ricky fixed him with the famous mad-guy Kelleher stare. Gardino held the gaze just fine. Which Ricky respected.

"I'll give you twenty-five percent if the buyer pays a hun-dred Gs or less. Thirty, if it's more than that."

Ricky said, "Over one fifty, I want half."

Gardino finally said, "Deal. You really know somebody can get his hands on that kind of money?"

Ricky finished his beer and, without paying, started for the door. "That's what I'm going to go work on right now."

Ricky walked into Mack's bar.

It was pretty much like Hanrahan's, four blocks away, but was busier, since it was closer to the convention center where hundreds of teamsters and union electricians and carpenters would take fifteen-minute breaks that lasted two hours. The neighborhood surrounding Mack's was better too: redeveloped town houses and some new buildings, expensive as shit, and even a Starbucks. Way fucking different from the grim, hustling combat zone that Hell's Kitchen had been until the '70s.

T.G., a fat Irishman in his mid-thirties, was at the corner table with three, four buddies of his.

"It's the Lime Rickey man!" T.G. shouted, not drunk, not sober—the way he usually seemed. Man used nicknames a lot, which he seemed to think was cute but always pissed off the person he was talking to, mostly because of the way he said it, not so much the names themselves. Like, Ricky didn't even know what a Lime Rickey was, some drink or something, but the sneery tone in T.G.'s voice was a putdown. Still, you had to have major balls to say anything back to the big, psycho Irishman.

"Hey," Ricky offered, walking up to the corner table, which was like T.G.'s office.

"The fuck you been?" T.G. asked, dropping his cigarette on the floor and crushing it under his boot.

"Hanny's."

"Doing what, Lime Rickey man?" Stretching out the nickname.

"Polishing me knob," Ricky responded in a phoney

brogue. A lot of times he said stuff like this, sort of putting himself down in front of T.G. and his crew. He didn't want to, didn't like it. It just happened. Always wondered why.

"You mean, polishing some *altar boy's* knob," T.G. roared. The more sober in the crew laughed.

Ricky got a Guinness. He really didn't like it but T.G. had once said that Guinness and whiskey were the only things real men drank. And, since it was called stout, he figured it would make him fatter. All his life, trying to get bigger. Never succeeding.

Ricky sat down at the table, which was scarred with knife slashes and skid marks from cigarette burns. He nodded to T.G.'s crew, a half-dozen losers who sorta worked the trades, sorta worked the warehouses, sorta hung out. One was so drunk he couldn't focus and kept trying to tell a joke, forgetting it halfway through. Ricky hoped the guy wouldn't puke before he made it to the john, like yesterday.

T.G. was rambling on, insulting some of the people at the table in his cheerful-mean way and threatening guys who weren't there.

Ricky just sat at the table, eating peanuts and sucking down his licorice-flavored stout, and took the insults when they were aimed at him. Mostly he was thinking about Gardino and the boats.

T.G. rubbed his round, craggy face and his curly red-brown hair. He spat out, "And, fuck me, the nigger got away."

Ricky was wondering which nigger. He thought he'd been paying attention, but sometimes T.G.'s train of thought took its own route and left you behind.

He could see T.G. was upset, though, and so Ricky muttered a sympathetic, "That asshole."

"Man, I see him, I will take that cocksucker out so fast."

He clapped his palms together in a loud slap that made a couple of the crew blink. The drunk one stood up and staggered toward the men's room. Looked like he was going to make it this time.

"He been around?" Ricky asked.

T.G. snapped, "His black ass's up in Buffalo. I just told you that. The fuck you asking if he's here?"

"No, I don't mean here," Ricky said fast. "I mean, you know, *around.*"

"Oh, yeah," T.G. said, nodding, as if he caught some other meaning. "Sure. But that don't help me any. I see him, he's one dead nigger."

"Buffalo," Ricky said, shaking his head. "Christ." He tried to listen more carefully, but he was still thinking about the boat scam. Yeah, that Gardino'd come up with a good one. And man, making a hundred thousand in a single grift—he and T.G.'d never come close to that before.

Ricky shook his head again. He sighed. "Got half a mind to go to Buffalo and take his black ass out myself."

"You the man, Lime Rickey. You the fucking man." And T.G. started rambling once again.

Nodding, staring at T.G.'s not-drunk, not-sober eyes, Ricky was wondering: How much would it take to get the fuck out of Hell's Kitchen? Get away from the bitching ex-wives, the bratty kid, away from T.G. and all the asshole losers like him. Maybe go to Florida, where Gardino was from. Maybe that'd be the place for him. From the various scams he and T.G. put together, he'd saved up about thirty thousand in cash. Nothing shabby there. But man, if he conned just two or three guys in the boat deal, he could walk away with five times that.

Wouldn't set him for good, but it'd be a start. Hell,

Florida was full of rich old people, most of 'em stupid, just waiting to give their money to a player had the right grift.

A fist colliding with his arm shattered the daydream. He bit the inside of his cheek and winced. He glared at T.G., who just laughed. "So, Lime Rickey, you going to Leon's, ain't you? On Saturday."

"I don't know."

The door swung open and some out-of-towner wandered in. An older guy, in his fifties, dressed in beltless tan slacks, a white shirt, and a blue blazer, a cord around his neck holding a convention badge, AOFM, whatever that was.

Association of . . . Ricky squinted. Association of Obese Ferret Molesters.

He laughed at his own joke. Nobody noticed. Ricky eyed the tourist. This never used to happen, seeing geeks in a bar around here. But then the convention center went in a few blocks south and after that, Times Square got its balls cut off and turned into Disneyland. Suddenly Hell's Kitchen was White Plains and Paramus, and the fucking yuppies and tourists took over.

The man blinked, eyes getting used to the dark. He ordered wine—T.G. snickered, wine in this place?—and drank down half right away. The guy had to've had money. He was wearing a Rolex and his clothes were designer shit. The man looked around slowly, and it reminded Ricky of the way people at the zoo look at the animals. He got pissed and enjoyed a brief fantasy of dragging the guy's ass outside and pounding him till he gave up the watch and wallet.

But of course he wouldn't. T.G. and Ricky weren't that way; they steered clear of busting heads. Oh, a few times somebody got fucked up bad—they'd pounded a college kid when he'd taken a swing at T.G. during a scam, and Ricky'd slashed the face of some spic who'd skimmed a thousand bucks of their money. But the rule was, you didn't make people bleed if you could avoid it. If a mark lost only money, a lot of times he'd keep quiet about it, rather than go public and look like a fucking idiot. But if he got hurt, more times than not he'd go to the cops.

"You with me, Lime Rickey?" T.G. snapped. "You're off in your own fucking world."

"Just thinking."

"Ah, thinking. Good. He's thinking. 'Bout your altar bitch?"

Ricky mimicked jerking off. Putting himself down again. Wondered why he did that. He glanced at the tourist. The man was whispering to the bartender, who caught Ricky's eye and lifted his head. Ricky pushed back from T.G.'s table and walked to the bar, his boots making loud clonks on the wooden floor.

"Whassup?"

"This guy's from out of town."

The tourist looked at Ricky once, then down at the floor.

"No shit." Ricky rolled his eyes at the bartender.

"Iowa," the man said.

Where the fuck was Iowa? Ricky'd come close to finishing high school and had done okay in some subjects, but geography had bored him crazy and he never paid any attention in class.

The bartender said, "He was telling me he's in town for a conference at Javits."

Him and the ferret molesters . . .

"And . . ." the bartender's voice faded as he glanced at the tourist. "Well, why don't *you* tell him?"

The man took another gulp of his wine. Ricky looked at

his hand. Not only a Rolex, but a gold pinky ring with a big honking diamond in it.

"Yeah, why don't you tell me?"

The tourist did—in a halting whisper.

Ricky listened to his words. When the old guy was through, Ricky smiled and said, "This is your lucky day, mister."

Thinking: Mine too.

A half hour later, Ricky and the tourist from Iowa were standing in the grimy lobby of the Bradford Arms, next to a warehouse at Eleventh Avenue and 50th Street.

Ricky was making introductions. "This's Darla."

"Hello, Darla."

A gold tooth shone like a star out of Darla's big smile. "How you doing, honey? What's yo' name?"

"Uhm, Jack."

Ricky sensed he'd nearly made up "John" instead, which would've been pretty funny, under the circumstances.

"Nice to meet you, Jack." Darla, whose real name was Sha'quette Greeley, was six feet tall, beautiful, and built like a runway model. She'd also been a man until three years ago. The tourist from Iowa didn't catch on to this, or maybe he did and it turned him on. Anyway, his gaze was lapping her body like a tongue.

Jack checked them in, paying for three hours in advance.

Three hours? thought Ricky. An old fart like this? God bless him.

"Y'all have fun now," Ricky said, falling into a redneck accent. He'd decided that Iowa was probably somewhere in the south.

Detective Robert Schaeffer could've been the host on one of

those FOX or A&E cop shows. He was tall, silver-haired, good-looking, maybe a bit long in the face. He'd been an NYPD detective for nearly twenty years.

Schaeffer and his partner were walking down a filthy hallway that stank of sweat and Lysol. The partner pointed to a door, whispering, "That's it." He pulled out what looked like an electronic stethoscope and placed the sensor over the scabby wood.

"Hear anything?" Schaeffer asked, also in a soft voice.

Joey Bernbaum, the partner, nodded slowly, holding up a finger. Meaning wait.

And then a nod. "Go."

Schaeffer pulled a master key out of his pocket, and drawing his gun, unlocked the door then pushed inside.

"Police! Nobody move!"

Bernbaum followed, his own automatic in hand.

The faces of the two people inside registered identical expressions of shock at the abrupt entry, though it was only in the face of the pudgy middle-aged white man, sitting shirt-less on the bed, that the shock turned instantly to horror and dismay. He had a Marine Corps tattoo on his fat upper arm and had probably been pretty tough in his day, but now his narrow, pale shoulders slumped and he looked like he was going to cry. "No, no, no . . ."

"Oh, fuck," Darla said.

"Stay right where you are, sweetheart. Be quiet."

"How the fuck you find me? That little prick downstairs at the desk, he dime me? I know it. I'ma pee on that boy next time I see him. I'ma—"

"You're not going to do anything but shut up," Bernbaum snapped. In a ghetto accent he added a sarcastic, "Yo, got that, girlfriend?"

"Man oh man." Darla tried to wither him with a gaze. He just laughed and cuffed her.

Schaeffer put his gun away and said to the man, "Let me see some ID."

"Oh, please, officer, look, I didn't—"

"Some ID?" Schaeffer said. He was polite, like always. When you had a badge in your pocket and a big fucking pistol on your hip you could afford to be civil.

The man dug his thick wallet out of his slacks and handed it to the officer, who read the license. "Mr. Shelby, this your current address? In Des Moines?"

In a quivering voice, he said, "Yessir."

"All right, well, you're under arrest for solicitation of prostitution." He took his cuffs out of their holder.

"I didn't do anything illegal, really. It was just . . . It was only a date."

"Really? Then what's this?" The detective picked up a stack of money sitting on the cockeyed nightstand. Four hundred bucks.

"I—I just thought . . ."

The old guy's mind was working fast, that was obvious. Schaeffer wondered what excuse he'd come up with. He'd heard them all.

"Just to get some food and something to drink."

That was a new one. Schaeffer tried not to laugh. You spend four hundred bucks on food and booze in this neighborhood, you could afford a block party big enough for fifty Darlas.

"He pay you to have sex?" Schaeffer asked Darla.

She grimaced.

"You lie, baby, you know what'll happen to you. You're honest with me, I'll put in a word."

"You a prick too," she snapped. "All right, he pay me to do a round-the-world."

"No . . ." Shelby protested for a moment but then he gave up and slumped even lower. "Oh, Christ, what'm I gonna do? This'll kill my wife . . . and my kids . . ." He looked up with panicked eyes. "Will I have to go to jail?"

"That's up to the prosecutor and the judge."

"Why the hell'd I do this?" he moaned.

Schaeffer looked him over carefully. After a long moment he said, "Take her downstairs."

Darla snapped, "Yo, you fat fuck, keep yo' motherfuckin' hands offa me."

Bernbaum laughed again. "This mean you ain't my girl-friend no more?" He gripped her by the arm and led her outside. The door swung shut.

"Look, detective, it's not like I robbed anybody. It was harmless. You know, victimless."

"It's still a crime. And don't you know about AIDS, hepatitis?"

Shelby looked down again. He nodded. "Yessir," he whispered.

Still holding the cuffs, Schaeffer eyed the man carefully. He sat down on a creaky chair. "How often you get to town?"

"To New York?"

"Yeah."

"Once a year, if I've got a conference or meeting. I always enjoy it. You know what they say, 'It's a nice place to visit.'" His voice faded, maybe thinking that the rest of that old saw—"but you wouldn't want to live there"—would insult the cop.

Schaeffer asked, "So, you got a conference now?" He pulled the badge out of the man's pocket, read it.

"Yessir, it's our annual trade show. At the Javits. Outdoor furniture manufacturers."

"That's your line?"

"I have a wholesale business in Iowa."

"Yeah? Successful?"

"Number one in the state. Actually, in the whole region." He said this sadly, not proudly, probably thinking of how many customers he'd lose when word got out about his arrest.

Schaeffer nodded slowly. Finally he put the handcuffs away.

Shelby's eyes narrowed, watching this.

"You ever done anything like this before?"

A hesitation. He decided not to lie. "I have. Yessir."

"But I get a feeling you're not going to again."

"Never. I promise you. I've learned my lesson."

There was a long pause.

"Stand up."

Shelby blinked then did what he was told. He frowned as the cop patted down his trousers and jacket. With the guy not wearing a shirt, Schaeffer was ninety-nine percent sure the man was legit, but had to make absolutely certain there were no wires.

The detective nodded toward the chair and Shelby sat down. The businessman's eyes revealed that he now had an inkling of what was happening.

"I have a proposition for you," Schaeffer said.

"Proposition?"

The cop nodded. "Okay. I'm convinced you're not going to do this again."

"Never."

"I could let you go with a warning. But the problem is, the situation got called in."

"Called in?"

"A vice cop on the street happened to see you go into the hotel with Darla—we know all about her. He reported it and they sent me out. There's paperwork on the incident."

"My name?"

"No, just a John Doe at this point. But there *is* a report. I could make it go away but it'd take some work and it'd be a risk."

Shelby sighed, nodding with a grimace, and opened the bidding.

It wasn't much of an auction. Shelby kept throwing out numbers and Schaeffer kept lifting his thumb, more, more . . . Finally, when the shaken man hit $150,000, Schaeffer nodded.

"Christ."

When T.G. and Ricky Kelleher had called to say that he'd found a tourist to scam, Ricky told him the mark could go six figures. That was so far out of those stupid micks' league that Schaeffer had to laugh. But sure enough, he had to give the punk credit for picking out a mark with big bucks.

In a defeated voice Shelby asked, "Can I give you a check?"

Schaeffer laughed.

"Okay, okay . . . but I'll need a few hours."

"Tonight. Eight." They arranged a place to meet. "I'll keep your driver's license. And the evidence." He picked up the cash on the table. "You try to skip, I'll put out an arrest warrant and send that to Des Moines too. They'll extradite you and *then* it'll be a serious felony. You'll do real time."

"Oh, no, sir. I'll get the money. Every penny." Shelby hurriedly dressed.

"Go out by the service door in back. I don't know where the vice cop is."

The tourist nodded and scurried out of the room.

In the lobby by the elevator the detective found Bernbaum and Darla sharing a smoke.

"Where my money?" the hooker demanded.

Schaeffer handed her two hundred of the confiscated cash. He and Bernbaum split the rest, a hundred fifty for Schaeffer, fifty for his partner.

"You gonna take the afternoon off, girlfriend?" Bernbaum asked Darla.

"Me? Hell no, I gots to work." She glanced at the money Schaeffer'd given her. "Least till you assholes start paying me fo' not fuckin' same as I make *fo'* fuckin'."

Schaeffer pushed into Mack's bar, an abrupt entrance that changed the course of at least half the conversations going on inside real fast. He was a crooked cop, sure, but he was still a cop, and the talk immediately shifted from deals, scams, and drugs to sports, women, and jobs. Schaeffer laughed and strode across the room. He dropped into an empty chair at the scarred table, muttered to T.G., "Get me a beer." Schaeffer being about the only one in the universe who could get away with that.

When the brew came he tipped the glass to Ricky. "You caught us a good one. He agreed to a hundred fifty."

"No shit," T.G. said, cocking a red eyebrow. The split was Schaeffer got half and then Ricky and T.G. divided the rest equally. "Where's he getting it from?"

"I dunno. His problem."

Ricky squinted. "Wait. I want the watch too."

"Watch?"

"The old guy. He had a Rolex. I want it."

At home Schaeffer had a dozen Rolexes he'd taken off

marks and suspects over the years. He didn't need another one. "You want the watch, he'll give up the watch. All he cares about is making sure his wife and his corn-pone customers don't find out what he was up to."

"What's corn-pone?" Ricky asked.

"Hold on," T.G. snarled. "Anybody gets the watch, it's me."

"No way. I saw it first. It was me who picked him—"

"My watch," the fat Irishman interrupted. "Maybe he's got a money clip or something you can have. But I get the fucking Rolex."

"Nobody has money clips," Ricky argued. "I don't even want a fucking money clip."

"Listen, little Lime Rickey," T.G. muttered. "It's mine. Read my lips."

"Jesus, you two are like kids," Schaeffer said, swilling the beer. "He'll meet us across the street from Pier 46 at 8 tonight." The three men had done this same scam, or variations on it, for a couple of years now but still didn't trust each other. The deal was they all went together to collect the payoff.

Schaeffer drained the beer. "See you boys then."

After the detective was gone they watched the game for a few minutes, with T.G. bullying some guys to place bets, even though it was in the fourth quarter and there was no way Chicago could come back. Finally, Ricky said, "I'm going out for a while."

"What, now I'm your fucking babysitter? You want to go, go." Though he still made it sound like Ricky was a complete idiot for missing the end of game that only had eight minutes to run.

Just as Ricky got to the door, T.G. called in a loud voice, "Hey, Lime Rickey, my Rolex? Is it gold?"

Just to be a prick.

* * *

Bob Schaeffer had walked a beat in his youth. He'd investigated a hundred felonies, he'd run a thousand scams in Manhattan and Brooklyn. All of which meant that he'd learned how to stay alive on the streets.

Now, he sensed a threat.

He was on his way to score some coke from a kid who operated out of a newsstand at Ninth and 55th, and he realized he'd been hearing the same footsteps for the past five or six minutes. A weird scraping. Somebody was tailing him. He paused to light a cigarette in a doorway and checked out the reflection in a storefront window. Sure enough, he saw a man in a cheap gray suit, wearing gloves, about thirty feet behind him. The guy paused for a moment and pretended to look into a store window.

Schaeffer didn't recognize the guy. He'd made a lot of enemies over the years. The fact he was a cop gave him some protection—it's risky to gun down even a crooked one—but there were plenty of nuts jobs out there.

Walking on. The owner of the scraping shoes continued his tail. A glance in the rearview mirror of a car parked nearby told him the man was getting closer, but his hands were at his side, not going for a weapon. Schaeffer pulled out his cell phone and pretended to make a call, to give himself an excuse to slow up and not make the guy suspicious. His other hand slipped inside his jacket and touched the grip of his chrome-plated Sig Sauer 9mm automatic pistol.

This time the guy didn't slow up.

Schaeffer started to draw.

Then: "Detective, could you hang up the phone, please?"

Schaeffer turned, blinked. The pursuer was holding up a gold NYPD shield.

The fuck is this? Schaeffer thought. He relaxed, but not much. Snapped the phone closed and dropped it into his pocket. Let go of his weapon.

"Who're you?"

The man, eyeing Schaeffer coldly, let him get a look at the ID card next to the shield.

Schaeffer thought: Fuck me. The guy was from the department's Internal Affairs Division—the boys that tracked down corrupt cops.

Still Schaeffer kept on the offensive. "What're you doing following me?"

"I'd like to ask you a few questions."

"What's this all about?"

"An investigation we're conducting."

"Hello," Schaeffer said sarcastically. "I sort of figured that out. Give me some fucking details."

"We're looking into your connection with certain individuals."

"'Certain individuals.' You know, not all cops have to talk like cops."

No response.

Schaeffer shrugged. "I have 'connections' with a lotta people. Maybe you're thinking of my snitches. I hang with 'em. They feed me good information."

"Yeah, well, we're thinking there might be other things they feed you. Some *valuable* things." He glanced at Schaeffer's hip. "I'm going to ask you for your weapon."

"Fuck that."

"I'm trying to keep it low key. But you don't cooperate, I'll call it in and we'll take you downtown. Then everything'll all be public."

Finally Schaeffer understood. It was a shakedown—only

this time he was on the receiving end. And he was getting scammed by Internal Affairs, no less. This was almost fucking funny, IAD on the take too.

Schaeffer gave up his gun.

"Let's go talk in private."

How much was this going to cost him? he wondered.

The IAD cop nodded toward the Hudson River. "That way."

"Talk to me," Schaeffer said. "I got a right to know what this's all about. If somebody told you I'm on the take, that's bullshit. Whoever said it's working some angle." He wasn't as hot as he sounded; this was all part of the negotiating.

The IAD cop said only, "Keep walking. Up there." He pulled out a cigarette and lit it. Offered one to Schaeffer. He took it and the guy lit it for him.

Then Schaeffer froze. He blinked in shock, staring at the matches. The name on them was *McDougall's Tavern*. The official name of Mack's—T.G.'s hangout. He glanced at the guy's eyes, which went wide at his mistake. Christ, he was no cop. The ID and badge were fake. He was a hit man, working for T.G., who was going to clip him and collect the whole hundred fifty Gs from the tourist.

"Fuck," the phony cop muttered. He yanked a revolver out of his pocket, then shoved Schaeffer into a nearby alley.

"Listen, buddy," Schaeffer whispered, "I've got some good bucks. Whatever you're being paid, I'll—"

"Shut up." In his gloved hands, the guy exchanged his gun for Schaeffer's own pistol and pushed the big chrome piece into the detective's neck. Then the fake cop pulled a piece of paper out of his pocket and stuffed it into the detective's jacket. He leaned forward and whispered, "Here's the message, asshole: For two years T.G.'s been setting up everything, doing all the work, and you take half the money. You've fucked with the wrong man."

"That's bullshit," Schaeffer cried desperately. "He needs me! He couldn't do it without a cop! Please—"

"So long—" He lifted the gun to Schaeffer's temple.

"Don't do it! Please, man, no!"

A scream sounded from the mouth of the alley. "Oh my god!" A middle-aged woman stood twenty feet away, staring at the man with the pistol. Her hands were to her mouth. "Somebody call the police!"

The hit man's attention was on the woman. Schaeffer shoved him into a brick wall. Before he could recover and shoot, the detective sprinted fast down the alley.

He heard the man shout, "Goddamn it!" and start after him. But Hell's Kitchen was Bob Schaeffer's hunting grounds, and in five minutes the detective had raced through dozens of alleys and side streets and lost the killer.

Once again on the street, he paused and pulled his back-up gun out of his ankle holster, slipped it into his pocket. He felt the crinkle of paper—what the guy had planted on him. It was a fake suicide note, Schaeffer confessing that he'd been on the take for years and he couldn't handle the guilt anymore. He had to end it all.

Well, he thought, that was partly right.

One thing was fucking well about to end.

Smoking, staying in the shadows of an alley, Schaeffer had to wait outside Mack's for fifteen minutes before T.G. Reilly emerged. The big man, moving like a lumbering bear, was by himself. He looked around, not seeing the cop, and turned west.

Schaeffer gave him half a block and then followed.

He kept his distance, but when the street was deserted he pulled on gloves and fished into his pocket for the pistol he'd just gotten from his desk. He'd bought it on the street years ago—a cold gun, one with no registration number stamped on the frame. Gripping the weapon, he moved up fast behind the big Irishman.

The mistake a lot of shooters make during a clip is they feel they've gotta talk to their vic. Schaeffer remembered some old Western where this kid tracks down the gunslinger who killed his father. The kid's holding a gun on him and explaining why he's about to die, you killed my father, yadda, yadda, yadda, and the gunslinger gets this bored look on his face, pulls out a hidden gun, and blows the kid away. He looks down at the body and says, "You gonna talk, talk. You gonna shoot, shoot."

Which is just what Robert Schaeffer did now.

T.G. must've heard something. He started to turn. But before he even caught sight of the detective, Schaeffer parked two rounds in the back of the fat man's head. He dropped like a bag of sand. The cop tossed the gun on the sidewalk—he'd never touched it with his bare hands—and, keeping his head down, walked right past T.G.'s body, hit Tenth Avenue, and turned north.

You gonna shoot, shoot.

Amen . . .

It took only one glance.

Looking into Ricky Kelleher's eyes, Schaeffer decided he wasn't in on the attempted hit.

The small goofy guy, with dirty hair and a cocky face, strode up to the spot where Schaeffer was leaning against a wall, hand inside his coat, near his new automatic. But the loser didn't blink, didn't show the least surprise that the cop was still alive. The detective had interviewed suspects for years and he now concluded that the asshole knew nothing about T.G.'s plan.

Ricky nodded, "Hey." Looking around, asked, "So where's T.G.? He said he'd be here early."

Frowning, Schaeffer asked, "Didn't you hear?"

"Hear what?"

"Damn, you didn't. Somebody clipped him."

"T.G.?"

"Yep."

Ricky just stared and shook his head. "No fucking way. I didn't hear shit about it."

"Just happened."

"Christ almighty," the little man whispered. "Who did it?"

"Nobody knows yet."

"Maybe that nigger."

"Who?"

"Nigger from Buffalo. Or Albany. I don't know." Ricky then whispered, "Dead. I can't believe it. Anybody else in the crew?"

"Just him, I think."

Schaeffer studied the scrawny guy. Well, yeah, he *did* look like he couldn't believe it. But, truth was, he didn't look *upset*. Which made sense. T.G. was hardly Ricky's buddy; he was a drunk loser bully.

Besides, in Hell's Kitchen the living tended to forget about the dead before their bodies were cold.

Like he was proving this point, Ricky said, "So how's this going to affect our, you know, arrangement?"

"Not at all, far as I'm concerned."

"I'm going to want more."

"I can go a third."

"Fuck a third. I want half."

"No can do. It's riskier for me now."

"Riskier? Why?"

"There'll be an investigation. Somebody might turn up something at T.G.'s with my name on it. I'll have to grease more palms." Schaeffer shrugged. "Or you can find yourself another cop to work with."

As if the Yellow Pages had a section, "*Cops, Corrupt.*"

The detective added, "Give it a few months. After things calm down, I can go up a few more points then."

"To forty?"

"Yeah, to forty."

The little man asked, "Can I have the Rolex?"

"The guy's? Tonight?"

"Yeah."

"You really want it?"

"Yeah."

"Okay, it's yours."

Ricky looked out over the river. It seemed to Schaeffer that a faint smile crossed his face.

They stood in silence for a few minutes and, right on time, the tourist, Shelby, showed up. He was looking terrified and hurt and angry, which is a fucking tricky combination to get into your face all at one time.

"I've got it," he whispered. There was nothing in his hands—no briefcase or bag—but Schaeffer had been taking kickbacks and bribes for so long that he knew a lot of money can fit into a very small envelope.

Which is just what Shelby now produced. The grim-faced tourist slipped it to Schaeffer, who counted the bills carefully.

"The watch too." Ricky pointed eagerly to the man's wrist.

"My watch?" Shelby hesitated and, grimacing, handed it to the skinny man.

Schaeffer gave the tourist his driver's license back. He pocketed it fast then hurried east, undoubtedly looking for a taxi that'd take him straight to the airport.

The detective laughed to himself. So, maybe New York ain't such a nice place to visit, after all.

The men split the money. Ricky slipped the Rolex on his wrist but the metal band was too big and it dangled comically. "I'll get it adjusted," he said, putting the watch into his pocket. "They can shorten the bands, you know. It's no big deal."

They decided to have a drink to celebrate and Ricky suggested Hanny's since he had to meet somebody over there.

As they walked along the avenue, blue-gray in the evening light, Ricky glanced at the placid Hudson River. "Check it out."

A large yacht eased south in the dark water.

"Sweet," Schaeffer said, admiring the beautiful lines of the vessel.

Ricky asked, "How come you didn't want in?"

"In?"

"The boat deal."

"Huh?"

"That T.G. told you about. He said you were going to pass."

"What the fuck're you talking about?"

"The boat thing. With that guy from Florida."

"He never said anything to me about it."

"That prick." Ricky shook his head. "Was a few days ago.

This guy hangs at Hanny's? He's who I'm gonna meet. He's got connections down in Florida. His crew perps these confiscated boats before they get logged in at the impound dock."

"DEA?"

"Yeah. And Coast Guard."

Schaeffer nodded, impressed at the plan. "They disappear *before* they're logged. That's some smart shit."

"I'm thinking about getting one. He tells me I pay him, like, twenty Gs and I end up with a boat worth three times that. I thought you'd be interested."

"Yeah, I'd be interested." Bob Schaeffer had a couple of small boats. Had always wanted a really nice one. He asked, "He got anything bigger?"

"Think he just sold a fifty-footer. I seen it down in Battery Park. It was sweet."

"Fifty feet? That's a million-dollar boat."

"He said it only cost his guy two hundred or something like that."

"Jesus. That asshole, T.G. He never said a word to me." Schaeffer at least felt some consolation that the punk wouldn't be saying *anything* to *anyone* from now on.

They walked into Hanrahan's. Like usual, the place was nearly deserted. Ricky was looking around. The boat guy apparently wasn't here yet.

They ordered boiler makers. Clinked glasses, drank.

Ricky was telling the old bartender about T.G. getting killed, when Schaeffer's cell phone rang.

"Schaeffer here."

"This's Malone from Homicide. You heard about the T.G. Reilly hit?"

"Yeah. What's up with it? Any leads." Heart pounding

fast, Schaeffer lowered his head and listened real carefully.

"Not many. But we heard something and we're hoping you can help us out. You know the neighborhood, right?"

"Pretty good."

"Looks like one of T.G.'s boys was running a scam. Involved some tall paper. Six figures. We don't know if it had anything to do with the clip, but we want to talk to him. Name of Ricky Kelleher. You know him?"

Schaeffer glanced at Ricky, five feet away. He said into the phone, "Not sure. What's the scam?"

"This Kelleher was working with somebody from Florida. They came up with a pretty slick plan. They sell some loser a confiscated boat, only what happens is, there is no boat. It's all a setup. Then when it's time to deliver, they tell the poor asshole that the feds just raided 'em. He better forget about his money, shut up, and go to ground."

That little fucking prick . . . Schaeffer's hand began shaking with anger as he stared at Ricky. He told the Homicide cop, "Haven't seen him for a while. But I'll ask around."

"Thanks."

He disconnected and walked up to Ricky, who was working on his second beer.

"You know when that guy's going to get here?" Schaeffer asked casually. "The boat guy?"

"Should be any time," the punk said.

Schaeffer nodded, drank some of his own beer. Then he lowered his head, whispered, "That call I just got? Don't know if you're interested but it was my supplier. He just got a shipment from Mexico. He's gonna meet me in the alley in a few minutes. It's some really fine shit. He'll give it to us for cost. You interested?"

"Fuck yes," the little man said.

The men pushed out the back door into the alley. Letting Ricky precede him, Schaeffer reminded himself that after he'd strangled the punk to death, he'd have to be sure to take the rest of the bribe money out of his pocket.

Oh, and the watch too. The detective decided that you really couldn't have too many Rolexes after all.

Detective Robert Schaeffer was enjoying a grande mocha outside the Starbucks on Ninth Avenue. He was sitting in a metal chair, none too comfortable, and he wondered if it was the type that outdoor furniture king Shelby distributed to his fellow hicks.

"Hey there," a man's voice said to him.

Schaeffer glanced over at a guy sitting down at the table next to him. He was vaguely familiar and even though the cop didn't exactly recognize him, he smiled a greeting.

Then the realization hit him like ice water and he gasped. It was the fake Internal Affairs detective, the guy T.G. had hired to clip him.

Christ!

The man's right hand was inside a paper bag, where there'd be a pistol, of course.

Schaeffer froze.

"Relax," the guy said, laughing at the cop's expression. "Everything's cool." He extracted his hand from the bag. No gun. He was holding a raisin scone. He took a bite. "I'm not who you think I am."

"Then who the fuck are you?"

"You don't need my name. I'm a private eye. That'll do. Now listen, we've got a business proposition for you." The PI looked up and waved. To Schaeffer he said, "I want to introduce you to some folks."

A middle-aged couple, also carrying coffee, walked outside. In shock, Schaeffer realized that the man was Shelby, the tourist they'd scammed a few days ago. The woman with him seemed familiar too. But he couldn't place her.

"Detective," the man said with a cold smile.

The woman's gaze was chill too, but no smile was involved.

"Whatta you want?" the cop snapped to the private eye.

"I'll let them explain that." He took a large bite of scone.

Shelby's eyes locked onto Schaeffer's face with a ballsy confidence that was a lot different from the timid, defeated look he'd had in the cheap hotel, sitting next to Darla, the used-to-be-a-guy hooker. "Detective, here's the deal: A few months ago my son was on vacation here with some friends from college. He was dancing in a club near Broadway and your associates T.G. Reilly and Ricky Kelleher slipped some drugs into his pocket. Then you came in and busted him for possession. Just like with me, you set him up and told him you'd let him go if he paid you off. Only Michael decided you weren't going to get away with it. He took a swing at you and was going to call 911. But you and T.G. Reilly dragged him into the alley and beat him so badly he's got permanent brain damage and is going to be in therapy for years."

Schaeffer remembered the college kid, yeah. It'd been a bad beating. But he said, "I don't know what you're—"

"Shhhhh," the private eye said. "The Shelbys hired me to find out what happened to their son. I've spent two months in Hell's Kitchen, learning everything there is to know about you and those two pricks you worked with." A nod toward the tourist. "Back to you." The PI ate some more scone.

The husband said, "We decided you were going to pay for what you did. Only we couldn't go to the police—who knew how many of them were working with you? So my wife and I and our other son—Michael's brother—came up with an idea. We decided to let you assholes do the work for us; you were going to double-cross each other."

"This is bullshit. You—"

The woman snapped, "Shut up and listen." She explained: They set up a sting in Hanny's bar. The private eye pretended to be a scam artist from Florida selling stolen boats and their older son played a young guy from Jersey who'd been duped out of his money. This got Ricky's attention, and he talked his way into the phony boat scam. Staring at Schaeffer, she said, "We knew you liked boats, so it made sense that Ricky'd try to set you up."

The husband added, "Only we needed some serious cash on the table, a bunch of it—to give you losers some real incentive to betray each other."

So he went to T.G.'s hangout and asked about a hooker, figuring that the three of them would set up an extortion scam.

He chuckled. "I kept *hoping* you'd keep raising the bidding when you were blackmailing me. I wanted at least six figures in the pot."

T.G. was their first target. That afternoon the private eye pretended to be a hit man hired by T.G. to kill Schaeffer so he'd get all the money.

"You!" the detective whispered, staring at the wife. "You're the woman who screamed."

Shelby said, "We needed to give you the chance to escape—so you'd go straight to T.G.'s place and take care of him."

Oh lord. The hit, the fake Internal Affairs cop . . . It was all a setup!

"Then Ricky took you to Hanrahan's, where he was going to introduce you to the boat dealer from Florida."

The private eye wiped his mouth and leaned froward. "*Hello*," he said in a deeper voice. "*This's Malone from Homicide.*"

"Oh fuck," Schaeffer spat out. "You let me know that Ricky'd set me up. So . . ." His voicc faded.

The PI whispered, "You'd take care of him too."

The cold smile on his face again, Shelby said, "Two perps down. Now we just have the last one. You."

"What're you going to do?" the cop whispered.

The wife said, "Our son's got to have years of therapy. He'll never recover completely."

Schaeffer shook his head. "You've got evidence, right?"

"Oh, you bet. Our older son was outside of Mack's waiting for you when you went there to get T.G. We've got real nice footage of you shooting him. Two in the head. Real nasty."

"And the sequel," the private eye said. "In the alley behind Hanrahan's. Where you strangled Ricky." He added, "Oh, and we've got the license number of the truck that came to get Ricky's body in the dumpster. We followed it to Jersey. We can implicate a bunch of very unpleasant people, who aren't going to be happy they've been fingered because of you."

"And, in case you haven't guessed," Shelby said, "we made three copies of the tape and they're sitting in three different lawyers' office safes. Anything happens to any one of us, and off they go to Police Plaza."

"You're as good as murderers yourself," Schaeffer muttered. "You used me to kill two people."

Shelby laughed. "*Semper Fi* . . . I'm a former Marine and

I've been in two wars. Killing vermin like you doesn't bother me one bit."

"All right," the cop said in a disgusted grumble, "what do you want?"

"You've got the vacation house on Fire Island, you've got two boats moored in Oyster Bay, you've got—"

"I don't need a fucking inventory. I need a number."

"Basically your entire net worth. Eight hundred sixty thousand dollars. Plus my hundred fifty back . . . And I want it in the next week. Oh, and you pay his bill too." Shelby nodded toward the private eye.

"I'm good," the man said. "But very expensive." He finished the scone and brushed the crumbs onto the sidewalk.

Shelby leaned forward. "One more thing: my watch."

Schaeffer stripped off the Rolex and tossed it to Shelby.

The couple rose. "So long, detective," the tourist said.

"Love to stay and talk," Mrs. Shelby added, "but we're going to see some sights. And then we're going for a carriage ride in Central Park before dinner." She paused and looked down at the cop. "I just love it here. It's true what they say, you know. New York really *is* a nice place to visit."

THE NEXT BEST THING

BY JIM FUSILLI

George Washington Bridge

He was a nasty bastard and everybody knew it, but she fell for him anyway. He had blue, blue eyes and he knew how to take his time and, of course, she loved the way he played piano. She thought everybody loved the way he played piano.

She didn't know he'd been run out of Kansas City and that he worked in Jersey because he couldn't cut it on 52nd Street, up at Minton's or at the Café Bohemia in the Village. One time, she followed him to Broadway, knowing Bud Powell was playing Birdland, and she cozied up to him at the bar between sets and slid her hand onto his broad shoulder. He turned hard, his face going blank with a pure, powerful rage. Taking it simple, figuring he didn't want her catching him doing something or hearing something he didn't want her to know, she slid off the stool, pushed through the chattering crowd and walked back downtown, and she never asked why. She was learning it was better to let him be.

They were in Hell's Kitchen, and she wore a slip, and his scent surrounded her like mist, and one evening she said, "Maxie, do you ever—"

"No," he said as he brushed his shoes. Maxie put on his shoes before his trousers, and she liked that too.

Later, he slipped the straight razor into its leather sheath, dusted his face and neck with Pinaud talc, and headed out to

Port Authority for the 8:05 bus to Fort Lee. Three sets at the Continental Lounge for six bucks a night and whatever ended up in the brandy snifter. He would've done better in tips if he wasn't such a nasty bastard. He had those blue, blue eyes.

Maxie had his shot, but it didn't take, and soon he was just another guy with his hat in his hand.

He wasn't going to get a gig in New York City. He knew that before he caught the train. His old man called it from the day Maxie was born. A gristled rail, an Okie to his soul, he used to sit by the Franklin stove, wind whistling through the shack, and as firelight danced on his sorrowful face, he'd say, "Man was born to fail, son. There ain't no way around that."

Thumbing, he made his way to Missouri, thinking it'd be all right. But Bird told him kindly he couldn't play, so he hustled and found work with the Benny Walters band, passing through K.C., their pianist coming down with shingles. But soon every musician and big-time booking agent was hearing how Maxie had taken off Bippy Brown's left ear with a .22. Bippy had a mouth on him, but it was Maxie who got the gate, Benny bouncing him in a diner outside Chickasha. Maxie could've walked home.

He'd arrived at Pennsylvania Station with thirty-eight cents in his pocket, figuring if he was going to fail, he'd make it look like he failed at the top.

Big, big city, he thought, as he stepped into the sun, catching a breeze from the IND running below. Buzz buzz buzz, and he looked up at the Empire State, and then at the Western Union Telegraph building in the distance. Yeah, a real metropolis, he thought, as he spit through his teeth onto

Eighth Avenue. They got a bank on every corner.

A merciless winter and he caught a cold, and she made him hot lemonade and brought a therapeutic lamp to his two-room flat.

By then, he was set at the Continental, and she thought he'd hung the moon.

He'd sleep until 11 and walk until supper, and sometimes she'd eat with him. He liked the steam-table dives, so she said she did too.

He was the first man she knew who didn't babble about her red hair or the birthmark under her left breast. He hadn't hit her, at least not yet, and somebody taught him to keep himself neat, and that was new too. She thought there might be more to him, even after the lanky Mexican woman from downstairs started dropping in, leading with sympathy when she'd asked for none.

At night, she'd go up to the Gaiety for a rye and ginger ale, killing time before he returned from Jersey, and pretty soon the stories, all with the ring of truth. Maxie lifted a gold-plated lighter from the bouncer at the Onyx, Maxie took a sap to the doorman at the Stuyvesant Casino, Maxie tore up a joint on the Bowery over a ten-cent pig's feet-and-potato dish.

The black-eyed Mexican beauty said Maxie was itching to get himself killed.

"Honey," Maria said, "this man hate himself. You can no love somebody who hate himself."

She ran her fingers through Mitzi's red hair, called her Margarita.

Slumped on the divan, Mitzi listened, listened, and she rested her head against Maria's hip.

She's right, she thought. Ain't it always the way?

Maria kissed the top of her hair, traced her ear with her thumb.

Mitzi heard Maria singing through the floorboard. Always something sweet, proud, and tragic. Always in Spanish.

Soon, they were spending afternoons in Maxie's bed, Maria toying with the tufts of hair below Mitzi's baby paunch, Maria exploring; the two of them soaking through the sheets. Mitzi arching her back, tingling like her soul was being stroked, smiling as she wiped away warm tears, as she met soothing kisses from Maria's salty lips.

Later, after barefoot Maria slipped away, Mitzi quickly washed her face, washed under her arms, brushed her teeth with his Ipana powder. She sprinkled Pinaud talc on the pillows and opened the windows wide.

The rubes under the George Washington Bridge didn't know a damned thing about much, most of all music, so he gave them some Van Heusen Sinatra brought to life. The rest of the time he riffed on the chords to "I Got Rhythm" and the I-IV-V blues Jay McShann showed him, figuring that right there covered most modern jazz.

When they applauded, he saw chimps, the kind they teach to roller-skate, to wear a fez and smoke a cigar.

He let his mind drift when he played, and he was back in K.C. with all that dough, telling them how he made it at the Three Deuces, up at Small's Paradise, stared down the shadow of the great Tatum, knocked Al Haig on his ass.

He'd already decided it was going to be one of those banks, all marble, cathedral ceilings, gold-leaf lettering on the windows, pens on chains.

Payday, early, before they came by to cash their checks,

while the vault still swelled with dough. And a crowd on the street so the weary ex-cop drowsing amid all that marble and all that money don't come out blazing.

Every day he walked until supper, and in time he scoured the city.

And he found it: the North River Savings Bank, a block west of Macy's and Gimbel's, maybe a thousand people working between the two. The bank had a piano in the lobby, some heeb with glasses murdering Richard Rodgers.

Maxie followed the little guy home.

A stretch of cord flung like he was roping a calf. Stomped him into shock, his wrists wrecked, elbows all but ground to dust.

He quit the Continental, calling from a booth in the bank's lobby.

Maria was looking to borrow the iron, and she knew Maxie was gone, hearing his brood steps on the stairs.

She let herself in, and she found Mitzi hunched over the bed, angrily cramming clothes into a cardboard suitcase. Crying like she should've known better.

"Margarita?" Maria said, shutting the door. "Mi *amor*, what?"

"No, no . . ."

Maria turned her, wrapped her arms around her, waited until she lifted her chin.

"What? What did he do?"

"He—oh Maria, he—"

A man at the bank, a vice president, a sucker for redheads, always was. Liked a good time, and didn't mind laying out for quality. Winked at Maxie when he said he liked to come and go, and Maxie winked when he passed it on.

"A vice president . . ." Maria thought about it. "That son of a bitch."

Mitzi whimpered.

Maria never liked him. A musician who didn't have records and didn't play the radio, not even to study, did not love music and did not have pride for his own gifts.

Going after the money: it's what they did when they knew their talent fell short.

"You are nobody's whore," Maria said, as she kissed her tears.

Not for a good long while, Mitzi thought. Not since Maxie.

Maria nudged her toward the divan.

Mitzi, one, two, three steps and everything moving under red rayon.

"You go no place," Maria began, kneeling now. "Here is you home."

She murdered English, but she was damned smart and she saw it in Technicolor. Jazzman takes a gig in a bank, cozies up to a vice president, maybe the one with the key to the vault, the combination. Mr. Moneybags.

"This vice president. He is a married man?"

Mitzi wiped her nose on the back of her hand. "I guess. Maxie says he's got a pencil mustache."

Maria looked into her hazel eyes, gave her nipple a playful twist. "It's the woman's curse. To fall for the stupid man."

"Oh Maria," she moaned, "ain't I ever going to learn?"

"I tell you, *chica*. Leave everything to me."

Mitzi leaned back, stared at the tin ceiling. She expected Maria's hand on her thigh, thinking what a man might do, claiming his reward.

Instead, Maria stood, went for the bottle of rye in the kitchenette, the Hoffman's ginger ale on the window sill.

Mitzi opened her eyes. "Maria . . . ?"

"Margarita," she said, "I tell you: Leave everything to me."

He started showing up a half hour before the bank opened, and the tellers liked his serenade almost as much as his blue, blue eyes, and he brought black coffee for Puckett, knowing the ex-cop made him for the nasty bastard he'd become.

Puckett had to piss before he took a second sip.

"You holding out on me, Maxie?" asked the vice president, jaunty when he passed the Steinway. "Keeping that redhead for yourself?"

"Looking for twins, Mr. Minthorn," he replied, toying with the waltz from "Carousel," playing it in 4/4 time.

Maxie broke for lunch at 2 o'clock.

Maria walked in eight minutes later.

Seated beside Minthorn's desk, legs crossed, with his eyes fixed on the underside of her brown thigh, she made her pitch.

"But a man like you knows this," she added. "A man in your position."

Flattery, and the way she said "position": lips pursed, her tongue peeking between her teeth for the little hiss.

And Minthorn knew she was right. A bunch of people from Macy's and Gimbel's who cashed their checks were from the islands, janitors and bus boys and such, and they needed to bank somewhere. To have someone to greet them in Spanish, to help them, a gentle twist of the arm . . .

"Whatever it is you invest, you make back quick," she said.

"And someone as lovely as yourself to grace our branch . . ."

Maria pretended to blush, bringing her tapered fingers to her throat.

He hired her immediately, hoping her sense of propriety would wither in time.

She waited outside the bank on Eighth Avenue, shivering as the lunchtime crowd rushed by, their shopping bags brimming.

Coming back from Child's, Maxie turned onto the avenue, topcoat collar high, and he looked right at her as he pushed the revolving door to enter the heated lobby.

She saw he hadn't recognized her, and she knew it was going to be all right.

Find where Maxie kept his gun, look at the spot every morning when he leaves for the bank, and tell Maria when the piece was gone. Find where Maxie kept the gun, look at the spot every morning, and tell Maria . . .

The butterflies in her belly, prickle in her neck and chest, the way time stood still when she was gone: They all told Mitzi that she'd do whatever Maria said.

Never occurred to her that Maria might do her wrong like everybody else she'd fallen for.

Maxie's gun rested beneath his array of socks, each pair rolled in a tight ball, diamonds on the ankles.

And then it was gone.

Wrapped in a thirsty robe, Mitzi went downstairs, drawing toward Maria's lilting voice.

"It's gone," she said.

Maria in a black slip, and she was rolling up her hose. "He leave the same time?"

Mitzi nodded, and she watched as Maria went to her closet, brought out a dress in indigo-blue.

"Is it going to be today?" Mitzi asked.

"No, no, *mi amor,*" she replied as she slipped into the garment, stole a glance at the clock on the nightstand. "The money comes late this afternoon. Tomorrow. Has to be."

"Should I be . . . Should I be scared?"

Maria wasn't due at the bank until 10, but she found Minthorn liked it if she showed up early.

"No, you just do what we said."

Maria pecked her cheek, then erased the lipstick trace. "Margarita, don't think," she said. "Don't worry."

"Okay, Maria."

A moment later, Mitzi was alone.

She sprayed Maria's perfume into the air, and stood beneath the cloud of flowers, summer songs, a feathery sway. For the rest of the day, Maria's scent clung to her fingertips and her red hair.

Mitzi felt like a heel stealing Maxie's valise, but Maria said he wasn't going to need it, and besides, he left it behind, dumping it like he was dumping her.

He took his razor, though. Took his ties, a shirt, two pairs each of boxers and those diamond socks too, and she saw him packing the night before last, one eye open under the covers, carefully stuffing the duffel he'd bought. Spent a long time looking at his cocoa suit in the closet, fingering the sleeve, and she knew he hated like hell to leave it behind.

Mitzi lifted the slacks, figuring what the hell.

Kerchief knotted under her chin, she went down the stairs, everything she owned in the valise but the therapeutic lamp and her old cardboard suitcase, and she was thinking a handful of talc might've captured the sweat soaking under her arms, running along her ribs.

She looked at Maria's door.

Maria said Pennsylvania Station, 9:18. Track 101,

Baltimore, and to stay put even if the seat next to her was empty when the train pulled out.

Maria had given her a ticket, and as Mitzi stepped onto the avenue, the cold stinging her face, she tapped her pocket, felt the envelope. Tapped it twice more for luck.

Baltimore to D.C. to Shreveport via Roanoke, Chattanooga, and Birmingham.

Maria said she always wanted to drive to Texas, said they'd cross the border at Eagle Pass. Said she had a brother in Salinas.

Baltimore would've been enough for Mitzi, leaning into the wind, a bitty thing under buildings pricking the clouds. She'd never been south of Battery Park.

Maxie had ice-water veins, never regretted shooting off Bippy Brown's ear and now he didn't give a damn about nothing. In less than an hour, he'd be back at the Hotel New Yorker using his real name, Mr. H.J. Blubaugh, having them deliver eggs, sunny-side up, and hash browns too.

Puckett thanked him for the container of black joe, and Maxie sat on the piano bench to remove his galoshes, putting his hat and topcoat on the case, wondering if he was going to have to kill anybody to get it done.

Wick, the senior teller, was already at her station, puckered lips, rouge, and all business, and then the Mexican broad entered, head held high.

The ex-cop walked across the lobby, falling in behind the Mexican on his way to the can.

Maxie eased the gun from the piano bench and dropped it into the side pocket of his blue suit jacket. As he went toward the locker room, he saw Minthorn opening the vault door, grunting.

The Mexican broad was sitting at her desk under the stairs, and she was still wearing her coat.

Puckett pissing away behind a door to the men's room.

Maxie opened his locker and saw that his duffel bag was gone, and his clothes.

On the shelf, a record: "Moonlight and You" by the Benny Walters Orchestra, cornet solo by Bippy Brown, back when he had two ears.

Maxie felt a jolt, but he already had it spent. "Fuck it," he said, charging out.

Puckett thought he heard someone call his name.

Passing Minthorn and the open vault, Maxie marched around the counter, and the tellers looked at him, wondering, thinking, *Maxie . . . ?*

He grabbed the startled Wick by the meat of her arm, yanked her off the stool, rammed the .38 against her spine, and told her he didn't give a shit if he had to kill her now or later, just keep her mouth shut.

She said, "See here, Maxie—"

Maxie, a nasty bastard, didn't have a free hand to clap her, so he bit her hard on the back of her neck, drawing blood.

"Ready to shut it now?" he said, as he spit to the side.

They advanced toward Minthorn, who was stacking the cart with thick packets of bills and a fat bag of coins.

Puckett backed out of the toilet, and then he looked at Maria who, with a wide-eyed nod of her head and a sideways glance, told the ex-cop what was going on.

Puckett drew his side arm, held it shoulder high. He stayed under the stairs as Maxie and Wick passed the final teller.

"Minthorn," Maxie said.

The vice president turned and, no panic, lifted his hands

in the air. And then he said, "Maxie, let her go. Maxie, she's got three kids."

Maxie released Wick's arm, grabbed her hair by the bun. Wick hissed, but didn't scream, blood dribbling.

"Maxie, for Christ's sake, take the money. Just let her—"

Puckett squeezed the trigger.

Out of the corner of his blue, blue eyes, Maxie saw it, saw how the whole thing was going to end.

The bullet in the air, and he remembered it was Bird who gave him his nickname. Bird dubbed him Mum, since he didn't yap much, and then Bird, as well read as anybody and twice as quick, upped it to Maximum, calling him Maxie.

He loved Bird, and he hightailed it to K.C. full of hope, thinking he could play, thinking what he'd learned in the basement of the Kingdom Hall—

Puckett's shot took off the back of Maxie's head.

Wick went to her knees, the red mist finding her easy, and Minthorn charged out of the safe to catch her, failing when he bumped the cart.

Maxie collapsed to the marble floor like somebody cut his strings.

Minthorn took Wick in his arms. "Muriel?"

She told him she was okay, and the color rushed back to her face.

Puckett holstered his gun and pushed back the swinging door.

Maxie's blood was spreading fast.

Minthorn said, "Muriel, let's get the girls into my office." Looking at the ex-cop, "Frank, don't trip the alarm. Just keep the front door locked and wait for them outside. I'll make the call."

"Sure thing, Mr. Minthorn," he said as he turned, started

toward the piano bench, the revolving door on Eighth, steam still rising from his coffee container.

Minthorn shepherded Wick and the quaking tellers, and then they were all inside, grateful they no longer had to see Maxie, the nasty bastard, with the side of his skull blown off, his blue, blue eyes rolled up into his head.

Minthorn pulled the blinds all around his office, cutting the light until he reached the desk lamp.

On cue, Maria took Maxie's empty duffel bag from her drawer and went to the open vault, as Minthorn had agreed.

Minthorn, spent and on his side last night at the Hotel Martinique, and Maria, naked beneath his shirt on the chaise, telling him about Cuba. After a stopover in Miami, she said, they'd lounge on golden beaches, rum concoctions in their hands, and there wasn't a banker on the entire island who would fail to believe he'd won the $202,000 at the casinos.

She stretched out her long legs, giving him a peek at the dark patch under the shirt front, and Minthorn quivered at the thought of her on white sheets after a day in the sun.

Referencing Maxie, she said, "He won't know what to do when he has to face a man like you, Morris."

There was no counting how many ways a line like that would work on a dope like Minthorn.

The 9:18 to Baltimore lurched forward, jostling the last of the passengers to board. Mitzi turned one last time to the rear. Maxie's valise sat next to her atop the empty seat on the aisle.

She's not coming, Mitzi thought, as she wrapped her kerchief around her finger, unwrapped it, all but tied it in knots. I'm sent off, again, only this time it's to Baltimore with two dollars and change in my purse.

Ain't it always the way?

She started thinking she'd get off in Newark, grab a couple of bucks on a refund, figuring they had a subway or some kind of ferry would take her back to Hell's Kitchen, knowing Maxie was paid up until New Year's.

As the clattering train began to find its pace, she thought, maybe there's a guy in Baltimore. There's got to be. A real nice guy, and she's new in town, and he can see she's had it rough. He's got a job, something regular, and he's kind. Buys her a drink, then the blue-plate special, a refill on the coffee, and everybody in the diner says he's kind, a gentleman—

"Excuse me, miss. I can have this seat?"

Maria smiled, looking down.

She seemed awfully composed, considering.

"I can put your valise with mine," she said.

Brand new, brown leather, and without a single scratch.

Mitzi figured the money was locked inside.

"Okay," Mitzi said, and she watched Maria allow the porter to hoist the two pieces, and her coat, into the overhead compartment.

"Your coat now, miss?" asked the colored porter, sharp in a black bow tie and vest.

"No," Mitzi said, as Maria nestled next to her. "If you don't mind, I'll keep it."

They met sunlight in Jersey, and Mitzi leaned over, whispered, "Did you hurt him?"

Maria looked at the red trim on the seat in front of them. "No, *chica,* I did not."

"The money . . ."

Outside, miles of tracks on all sides, maybe twenty ways to come and go.

Maria tapped Mitzi's hand. She'd booked a sleeper for the overnight to Birmingham, and they'd count the dough on the bed, if the girl insisted.

Maria figured it was $200,000, seeing that she left the coins.

Minthorn thought she was waiting at the Hotel Martinique. He said he'd arrive around noon, passport in his pocket.

She told him she had a brother in Camagüey.

Her turn to whisper, Maria said, "The next tunnel I'm going to kiss you, Margarita. I'm going to kiss you until you no can breathe."

Mitzi blushed.

"There is no one between us now, baby," Maria added. "Now you are mine alone."

They rode in silence for a stretch, pulling into Newark, pulling out. "Trenton next," bellowed the roly-poly man.

Factories on either side, most of the way. Mitzi wondering if they had an ocean in Baltimore. Be nice to swim in an ocean.

She didn't know what to call the feeling inside. No, but it was like it was all the other times at the start. She wondered if it could be different in the long run.

"Maria? Maria, will you be nasty?"

"*Que?*"

"I mean, are you ever nasty?"

Maria looked at her with her black, black eyes.

"I told you, Margarita: Don't think and don't worry," she said softly. "Leave everything to me."

Mitzi studied her, trying to figure out how she could ignore the passing scenery, puffy smoke billowing from towering chimneys, a silver airplane growing bigger. Christmas lights, and little backyards with snowmen, coal buttons, car-rots, corncob pipes.

TAKE THE MAN'S PAY

BY ROBERT KNIGHTLY

Garment District

Sergeant Thomas Cippolo, desk sergeant at Midtown South, peers over his half-moon reading glasses at Detective Morrie Goldstein and his handcuffed prisoner as they enter the precinct.

"What's up wit' Charlie Chang?" he asks.

"Chang?"

"Yeah." Cippolo starts his various chins in motion with a vigorous shake of his head. "Charlie Chang. The dude made all those movies with Number One Son."

"That's *Chan,* ya moron," Goldstein replies without relaxing his grip on the arm of his prisoner. "Charlie Chan." Goldstein is a massive man, well over six feet tall with broad sloping shoulders that challenge the seams of an off-the-rack suit from the Big & Tall shop at Macy's. "Anyway, he's not Chinese. He's a Nip. Hoshi Taiku."

"A Nip?"

"Yeah, like Nipponese. From Japan." Goldstein notes Cippolo's blank stare, and sighs in disgust. "The Japanese people don't call their country Japan. They call it Nippon. Ain't that right, Hoshi?"

Taiku does not speak. Though he's been in the United States for three days and has only the vaguest notion of the American criminal justice system, he's heard about Abner Louima and wouldn't be surprised if the giant policeman strung him up by his toes.

Goldstein steers Taiku around Cippolo's desk and up a flight of stairs to a large room jammed with desks set back-to-back. A few of the desks are occupied by detectives who look up from their paperwork to watch Goldstein direct his prisoner to a small interview room. They do not speak. The windowless interview room contains a table and two metal chairs, one of which is bolted to the floor. The table and chairs are gray, the floor tiles brown, the walls a dull institutional yellow. All are glazed with decades of accumulated grime, even the small one-way mirror in the wall opposite the hump seat.

"That feel better?" Goldstein removes Taiku's handcuffs, then flips them onto the table where they settle with an echoing clang. "Okay, that's your chair." He points to the bolted-down chair. "Take a seat."

Hoshi Taiku is a short middle-aged man with a round face that complements his soft belly. From his seated position, looking up, Goldstein appears gigantic and menacing. Curiously, this effect remains undiminished when Goldstein draws his own chair close, then settles down with an appreciative sigh.

"My back," he explains. "When I gotta stand around, it goes into spasm. I don't know, maybe I should get myself one of those supports. I mean, standing around is all I ever fuckin' do." He removes a cheap ballpoint pen, a notebook, and a small tape recorder from his jacket pocket and sets them on the table.

"First thing I gotta do is explain your rights. Understand?"

Taiku does not reply. Instead, his gaze shifts to the wall on the other side of the room, a small act of defiance which elicits a triumphant smile from Goldstein. Goldstein has bet Sergeant Alex Mowrey $25 that Taiku will crack before 1 o'clock in the afternoon. It is now 10:30 in the morning.

Goldstein lays his hand on Hoshi's shoulder, and notes a barely detectable shudder run along the man's spine. "Hoshi, listen to me. You chatted up the desk clerk, the bartender in the Tiger Lounge, and a barmaid named Clara. I know you know how to speak English, so please don't start me off with bullshit. It's inconsiderate."

After a moment, Hoshi bows, a short nod that Goldstein returns.

"Okay, like I already said, you got certain rights which I will now carefully enumerate. You don't have to speak to me at all if you don't want to, plus you can call a lawyer whenever you like. In fact, if you're broke, which I doubt very much, the court will appoint a lawyer to represent you. But the main thing, which you should take into your heart, is that whatever you say here is on the record. Even though you haven't been arrested and you might never be. You got it so far?"

Goldstein acknowledges a second bow with a squeeze of Taiku's bony shoulder, then releases his grip, leans back in the chair, and scratches his head. In contrast to his body, Goldstein's oval skull is very small and rises to a definite point in the back, a sad truth made all the more apparent by a hairline the stops an inch or so above his ears.

"So it's up to you, Hoshi," he finally declares. "What you're gonna do and all. You say the word, tell me you don't wanna clear this up, I'll put you under arrest, and that'll be that."

"No lawyer." Despite a prodigious effort, the words come out, "'No roy-uh.'"

"Okay, then you gotta sign this." Goldstein takes a standard Miranda waiver from the inside pocket of his jacket, then spreads it on the table as if unrolling a precious scroll. "Right here, Yoshi. Right on the dotted line."

A moment later, after Yoshi signs, a knock on the door precedes the entrance of Detective Vera Katakura.

"The lieutenant wants you in his office."

"Now?" Goldstein is incredulous.

"Not now, Morris. Ten minutes ago."

When he returns a few minutes later, Hoshi Taiku, though unattended, is sitting exactly as Goldstein left him, has not, in fact, moved at all.

"I'm gonna be a while," the detective explains. "I gotta take you downstairs. Stand up."

Re-cuffed, Hoshi is led across the squad room to a narrow stairway at the rear of the building, then down two flights to the holding cells in the basement.

"What you got here, Morrie?" Patrolman Brian O'Boyle asks when Goldstein approaches his desk. O'Boyle has been working lockup since he damaged his knee chasing a suspect ten years before. He sits with his feet on his desk, perusing a worn copy of *Penthouse* magazine.

"Gotta stash him for a while," Goldstein explains. He lays his service automatic on O'Boyle's desk, then grabs a set of keys. "Don't get up."

Goldstein leads Taiku through a locked door, then down a corridor to a pair of cells. The cells are constructed of steel bars, two cages side-by-side.

"Yo, Detective Goldstein, wha'chu doin'? You bringin' me some candy?"

"That you, Speedo Brown? Again?"

"Yeah. Ah'm real popular these days."

Taiku's arm tightens beneath Goldstein's grip and his steps shorten. Speedo Brown is every civilian's nightmare, a bulked-up black giant with a prison-hard glare that overwhelms his bantering tone.

"Put your eyes back in your head, Speedo. I'm stashin' Hoshi outta reach."

"That the bitch cell," Speedo protests as Goldstein unlocks the cell adjoining his. "Can't put no man in the bitch cell lessen he a bitch. You a bitch, man? You some kinda Chinatown bitch? You Miss Saigon?"

Goldstein pushes Taiku into the cell, locks the door, then turns to leave. "C'mon, baby," he hears Speedo coo as he walks off, "bring it on over here. Let Speedo bus' yo cherry."

Hoshi Taiku perches on the edge of a narrow shelf bolted to the wall at the rear of his cell. He stares out through the bars, his face composed as he studiously ignores the taunts of Speedo Brown. But he cannot compose his thoughts. He has disgraced his family and betrayed his nation. In the ordinary course of events, he would already have lost everything there is to lose. But not here in this land of barbarians. No, in the land of the barbarians there is a good deal more to lose, as Speedo Brown's words make clear.

"You come to Rikers Island, ahm gonna own yo sorry ass. I got friends in Rikers, git you put up in my cell. You be shavin' yo legs by sunrise."

Taiku thinks of home, of Kyoto, of his wife and children. If he is arrested, they will be shunned by their neighbors, his disgrace falling on them as surely as if they'd committed the act themselves. But he has not been arrested, has not, in fact, even been questioned, a state of affairs he finds unfathomable. In Japan, in Kyoto, he would already have done what is expected of anyone arrested for a crime. He would have confessed, then formally apologized for upsetting the harmony of Japanese society. That was what you did when you were taken into custody: You accepted your unworthiness, took it upon yourself, the consequences falling across your shoulders like a yoke.

But he is not at home, he reminds himself for the second time, and there are decisions to make, and make soon. Should he speak to the detective? If so, what should he say? Is it dishonorable to lie to the barbarians who bombed Hiroshima and Nagasaki? Who occupied Japan? Who humiliated the emperor? Taiku no longer believes that Goldstein will hurt him, not physically. That's because Goldstein has made the nature of his true threat absolutely clear: Talk or face immediate arrest and Speedo Brown, or someone just like him. Well, talk is one thing, truth another . . .

Taiku's thoughts are interrupted by the appearance of Patrolman O'Boyle. He is walking along the hallway, a prisoner in tow, a female prisoner.

"Up ya go, Taiku," O'Boyle orders. "You're movin'."

"Thank you, Lord," Speedo Brown cries.

O'Boyle cuffs his prisoner to the bars of Taiku's cell, then unlocks the door and motions Taiku forward. Already on his feet, Taiku finds that his legs do not respond to his will, that his heart has dropped into his feet, that he has a pressing need to immediately void his bladder. He has never known such fear, has not, prior to this moment, known that human beings had the capacity to be this afraid.

"You wanna hustle it up, Tojo? I don't got all day."

Again, Taiku wills himself to move, again he fails.

"Lemme put it this way, Taiku. If I gotta call in backup

and extract you from that cell, I'm gonna carve your little Jap ass into sushi. You *comprende?*"

Taiku's mouth curls into a little circle, then he finally speaks, "Man threaten me."

The word "threaten" emerges as "fletta," which only adds to the humiliation Taiku feels at that moment. He has begged an inferior, a foreigner, to protect him.

"What?"

"Man threaten me."

"Who *fletta*, you? Speedo?" O'Boyle glances at Speedo Brown, then laughs before answering his own question. "Little Speedo? He wouldn't hurt a fly. Would ya, Speedo?"

"Never hurt a fly in my life, but I'm hell on Japanese beetles."

"I am Japanese citizen. You must . . . protect me." Taiku chokes on his own demand. A shudder runs through his body. If he'd had the means, he would have killed himself before speaking those words.

"Whatta ya think, Speedo? Should I *ploteck* him?"

"You jus' leave the boy in my hands, officer. Ain' nobody gonna hurt him. Leastways, nobody but me."

O'Boyle chuckles and shakes his head. "Awright, Tojo. You can wait for Goldstein out by the desk. Bein' as you're a Jap citizen and you ain't been charged with a crime, I guess it's my beholden duty to save you from the big bad wolf."

"I'm really sorry," Goldstein apologizes for the second time. "A couple of uniforms picked up a rapist I been after for six months. I hadda make sure he got hit with enough counts to catch a high bail. The asshole, he goes out on the streets, he's gonna rape someone else."

They are sitting in the interview room they left an hour

before, on either side of the gray table. Goldstein's pen, pad, and tape recorder are laid out in a neat row. "We're goin' on the record now." Goldstein sets the tape recorder on end, starts it running, then suddenly shuts it off and pushes it to the side.

"Ya know something, Hoshi? I don't think we need to get formal. For right now, let's just keep this between the two of us. Whatta ya say?"

Goldstein acknowledges Hoshi Taiku's nod with one of his own, then gets to work. "Okay, why don't we start at the beginning. Why don't you tell me, in your own words, exactly what happened at the hotel this morning."

Taiku draws a breath and feels his command of English, modest at the best of times, slip away. He fears that when he speaks, he will appear a clown to the detective whose eyes never leave his own. Still, he knows he must speak.

"Girl jump," he finally says. "She whore."

"Whore?"

"She whore," Taiku repeats.

"A prostitute? That's what you're saying?"

"Yes."

"You devil. So, how'd you meet her?" Goldstein shakes his head and mock-punches Taiku's arm. "And by the way, her name was Jane Denning. She was twenty-eight years old and had a kid in fourth grade at Holy Savior in Brooklyn."

Bit by bit, with Goldstein in no seeming rush, Taiku's story emerges. First, before leaving Japan, he was handed a business card from the Monroe Escort Service by a superior who'd been quick to explain that Monroe's specialty was large-breasted, blond-all-over blondes. Taiku had accepted the business card, not because he wished to enjoy the favors of a blond-all-over blonde, but only because a refusal would result in his superior's losing face. He'd bowed, put the card in his wallet, and had forgotten about it until a dinner meeting was canceled at the last second and he found himself consigned to a long evening in his room at the Martinique Hotel. Jane Denning (who'd called herself Inga Johannson) had arrived an hour later.

"Did you get what you paid for?" Goldstein asks. He hasn't stopped grinning (nor have his eyes strayed from Taiku's) since Taiku began his story.

"What you say?"

"You know." Goldstein cups his hands against his chest. "Did she have a big pair? Was she blond all over?"

Taiku recoils. He cannot divine the motive behind the question; the cultural differences are too vast. Policemen in Japan maintained a supremely disapproving countenance at all times. Goldstein looks as if he's about to drool.

"*Hai.* Girl okay."

"How many times you do her?" Goldstein arches his back and grunts. "I mean, it was an all-nighter, right? You took her for the whole night?"

"Yes. All night."

"So, how many times you do her?"

Taiku has had enough. He expects foreigners to be offensive, and knows he has to make allowances. But this is too much. Next Goldstein will ask him to describe what they did. "This not your business."

Goldstein's eyes narrow, but do not waver. "Awright," he waves his hand in a vague circle. "Go on, Hoshi."

They'd had sex, Taiku admits, then he'd gone to sleep. He'd slept through the night and when he'd awakened the next morning, found himself alone in the bed. His first thought was that he'd been robbed, but his wallet, with his cash and credit cards, was where he'd left it in the pocket of his trousers. Then a cool breeze had drawn his attention to an open window, which he'd closed without thinking to look down. It was only after he'd showered and dressed, after Goldstein knocked on his door, after a long, repeated explanation, that he'd finally understood. Inga Johannson had used the window to make her final exit.

The story is simple and carefully rehearsed, but Taiku's voice drops in pitch and volume as he proceeds. He is lying and certain that Goldstein knows it, certain also that he has to maintain the lie if he hopes to see his country and his family any time in the near future. But the need to confess, prompted by shame and disgrace, is very strong as well. And then there is the likelihood that even should he be released, he will neither be welcomed in his country, nor embraced by his family.

"Look," Goldstein declares after a long moment of silence, "just for the record, is this the woman who came to your hotel room?"

Goldstein dips into the breast pocket of his jacket to remove a small photo of a young woman kneeling behind a toddler. The child, a boy, is looking over his shoulder and up at his mother while she faces the camera squarely. The broad smile on her face appears to be spontaneous and genuine.

Taiku stares at the photo, remembering the heavily made-up prostitute who'd emerged from the bathroom in her transparent lingerie, who'd run her tongue over her lips and her fingertips over her belly as if possessed. "Tell me what you want me to do," she'd said. "Just tell me."

"*Hai.* This her."

"We found it in her wallet. Good thing, too, because the way she came down on her face . . . Wait a second."

Goldstein's fingers return to his breast pocket, this time removing a Polaroid taken a few hours before. He lays the photo on the table. "A fuckin' mess, huh?"

At first, Taiku sees only a large pool of blood spreading from a headless torso. But as he continues to stare down, he finally discerns the outlines of a flattened human skull made even more obscure by a semi-detached scalp.

Goldstein's tone, when he begins to speak, is matter-of-fact. "You did okay for an amateur, Hoshi. First, you washed up the bathroom pretty good. Then you dumped the dirty towels, her makeup, and her syringe in a plastic bag which you took from the waste basket. Then you carried the bag down two flights, and you tossed it in a service cart without being seen. The only problem is, it's not gonna help ya, not one bit, and what you're doin' here, lyin' to me and all, is only makin' things a lot worse."

Taiku finds that he can't tear his eyes from the photo on the table. Not because the gore holds him prisoner, but because he can no longer face Goldstein's steady gaze. It's ridiculous, of course; sooner or later he will have to look up. Still, he's relieved, at least initially, when Goldstein continues to speak.

"The way I see it, you wake up, find the bed empty, maybe check your wallet, then head into the bathroom, where you discover Jane Denning overdosed on heroin. Giving you the benefit of the doubt, you think she's dead. Maybe she's not breathing, maybe her skin is cool to the touch, maybe you can't find a pulse. Either way, you don't want her discovered in your room. Call it a culture thing. A dead whore brings dishonor on your company, your country, your family, yourself. You just can't let that happen. You tell yourself that nobody saw her come up to your room, that the cops will take it for a suicide, that nobody will lose any sleep over a dead whore, that by the time the police figure it out, you'll be ten thousand miles away.

"Not a bad plan, when I think about it. And if Jane hadn't been tight with the hotel detective, it might've worked, too. But she was well known to Mack Cowens, who was most likely bein' paid off, and she told him where she was goin'."

Goldstein pauses long enough to yawn. The squeal had come through at 7:30, at the end of his tour, and it's now a little after noon. He wants his home and his wife and his bed, but the way it is, he won't finish the paperwork for many hours.

"Awright, back to the ball." He leans closer to Taiku, until his mouth is within a few inches of the smaller man's ear. "What you did, Hoshi, you bad boy, after due consideration, was open the window, haul her across the room, and toss her out. Then you closed . . ." Goldstein stopped, rubbed his chin, and nodded to himself. "Oh, yeah, something we couldn't figure out and I been wantin' to ask you. Did you wait for the crunch before you closed the window? You know, did you wait for her to hit the sidewalk? And another thing: Did you think about what would've happened if Jane landed on a pedestrian? I mean, it was pretty early, but what if some little kid had been walkin' along, mindin' her own business, maybe thinkin' about school or goin' to a party, and . . . *splat?* As it was, Hoshi, the few people down there who saw it happen, they're gonna carry that image into the grave. It's not fair and—"

The door opens at that moment, cutting Goldstein off in mid-sentence. He jerks back as though slapped. "What the fuck is this? I'm workin' here."

Vera Katakura endures the outburst without altering her stern expression. "You're wanted," she announces.

Goldstein's eyes squeeze shut for a moment, then, with a

visible effort, he slowly gets to his feet. "Keep an eye on this jerk," he commands. "I'll be back in five minutes."

Taiku watches the door close behind Goldstein, then turns to Vera Katakura. Though clearly Asian, she might be from any of a dozen countries. He guesses Chinese, maybe Korean, but it doesn't matter because . . .

"Stand up."

The simple demand, spoken in perfect Japanese, runs up Taiku's spine, an ice cube settling onto the back of his neck. As in a dream, he feels the muscles in his thighs flex, his knees bend, his body rising until he stares directly into Vera Katakura's unyielding black eyes. She doesn't speak, but she doesn't have to speak. He can see his disgrace at the very center of her pupils, a tiny shadow, a smudge, and he knows that his dishonor extends to all—and to each—of the Japanese people. He wants to bow, to bend forward until his back is parallel to the ground; he wants to acknowledge his shame, to shrivel up and die, a cockroach in a fire. Instead, though his knees tremble, he continues to stare into Vera's eyes until, without changing expression, she lifts her open palm to her shoulder, then cracks him right across the face.

"*Hai*," he says.

"She reduced him to a puddle," Goldstein declares, not for the first time. "The poor schmuck just melted on the spot." He turns to Vera Katakura, his partner for the last three years, and lifts his glass.

They are drinking in a hole-in-the-wall bar on Ninth Avenue, one of the last of its kind this close to Lincoln Center. Goldstein, Katakura, Brian O'Boyle, and First Grade Detective Speedo Brown.

It's been a very good day. A signed statement in hand

before 1, the paperwork completed by 2, a crowded press conference at 3:30 with Captain Anthony Borodski taking full credit for the successful investigation, though he hadn't arrived until after Hoshi Taiku was formally charged with murder. Mowrey had stood alongside his captain, there to field the questions that followed Borodski's official statement, while Goldstein and Katakura lounged at the rear of the dais, trying to appear at least vaguely interested.

"You were definitely right about one thing," O'Boyle says to Katakura. "You told me the poor bastard would beg to confess and beg he did."

Vera glances at Speedo Brown, who earned his nickname when he appeared at Captain Borodski's annual pool party in a tiny crimson bathing suit that fit his buttocks like a condom. "As you would, Brian, if you were in Taiku's position. For a Japanese male, Speedo Brown is the worst nightmare imaginable."

"I resent that," Speedo declares. "I'm really a very nice person when you get to know me."

They go on this way for another hour, with only Vera Katakura, who holds herself responsible, lending a passing thought to Hoshi Taiku. With malice aforethought, she'd signed, sealed, and delivered him into the hands of the state, plucking his strings as though playing a harp, effectively (and efficiently) consigning him to whatever nightmare awaited him on Rikers Island. Well, in fairness to herself, she hoped he'd asked for protective custody, or to get in touch with a lawyer, or with the Japanese embassy. An outraged embassy official had called the precinct ten minutes after the press conference ended. By that time, Taiku had already been arraigned and bail denied.

The saddest part, though it didn't seem to sadden her

comrades, was that if Jane Denning was dead before Taiku pushed her out the window, the worst charge he faces is unlawful disposal of a body, an E felony for which he will likely receive probation. It all depends on the autopsy results. If Hoshi catches a break, he'll be out within a week. If not, he'll sit until he is indicted and re-arraigned, until his lawyer makes an application for reduced bail, an application very likely to be denied.

"C'mon, Vera." Goldstein nudges his partner. "You got nothin' to say?"

Vera Katakura thinks it over for a moment, then sips at her third vodka tonic and shrugs. "You take the man's pay," she declares in a tone that brooks no contradiction, "you do the man's job."

THE LAUNDRY ROOM

BY JOHN LUTZ

Upper West Side

That it was blood didn't seem likely.

Possible, but not likely.

Laura Frain stood in the dim basement laundry room of her apartment building and studied the stained shirt beneath a sixty-watt bulb that should have been a hundred. The rust-red stain on Davy's blue collar looked as if it might be stubborn. And there was a similar stain on the shirt's right sleeve.

She glanced around the laundry room, as if she feared she wasn't alone. But she was alone. Most of the women in the building and not a few of the men didn't like coming to the basement room to use the aging, coin-operated washing machines and clothes dryers. Especially since Wash Up, a spacious and well-lighted laundromat, had opened down the block. The basement laundry room—smelling of mold and bleach—was oppressive, even spooky, with its dimness and shadows and slitlike windows that looked out on an air shaft and hadn't been washed in years. The truth was, she hated being there, but felt she had little choice.

The laundry room was one of the reasons she and Roger had rented the apartment, so she was determined to take advantage of the convenience. Besides, it was cheaper than a laundromat or dry cleaners.

Laura, her husband Roger, and their sixteen-year-old son

Davy had lived in the Upper West Side apartment for the past two years, after being displaced when their longtime apartment on West 89th Street had gone condo. The new apartment had finally begun to feel like home.

Like her husband, Laura was in her late thirties. She and Roger had only last month celebrated their seventeenth wedding anniversary. She smiled, thinking as she often did that she was part of an attractive family. She still had her dark good looks, her lush auburn hair, and bright blue eyes. And Roger, while never a handsome man in the conventional sense, was still trim and attractive in his homely, Lincolnesque way. Davy, of course, was beautiful, with Roger's craggy features and Laura's bold blue eyes and wavy dark hair. A heartbreaker, Davy, though he didn't date much.

Laura turned on the washer and listened to the ancient pipes rattle along the ceiling joists as the tub began to fill. She spread out the shirt with the stain facing up, stretching the material tight over the top of one of the nearby dryers, then reached for the aerosol can of spot remover. She sprayed the stain, then dipped a scrub brush into the warm water gushing into the machine, applied some soap to the brush's bristles, and began to work on the stain.

When it had completely disappeared, she started on the similar stain on the shirt sleeve. Red sauce of some kind, perhaps even a thick red wine. She scrubbed until that stain had disappeared too, then continued to scrub.

When the washer was almost filled, she put the shirt in by itself, so it would be good and clean.

Davy's shirt.

"David," he said.

The pretty blond girl looked at him and cocked her head

to the side to demonstrate she was curious. Her hair was combed straight back but ringlets had escaped to dangle in front of her ears and dance when she moved her head.

Davy smiled. "I thought you asked me my name." They were in a video arcade near Times Square, and it was noisy not only from the games but from the traffic sounds drifting in through the open door.

"You heard wrong," the girl said, but she returned his smile.

He shrugged and turned back to his Mounted Brigade game, swerving his horse right and lopping off the head of one of the charging Dragoons. An abbreviated shrill scream burst from the machine.

"Holly," he heard.

He turned back to face the girl. "A beautiful name."

She laughed cynically. "Yeah. So's David."

"You come in here often?" he asked, ignoring the trumpet signaling another charge.

"I don't come in here at all. I stopped in to get out of the rain."

He glanced outside and saw that a light summer drizzle had begun. People on the sidewalk were looking up at the sky in wary surprise, some of them opening umbrellas. Then he took a closer look at the girl—woman. She was older than he'd imagined, in her twenties. It was the renegade ringlets that threw him, and her clothes. She was dressed young, in tight jeans, a sleeveless Mets shirt, and dirty white jogging shoes. She had an angular, delicate look, emphasized by her swept back blond hair and the way she wore her makeup, heavily applied, with eyeliner that made her blue eyes even bluer. Both her ears were pierced in three places, and each piercing held a tiny fake diamond stud.

"Seen enough?" she asked.

He laughed. "Not by a long shot." He turned away from his video game so she'd know she had his full attention. They always liked that. "You go to NYU?"

"How'd you guess?"

"Your shirt."

She looked down at what she was wearing and gave him a quizzical look.

"NYU girls are Mets fans," he said.

"All of us?"

"Without exception."

"I actually like the Yankees."

"Okay. With one exception."

She gave him a different kind of smile this time. Kind of slow and lazy. It made her look even older. He liked that. "Let's get out of here," she said. "It's too fucking noisy."

"Just what I was thinking."

She widened her smile. "Yeah. I know what you were thinking."

"I got a call from the high school," Laura told Roger when he phoned from the office at Broadwing Mutual, where he sold all kinds of insurance over the phone and managed outstanding policies. Laura wasn't sure exactly what his job entailed, but he earned enough to support the family in reasonably good style—if they watched their pennies. "Davy's skipped his afternoon classes again."

"A habit."

"The school's concerned."

"He's a senior. He'll go away to college next year."

"If he graduates."

"He'll graduate, the tuition we pay the place."

"He's got to attend some classes."

"And he does attend some. Davy will always do at least enough to get by. That's the kind of kid he is. You worry too much, Laura."

Or not enough. "He probably won't be home in time for dinner, either. That seems to be the pattern."

"So he's out someplace having fun. He's a young man now. You want me to talk to him?"

"No." She knew her husband was bluffing. He wouldn't talk to their son even if she insisted. She'd known for years the kind of relationship Roger and Davy shared. The late night trips down the hall when Roger assumed she was asleep. The faint squeal of the hinge on Davy's bedroom door and—

"Laura?"

"I don't see any reason to talk to him," she said. "It probably wouldn't help, anyway."

"Davy'll be all right. I can just about guarantee it."

"Okay, I'll accept that guarantee."

"That's my girl."

"Will you be home for supper?"

"No, I've gotta work late. Be about 9 o'clock, I'm afraid."

"Okay, I'll see you then."

"Don't worry, Laura. Promise?"

"Sure," she said, and hung up the phone.

She hadn't mentioned the stained shirt to Roger. What would be the point?

They sat in the pocket park that was squeezed between two buildings on East 51st Street. The more they talked to each other, the more she thought they had a lot in common. Enough, anyway.

He was young, all right; Holly could see that even in the dim light from cars passing in the nearby street. But there was something about him, a deep sort of confidence despite his age, as if he'd been around. Maybe more than she had.

"Mind if I ask how old you are?"

He gave her a slow smile that got to her. "Sure, I mind. You afraid I'm jailbait?"

"No. Women don't think that way. Besides, you've got old eyes."

"You trust me to be old enough and I'll trust you."

"To do what?"

"To be gentle with me."

Holly laughed. "Listen, I've got nothing but booze at my place."

"We don't even need that."

She grinned. "C'mon, David. I might not even have that, but you can help me look."

"I'm good at finding things," he said, standing up from the bench. "Like, I found you."

Less than an hour later he slid the long blade of one of her kitchen knives in at the base of her sternum, then up at a sharp angle to the heart. He'd worked out that method from books and basic medical research on the Internet. When he withdrew the blade, it made a muffled scraping sound on her rib cage. It was a sound he liked and made a point to remember.

Holly died quickly on the kitchen floor, not even aware of falling. The last two years, her friends, her lovers, her neat but small apartment near the college, all of it slipped away from her so, so fast, somewhere in the darkness beneath her pain.

The last thing she saw as the light faded was David,

nude, standing near the sink, removing objects from the drawer where she kept the knives. *More knives.* There was a kind of studied purpose about the forward lean of his young body and his intense concentration, as if he were just beginning something rather than ending it.

"Another girl's been murdered and carved up down in the Village," Roger said, reading the folded *Times* as he sat at the kitchen table and sipped his coffee. "The news media's calling the killer the Slicer. Not very imaginative."

"I don't think I want to hear about this at breakfast," Laura said. She was sitting across from Roger, pouring milk over a bowl of cracked wheat cereal with raisins in it.

"The guy must be a frustrated surgeon. Or a butcher."

Laura stood up and stalked to the window, standing with her back very straight and staring out over the fire escape.

"Take it easy," Roger said. "I didn't mean to spook you."

Without turning around, she said, "Two weeks ago, the morning after another girl was killed the same way, I found what might be blood on Davy's shirt."

"So?"

"I found blood on his shirt this morning, too. Do you want me to show you?"

Roger picked up his cup, then paused, as if he'd changed his mind about coffee this morning. He placed the cup perfectly in its saucer. "No. I don't see the necessity."

"We could ask Davy if there's a necessity."

"Simple as that?"

"Yes." But she knew it really wasn't that simple. She was terrified of how Davy might reply. Even more terrified of what might follow. The media, the police and judges and juries, the system. Once the system, this city, had you by the throat, it shook and shook until there was nothing left of you. It might do that to Davy. To his family. Wasn't it always the family's fault? Over and over you heard that, how the killer was himself a victim.

Look at me. His mother. Look what I'm thinking. A victim and killer. Beautiful Davy.

It could be true. That terrified her more than anything.

Still, she had to know for sure.

"We could find out without telling Davy," she said.

"It's absurd even to think such a thing." Roger sounded angry now. She understood why.

"We can't simply do nothing. At least we can figure out what to do if we *must* do something."

"I don't follow you," Roger said, sipping his coffee and making a display of calm.

"I don't want you to follow me," Laura said. "I want you to follow Davy."

Two weeks later, when Davy emerged from his room after doing his homework, he said goodbye, then left for one of his unannounced destinations. This time neither Laura nor Roger pressed him for an explanation. Roger counted to twenty, then followed Davy.

"You'll phone me?" Holly said as her husband left the apartment.

"I'll phone you."

Roger followed his son to a subway station, then boarded a car behind Davy's and watched at each stop until he was among the passengers streaming out onto the platform.

Davy had gotten off at a stop in the Village. Roger hurriedly squeezed through incoming subway riders before the doors slid closed, then followed him up to the street.

It was a warm, pleasant evening, and plenty of people were out strolling the sidewalks and eating at outdoor cafés, so it was easy to keep Davy in sight without being noticed. He was unhurried yet seemed to walk with purpose, as if he knew where he was going rather than simply ambling around enjoying his surroundings.

Davy turned a corner, then made his way through a maze of narrow, crooked streets that were fairly dark but less crowded. Roger had to fall back, and it became more difficult to follow without being seen.

Suddenly Davy slowed and looked about, as if searching the block of old brick apartment buildings for an address. Roger picked up his pace, and from the other side of the street saw Davy enter the lighted vestibule of a beat-up structure whose bricks had years ago been painted white. Davy craned his neck slightly as if speaking into an intercom.

Roger jogged a few steps and saw that there was no inner door that needed to be buzzed open; Davy had simply announced himself. Roger watched his son take two wooden steps to a small landing and rap gently with his knuckles on the door to an apartment on his left. Moving closer still, Roger glimpsed a tall, thin, blond girl open the door and usher Davy inside.

Roger walked back across the street and studied the windows of what must be the front west ground-floor apartment, the one Davy had entered. There was protective iron grillwork over the windows. Shades were pulled, drapes drawn tightly shut. Only narrow angles of light made their way outside.

Feeling like an undercover cop—hoping a real undercover cop wouldn't notice him—Roger dug his cell phone out of his pocket and called Laura.

"He's in the Village visiting a tall blond girl—woman," he

said, then explained in detail his location and Davy's, and how they'd gotten there. "I just caught a glimpse of her, but she looked very pretty. Maybe in her twenties."

"You sound jealous."

That seemed an odd thing for Laura to say. *Was it in my voice?* "So what's our move now?" he asked. Laura seemed to have taken charge of the operation. "Should I bust in and yell for them to freeze?"

"You shouldn't make light of it," she said.

"Maybe we both *should.* All we've found out is Davy's visiting a girlfriend—if he's lucky."

"Remember the blood on his shirts."

"*If* it was blood."

"I'll come down there," Laura said. "I'm going to join you."

"What if Davy leaves before you get here?"

"If he does, let him leave. Don't let him see you."

"Then?"

"We'll go into that apartment building and ring a doorbell."

Roger didn't notice Laura at first. She must have walked close to the buildings, on his side of the street. He saw that she was wearing a dark jacket, jeans, and her jogging shoes.

"Is he still in there?" she asked.

"No. He left about ten minutes ago."

"How did he look?" Laura's eyes shone like a cat's in the dim reflected light of the streetlamp at the corner.

"He looked like he always looks. He seemed . . . calm." Laura was standing motionless, in a strangely awkward yet poised position. "I doubt if anything happened in there," Roger added, wondering himself how he could possibly hazard that guess.

"Let's find out." Laura started across the street.

Roger gripped her shoulder, stopping her. "And tell the woman what?"

"That we're Davy's parents."

"For God's sake, Laura!"

"We'll tell her we're taking a survey," Laura said. "Or that we're collecting food for charity." She walked out from beneath his hand and he fell in behind her as they crossed the street and entered the building.

The pale green vestibule was more brightly lit than it appeared from outside—which was reassuring—and smelled as if it had been recently painted. Even so, there was fresh graffiti on the wall above the mailboxes in crude black lettering: *God is watching over somebody else.*

"It has to be that one," Roger said, pointing up the stairs to the landing. He could see a brass letter and numeral, *1W*, on the door to the girl's apartment.

Laura pressed the brass button and they heard a distant buzzer inside the apartment.

There was no sound from the intercom.

They went up three wide wooden steps to the landing and waited at the door.

Nothing happened.

Laura knocked. Waited almost a full minute. Knocked again.

She glanced over at Roger.

"She didn't leave with Davy," he said. His voice was higher than he'd intended.

Laura turned the doorknob, pushed inward, and the door opened. She stepped inside, and Roger followed. For some reason he wanted to get in out of the hall now, didn't want to be seen.

There were two dead bolt locks and an unfastened brass chain on the door. The woman certainly hadn't locked herself in after Davy left.

They moved deeper inside the apartment, which was warm and comfortably furnished. The furniture was eclectic flea market but tasteful. There were art prints on the walls. A bookshelf was stuffed with paperbacks, most of them fiction.

They smelled the blood before they saw it. Roger felt as if his molars had turned to copper along the sides of his tongue, bringing saliva. He knew the stench was fresh blood even though he'd never before smelled it. Ancient knowledge.

The blond woman was sprawled in a wide circle of blood on the kitchen floor. Her long hair was fanned out and matted with blood. Her throat had been sliced almost deeply enough to have severed her head. Her breasts—

Roger had to turn away. He heard himself make a sobbing sound.

"We're leaving," Laura said. Her voice was so calm it frightened him.

"Jesus, Laura, we've gotta call the police. This—"

"Roger!"

"We've gotta tell somebody, no matter what. This is—"

"Don't touch anything on the way out."

He followed her. He touched nothing. In a dream. All in a dream. He saw Laura use her sleeve to wipe the outside doorknob after the door to the hall was closed behind them.

Out on the sidewalk, half a block away, they stopped, and Laura stooped low and vomited in a dark doorway.

Roger felt stronger than his wife now. At least he'd kept his food down. He pushed away a vivid image of the scene in the apartment kitchen and felt his own stomach roil. Swallowing a rising bitterness, he pulled his cell phone from his pocket.

"Don't do that," Laura said. "Not on a cell phone."

"If we don't call the police—"

"We'll call them from home. We've got to talk. Got to talk with Davy. You know what will happen if we call the police. To all of us."

"There's no *if* about it. We're going to call them. And maybe it should happen. Maybe we've all been partly to blame."

"*All* of us?" She stared at him, astounded.

He thought for the first time that what had happened tonight, what they'd just seen, might have unhinged her mind. "All right," he said, replacing the phone in his pocket. "We'll go home. We'll call from there."

That seemed to mollify her, but he knew the subject hadn't been dropped. They walked on to the subway stop and stood on the platform, which was now crowded. It must have been a while since the last train, so another should be due soon.

Even as he formulated the thought, a cool wash of air moved across the platform, pushed by an approaching train. A light appeared down the narrow, dark tunnel, and an increasing roar chased away all other sound. Everyone moved closer to where the speeding train would growl and squeal to a stop.

Roger was aware of Laura edging back behind him, which she did sometimes to protect her hairdo from the breeze of an approaching train.

When the train was no more than fifty feet away, he was surprised to feel her fists firm in the small of his back, and amazingly he was airborne, out and dropping, blinded by the brilliant light of the train, consumed by its thunder.

After the funeral, life, routine, settled back in. Roger had been dead less than six months, but Laura and Davy seldom spoke of him, and Laura and Roger's wedding photo was tucked away in a box of his possessions that someday Laura would put out curbside with the trash.

Davy was doing better in school now. The Slicer murders were happening less frequently, as if the killer were maturing and learning restraint. There was no sense of urgency about the murders now in the media. In fact, amidst all the ongoing mayhem of Manhattan, they were hardly news at all.

Laura rarely patronized dry cleaners or laundromats, choosing instead to do most of the family wash herself. She would spend hours in the basement laundry room, scrubbing diligently, removing stains, scrubbing them again and again to make sure they were removed.

Some of the stains never completely came clean, but they were hardly noticeable, so she didn't mind them. She didn't see that they made much difference.

FREDDIE PRINZE IS MY GUARDIAN ANGEL

BY LIZ MARTÍNEZ

Washington Heights

Freddie Prinze had been dead for four years when he spoke to me the first time. I was in my room in my family's apartment in Washington Heights, saying the Rosary, when he appeared. At first, I thought the dark spot on my wall was a shadow, and I closed my eyes tightly, trying to concentrate with fervor. I was preparing for my confirmation, and I knew that the ability to pray without distraction from the outside world was important.

He must have gotten impatient waiting for me to finish because he cleared his throat. I jumped at the sound, but for some reason I wasn't afraid to see him standing in my room in the fading January light. He winked at me. "Hey, *mamacita*," he said. "What's goin' on?"

I wasn't really sure how to talk to a celebrity, but he was just slouching against the wall, the way I'd seen him do in Ed Brown's garage on TV. He looked a lot taller in my room. In the living room, he was only about six inches high and sort of grayish on the old RCA. He also jumped up and down a lot because the vertical hold was busted. Here he was relatively still and looked like the older brother of one of my friends.

"Hi," I said shyly. I immediately wondered if he knew I was saying the Rosary twice because today was the fourth anniversary of his death.

"So what are you doing?" he asked.

I guessed that he couldn't read my mind after all. I breathed a little easier and held up the Rosary beads.

He nodded. "My mom does that all the time."

He seemed very much at ease, but my knees were shaking like Bill Cosby's Jell-O Pudding. I was glad I was kneeling so he couldn't see. Did he know I had a huge crush on him, still?

"I hear you're my number one fan," he said.

I wanted to die. I felt my face turning red-hot. "Who told you that?" I asked, trying to be cool, sending up a quick prayer that my brother wouldn't pick this moment to burst into my room.

He shrugged elaborately. "You know, you hear things when you're . . ."

"Dead?" I whispered.

"Yeah." He examined his fingernails.

"What's it like?" I asked.

"Being dead? It's not so bad," he said.

"I mean . . . heaven. What's heaven like? Do you get to meet all the saints?"

He snorted. "Naw. Haven't met any yet."

I was puzzled. This was not jibing with what the nuns had told me for the last eight years. An idea struck me. "Are you in, you know, purgatory?" I wondered if it was rude to ask, sort of like mentioning someone's deformity that you're not supposed to notice because it isn't polite.

"No, no. It doesn't really work that way."

"What do you mean?" I was stunned.

He seemed to lose interest all of a sudden. "Listen, Raquel, I don't have much time. I have to be getting back. I just came to tell you something important."

He looked at me to make sure he had my full attention. Like I could concentrate on anything else.

He pointed his finger at me. "You're going to have to make a decision soon, and it will affect the rest of your life."

I nodded importantly. At last, something I could understand. "I know. I have to choose a confirmation name. I want to take Frederika. After you, you know?" I looked at the floor.

"Aw, kid. Don't do this. I'm not—I wasn't that important, really. I mean, I'm flattered as hell that you think so much of me, but I'm not worth it. Really."

My eyes welled up. "I think you are." I couldn't speak above a whisper, and I couldn't look at him.

"No, no, come on. Hey. I wish I could give you a tissue, but I don't have any on me. Can you wipe your eyes on your sleeve and look at me? There you go. I hate to see anyone cry. Especially over me. I don't deserve it, believe me."

Now that I stopped sniffling, I got angry. "I think you do. You gave us all hope. You came from Washington Heights, and you made it. Everyone who has a TV saw that a Puerto Rican could be an important person."

"Most people thought I was Mexican because of the character I played on *Chico and the Man*," he said quietly. "And look at the kind of work Chico did on the show."

I thought I understood. It wouldn't be fitting for someone who would one day become a saint to brag. He must be practicing up by being modest with me. But I knew what he had done for me and countless others in el barrio. He was our symbol of possibilities.

I had another question. "Why'd you have to die so soon?"

There was no way to communicate to him the emptiness he left in my heart and soul when he abandoned me and all his other fans. Why couldn't he have waited until I was older and could handle his death better?

"Every life lasts exactly as long as it's supposed to," he said gently. "I was here just the right amount of time."

I hung my head and mumbled, "I wish you could have been here longer."

"No, come on. Anyway, I'm here now because I have something important to tell you. You listening? Okay, here it is: You're supposed to join the NYPD."

I didn't understand. "I'm only fourteen."

"Yeah, well, this is a little ahead of schedule, but trust me. This is what you need to do. Listen, I have to get going now. It was nice to meet you." He started to fade.

"Hey! Do you think you could say it before you go?"

"You mean, *Looooking goo . . . ?*"

The last sound was drowned out by the pounding in my ears, which receded long after Freddie had disappeared.

I couldn't understand why Freddie Prinze had told me to become a cop. There weren't a lot of female officers, and I certainly didn't know any Puerto Rican ones. It didn't make any sense. I considered that he might be wrong. But could a saint be wrong? He must be a saint, because I'd heard of the Virgin Mary appearing in people's oven windows, and she was certainly a saint if anyone was. He had the humility thing down, too, very important for those to be canonized.

But he had made those remarks about heaven and purgatory. Was it possible for a saint to be wrong? I didn't think so. I thought the saints were like the Pope, always right, even if other people didn't understand their logic.

I tested the waters with my mother. "Do you think saints can be wrong?" I asked her.

"Whaddaya talking about, wrong? Go wash up for supper," she told me.

When I broached the subject of my confirmation name with her, I knew I had to be well prepared to counter the inevitable argument. "I want to take the name Frederika, after Frederick of Utrecht," I said. "He was a Bishop who got stabbed to death during Mass in the year 838."

My mother didn't even glance away from her mending. "And you want to follow in his footsteps, maybe get stabbed to death on the street?" She finally looked up at me, narrowing her eyes. "Don't think I don't know what you're up to, young lady. *María.* You're going to take the name María," she said in a voice that would brook no further argument.

But I had to try once more. "Sister says that you're supposed to pick a saint's name if the saint means something to you personally."

"And this Frederick of Utrecht is a big idol for you, hmm? I think you didn't know who he was until you looked him up in a book." She shook her needle and thread at me. "I know which Frederick you're interested in, and believe me, he was no saint." My crush on Freddie Prinze was legendary.

"Maybe he will be one day," I said stubbornly.

"Oh, I don't think so, *mija,*" she said. "No, you'll take María, like a good girl, and that's final."

Sister Mary Claire wasn't any help, either. When I asked her how to go about proposing someone for canonization, she was immediately suspicious. She wanted to know who I had in mind, but I was cagey enough to pretend I was just asking in general. I don't think it was an accident that the priest came in right after that and talked to us for a whole day about piety and the Catholic woman's duty in the home.

* * *

I continued to pray for Freddie Prinze's soul and to say the Rosary twice every January 29, but he didn't come back the next year, even though I kept my eyes open long after I went to bed. I wracked my brain trying to remember the exact prayers that I had uttered in order to bring him back again. Each anniversary, I tried to repeat the magic formula, but it didn't work until the year I was eighteen.

I was on my knees in the bedroom saying the Rosary fast because it had become a ritual, but my mind was more on meeting my friends. It was a Friday night, and we were going to a party at a boy's house. I was thinking about the shoes I'd just bought when I saw Freddie standing against the wall.

This time, the first thing he said was, "Looooking good, *mamacita!* Whew, you've really grown up." He nodded approvingly.

I was flattered, but still a little mad that he'd ignored me for the last three years. I tried to play it cool. "What took you so long?" I asked.

"Where I am now, time doesn't work the same way it does here," he said. "Seems like it's been just a few weeks. That's why it's amazing that you're all grown up." He grinned.

I softened. I was thrilled to see him; why let my petty feeling of abandonment get in the way? "What's up?" I asked. I was dying to find out what he had to tell me this time.

"You still haven't joined the NYPD," he said. "I've been checking." He shook his finger at me.

"I'm not old enough yet. You have to be twenty-one."

"Oh. Right." He shrugged. "The time thing, you know?"

"You've been watching me?"

"Yeah. That's what I'm supposed to do."

"Like a guardian angel, you mean?"

He gave me a funny half-smile. "Something like that."

"So, do you see everything I do?" I worried about whether he observed me in the shower.

"Not everything, don't worry. But the important things."

I decided to test him. "Like what?"

He looked up at the ceiling. "Oh, I know about you and Julio Marquez down the block."

I blushed hard. I had experienced my first French kiss with Julio. I knew it was a sin, but I did it anyway. Then I went to Confession.

"Do you know other things, too?" I asked. "Like what horse is going to win?"

"Sometimes, yeah." He squirmed. "But don't ask me to tell you. I'm not supposed to."

I immediately thought of what I could do with the winnings from OTB. Get my family out of Washington Heights and away from the drug dealers, for one thing. "Please? Could you just tell me the winner for one race? I'd never ask you again, I promise."

"I'm really not supposed to," he said.

I rose. "Isn't there any way I could persuade you?"

He eyed me at chest level. "Um, I suppose just once wouldn't hurt." He beckoned me closer. I could feel his hot breath in my ear, but when I reached out to touch him, my hand hit the wall. "Okay, Broken Nose in the seventh at Aqueduct."

"Oh, thank you, thank you!" I clapped my hands together. I was already spending the money.

"Yeah, well." He cleared his throat. "You still need to become a police officer, okay?"

"I don't see why," I said. "It's not like it's what I really want to do or anything."

"What would you rather do?"

"I want to be an actress. I'm even going to Performing

Arts High School, just like you did." I couldn't keep the pride from my voice.

"Hey, kid, why do you wanna do that? No, no. It's not in the cards for you. You join the NYPD like I told you, okay?"

"I guess. But I thought that if I could have a TV show like yours . . ."

"That's not what's right for you, believe me. Now, I got something else to tell you, so listen up, 'cause I gotta go soon," he said.

"All right." I was disappointed about the acting. I still wanted to follow in his footsteps.

"Come on, don't sulk. This is important, so remember it, okay?"

I nodded to assure him that I was all ears.

"You're gonna meet someone called Jumbo. He's going to make you an offer, and it'll sound real good to you. *Don't take it*. If you do, you'll get into really bad trouble. You understand?"

"Don't accept Jumbo's offer," I repeated. "Who's Jumbo and what's he going to offer me?"

"No more time now. I gotta go." He began to fade.

"Wait! Will you come back again?"

"Count on it, *mami*," he said as he disappeared.

I broke open my piggy bank and counted the money. Not enough to bet on Broken Nose. On my way to the party, I picked up a copy of the *Post*, hoping to find the odds. Broken Nose wasn't listed, but a horse named Jumbo was running in the seventh. It reminded me of Freddie's warning, and I wondered about it again.

At the party, I tried to talk Julio and a few of my girl-friends into putting some money down on Broken Nose. I'd had a hot tip, I told them. Nobody believed me, especially when I couldn't tell them when the race was, just that it was the seventh.

I checked the paper the next day. Jumbo was the winner in the seventh race. If I had put down fifty bucks, I would have been so rich . . . I didn't even want to think about it. Why did Freddie give me the wrong tip? Maybe it was to keep me from gambling. He wasn't supposed to tell me, and if he did, I wasn't supposed to act on his tip. It must have been like a test. But for which one of us?

After I graduated from high school, I went to City College on a partial scholarship. I was so busy with my new life that I hardly ever thought about Freddie anymore. The first two years, I flew through the Rosary on the anniversary of his death, but the third year, I forgot to say it at all. I remembered two weeks later, but I was studying for a chemistry test and I didn't want to take the time to pray. Besides, I was still a little sore about Jumbo.

During my senior year, I got involved with a Spanish theater group. I felt alive on the stage. I was looking into having head shots taken and putting my sparse acting credits together for a resume. At the school job fair, I filled out an application for an agency that was holding a model and talent search.

It was hard to believe that the guy taking applications worked for a modeling agency. He was tall and gangly with big ears and a nose that looked as though it had been broken more than once. As soon as I stopped by the table to talk to him, he latched onto me, though. He wanted to know everything: about my background, my training, acting classes, which productions I had performed in. It was very flattering to be asked to go to his agency to meet with his boss, a woman who could get me a lot of bookings, he said. He also liked my friend Gabriela. We looked somewhat alike, and he thought he could get us photo shoots together, when they needed sisters or look-alikes. He wanted us to come to his studio for an initial photo shoot over the weekend.

Gabriela was enchanted. "Think about how much money we could make," she whispered.

But in the back of my mind, I wondered whether this man with the broken nose was the one that Freddie had warned me against. "I don't think it's a good idea. I mean, look at this guy. No way he's legit. He probably wants to get us to take off our clothes or something. Nah. I'm not going."

Gabriela kept pestering me but I wouldn't budge. She went by herself, and the next thing I knew, she was off to Florida to shoot a Coca-Cola commercial. She quit school because she got one booking after the next. She made so much money that she moved her mother to a house in Westchester. I tried to get her to convince her agent to let me try out for him, but she froze me out.

"You had your chance," she said. We didn't speak again after that.

I was kind of mad at Freddie, too, if you want to know the truth. Here he was supposed to be some kind of pre-saint or something, and he'd steered me wrong twice. What kind of guardian angel was he?

He showed up again that year. I didn't really want to have much to do with him, but it's kind of hard to ignore a dead guy who's standing in your room.

"Hey, *mami*, looooking good!" he said, leaning against the wall.

I thought his whole act was kind of immature. He obviously hadn't grown up much.

"Hey, *mamita,* what's the problem?" he asked me. "You're not happy to see me?"

"You gave me some bad advice," I said.

"Oh, yeah, yeah, the Jumbo and Broken Nose thing," he said. "That's why I'm here. I came to tell you that I got them mixed up. You don't have to worry about that guy Jumbo."

I curled my lip. "Jumbo was the *horse,*" I said. "The guy with the broken nose wanted to set me and my friend up as models. She made a zillion dollars, but I turned him down because of you." Something struck me. "What do you mean, you got them mixed up? How can you get this stuff wrong? You're in heaven, right? Don't you hear things from God?"

He laughed. "No, no, I don't get to talk to God. Like I told you before, it's not really the way you think it is up there."

I crossed my arms. "Well, how is it, then?"

"It's . . . hard to explain. It's just different, that's all."

"Well, anyway, why do you keep coming to visit me? I'm not saying the Rosary anymore, you know."

"The Rosary isn't like a magic trick. You didn't call me up by praying with your beads," he said.

"I didn't? Then how come you appeared?"

His voice was gentle. "I told you, it's my job."

I snickered. "All those years, you told everybody, *It's not my job.* Now you're saying different."

"That was just comedy. This is serious stuff. I've gotta watch over you or I won't be able to—well, it's sort of like getting a promotion. I have to do a certain number of things right before I can move up."

"I knew it! You are in purgatory, aren't you?"

"Naw. That's not exactly how it works. But listen, my time is almost up here. I have to remind you about your calling. The NYPD is where you belong."

"I'm not interested in police work at all."

"Do you remember praying for a vocation when you were younger, to see if you were supposed to be a nun?"

"What does that have to do with anything?"

"Try it again. You'll find out what you need through prayer. I gotta go. Don't forget, okay?"

He faded out, leaving me more confused than ever. I thought about it for a while, then hunted down my Rosary beads. *Okay, God,* I thought, *if I'm supposed to have some sort of vocation, then let me know what you want me to do.*

Nothing happened that night, but I thought I ought to give God more of a chance than that to show me His will. I said the Rosary every night, but I didn't receive any celestial direction.

On the fourteenth day, my father's younger sister Alma and her husband dropped by. They had a friend of my Uncle Juan's with them. Sal was an absolute doll. He had a mustache and dimples that flashed when he laughed, which was often. He told jokes that cracked everyone up. His hair was dark and wavy, and I longed to run my fingers through it even though he was almost twice my age. I sat on my hands to make sure they didn't jump out and touch him without my permission.

Tío Juan clapped Sal on the back repeatedly. They were celebrating his promotion from patrolman to sergeant. Juan kept saying how proud he was of Sal, one of the guys from the neighborhood making it: a good civil-service job, benefits, a pension. But I could hear the envy underneath my uncle's words. He was a baker, but he never managed to get into a union. He would speak about others in the family who had landed union jobs as though they had hit the lottery. It was clear that he thought his life would have been easier if he had made it like they did. When he started getting obnoxious, my aunt pulled him out the door.

Sal lingered behind, saying goodnight to everyone, thanking my father for his hospitality. "It was very nice to meet you," he said, looking into my eyes. His cheeks were made apple-round by his smile.

I wanted to touch his dimples, so I jammed my hands into the pockets of my jeans to keep them out of trouble.

He had been so easygoing and confident all evening that when he stuttered a little, I couldn't imagine what was wrong.

"I, uh, that is, do you think you might like—"

My father had had a few glasses of wine and was watching us from his chair in the living room. "Oh, for chrissake," he said, disgusted, "just ask her out already."

Sal blushed and grinned at the same time. "Really? Would that really be okay with you?"

My father leaned back in the chair, his eyes almost closed. He flapped his hand in Sal's direction, like, *Don't bother me.*

Sal cleared his throat. "Would you like to go—"

"Yes!" I said.

He laughed. "You don't even know what I was going to ask you."

Now it was my turn to blush.

He started again. "Would you like to go to a movie this weekend?"

I pretended to think it over. "Sounds good."

"I'll pick you up on Friday at 7."

"See you then," I said.

I dated Sal for three months before the attraction wore off. He was a gorgeous Latin male, but he was a Latin male. It was

1987, and the idea that I would be subservient because he was the guy grew old quickly.

After we broke up, I found myself missing the stories he told about his job. I didn't miss *him* too much, but the day I saw a sign on the subway advertising the next police exam, I realized that I'd been bitten by the bug. I signed up to take it, and I went into the Academy right after my college graduation.

I was glad for the time I'd spent with Sal—it was good preparation for all the crap I had to put up with from the other cops. But I just laid low and smiled through the practical jokes, even the nasty ones. After a while, they stopped. I was pulling my weight, and then some. I started making some good busts, and a few of the old hairbags even gave me some grudging respect. I bumped into Sal once or twice at rackets, and he always made sure to let me know that he was dating a busty blonde. I didn't care.

When I had five years on the job, I was assigned to a detail that focused on getting the homeless off the streets. The mayor wanted the city to look clean—he didn't actually want to clean it up, he just wanted it to *look* better temporarily for political reasons.

One night, after a tour that dragged into overtime, I staggered back to the studio apartment I was renting on the East Side, exhausted. All I wanted was to go to bed because I had to be up again in six hours to head back to work. I had just laid down when Freddie Prinze appeared—on the ceiling this time.

I groaned. "I'm really tired. Do we have to do this now?"

"Hey, what's the matter? You're not happy to see me?" He sounded genuinely hurt.

"No, no, it's great, really. I'm just very tired. Can you come back another time?" This dead guy in my house was just too much after the day I'd had.

"I have something important to tell you. That's why I show up, you know. It's my job to let you know this stuff."

I couldn't keep my eyes open one more second. "I'm sorry. I really have to go to sleep." I was out like a light.

The next thing I knew, I was sitting up in bed, only I was fourteen again. I looked down at my knobby knees and tried to figure out what was going on. Freddie was slouching against the wall in Ed's garage. What was my bed doing in California?

"It's a dream," Freddie said. "It doesn't have to make sense."

I didn't feel tired at all, so when he spoke, I was happy to listen. I even enjoyed his company.

"If you're too tired to stay awake, I'll just have to talk to you while you're sleeping," he said. "Here's the thing: You're gonna have to make a tough choice very soon. I don't want you going down the wrong path."

"What are you talking about?" I felt floaty and good.

"These homeless guys you're dealing with—one of them is going to try to hurt you. Your instinct will be to shoot him. *Do not shoot.* If you do, you'll regret it for the rest of your life. Think about this. It's the most important thing you're ever going to hear."

He started fading out, and then I wasn't aware of anything else until the alarm woke me. The noise startled me back into the world, and I wondered whether my dream had been real. I didn't have time to ponder it later that morning as I hustled homeless people into the converted trailers we had waiting for them.

Scraps of the dream came back to me as the day wore on. *Do not shoot. If you do, you'll regret it for the rest of your life.* I didn't need a guardian angel to tell me that. I'd been around long enough to know what happens to cops who shoot and kill somebody. They get really messed up.

We were almost ready to go back to the station house when one of the street guys pulled a knife out from under his seventeen layers of clothing and stuck it in my face. My adrenaline jump-started me, and I kicked out at the guy. He was wearing too much clothing for the blow to have any impact. It just made him madder. He slashed at my face with the knife. I felt a trickle down my cheek, and a moment later, fire blazed the same trail. I pulled my weapon.

All my police training screamed at me to shoot. My finger started to pull back on the trigger. I aimed at the lunatic's torso, just as I was taught at the range, but the view of my target was suddenly clouded. The sounds of the city were blocked out. All I could hear was the blood pounding in my ears. Each second felt like a month. Over the roar in my head, Freddie's words came back. *Don't shoot . . . You'll regret it . . .*

I lowered my gun. The crazed homeless guy jumped on top of me. Bulletproof vests aren't designed to stop knives, and mine didn't slow this one down.

The knife slid in between my ribs, and I felt as though someone had disconnected my electrical charger from the wall socket. My essence just drained away.

I had felt pain at first, but now I didn't. I noticed a cop lying on the ground, red blood staining the blue uniform. It was me, I realized. What was I doing down there?

Wait a minute, where was *down there?* Where was I?

I looked around. The street appeared the same as it had moments before, except that I was seeing it from above. Holy Christ, was I dead?

Freddie appeared. "How you doin'? You all right?"

"All right? I think I'm dead."

"Yeah, pretty much," he said and looked down. Paramedics were covering the dead cop—me—with a white sheet.

"Why'd you warn me against shooting?" I asked him. Then I realized that I didn't have to ask. I knew without his telling me that he was just doing his job as my guardian angel.

Then I knew something else. I wasn't supposed to be dead. Freddie had screwed it up.

"Yeah," he said, acknowledging my newfound understanding. "What did you expect?"

I thought about it. I really had no one to blame but myself for being dead. After all, what could I expect with Freddie Prinze as my guardian angel?

THE ORGAN GRINDER
BY MAAN MEYERS
Lower East Side

Antonio Cerasani rolled the mobile contraption over the broken cobble where Broome Street met Jefferson. The barrel organ had two wheels and handled like a pushcart. Every part of it gleamed in the bright sunshine. Even the country scene painted on its side seemed to glow with its own light.

He settled the cart as close to the curb as possible in the least of the refuse that layered the streets. With the cart in place, he began to crank the organ. Music poured from the barrel with sweet abundance, almost blocking out the other sounds: babes howling, the scraping of thick shoes on the asphalt pavement, metal-clad hooves and wheels clamoring on the cobblestones, passersby in screaming conversations. The cacophony of everyday life. But here the very intensity of it was an abomination.

Indifferent to the heat of the day, Tony wore heavy trousers, a vest, and a long brown coat. His shabby, dark brown hat sat atop his black hair. An enormous mustache hid his mouth. Only a wisp of smoke from the stub of the twisted black cigar gave any indication of where it was.

The bitter tang of the cigar almost wiped away the stench of horse shit. Almost. The organ grinder hated the smell from when he was a boy in Palermo and had to sleep in the stable of his father's padrone. New York was like a giant stable full of horse dung, particularly in this neighborhood where the White Wings, the street sweeping brigade, seldom ventured. Here the streets were ankle deep in dung and garbage, and the air, only barely modified by the briny reek of seaweed from the East River, was putrid with the rot of humanity.

"La Donna e Mobile" rolled from Tony's machine. He sang in a rich tenor voice. *Women are fickle, like a feather in the wind.*" And as always, the children on the street laughed and danced haphazardly to the organ grinder's music.

He searched the tenement windows where once-white sheets stirred languidly in the tepid breeze. Several pennies wrapped in paper dropped from the windows and landed at his feet. The organ grinder, never stopping his music, tipped his hat to his benefactors, collected the coins, and dropped them into his coat pockets.

One lone coin lay just beyond Tony's stretch, but he did not want to interrupt the flow of music for the moment it would take to claim it, lest he lose further pennies. Tony cranked and Verdi gushed, but no more coins rained down on him.

There came a loud braying, as of animals. Shouting. Blaspheming. Pounding feet. Racing toward the organ grinder were four boys, arms slender as the sticks they carried, their clothes ragged and dirty.

Tony knew these demon boys; they lived on the street. They would steal the nails from the Savior's cross. He stopped playing. The noise of the streets held sway again. He bent to retrieve the last coin, his coin, when with a cruel twitch of his ass, the largest of the boys bumped Tony, knocking the organ grinder into his organ, setting it trembling, akilter. He grabbed at the cart for balance, but misjudged and sank to his knees in the gutter filth.

Screeching with laughter, Butch Kelly leaned over and scooped up Tony's errant penny. The runt of the lot, Patsy Hearn, stuck his tongue through his scabby lips and gave the organ grinder a razzberry.

Tony's hands were in wild motion. His left felt for the coin no longer there, his right worked at steadying the cart. He struggled to his feet and brushed what offal he could from his trousers. Rage surged, all but suffocating him. He shook his fist at the rampaging youths and damned them, their forms and faces indelible in his mind.

The organ grinder knew that he could not pursue these filthy little devils. If he did, one would surely circle back and steal his organ. He was not so green a horn to let that happen. No. He clamped his teeth tighter on the twisted cigar.

The boys had shown disrespect. Antonio Cerasani from Ciminna, a village on a hill in north-central Sicily, never forgot an insult.

Anyone watching the rude boys would have seen them running along Jefferson down to South Street. Here the East River and the docks stopped their straightaway rush. Nine or ten blocks farther south was the bridge to Brooklyn. It was their playground, all of it.

The four, dressed alike in tattered knickerbockers and vests, their broken shoes wrapped with cloth and cord, ducked past horse carts and drays, shouting to each other, snatching food from pushcarts, brandishing their broomsticks, jabbing, threatening anyone in their path. Frequently they used their sticks to knock a hat from an unsuspecting head.

At South Street, the broken pavement created a channel that cut through the sidewalk and ran into an empty, filth-ridden lot on Jefferson. South Street and the streets leading to it and the harbor were overlaid with a sludge different from elsewhere in the city. This filth bore elements of tar and seawater, for the East River, like its sister the Hudson over to the west, was not truly a river but rather a tidal estuary.

Ships dotted the harbor. The boys could hear the water lapping at the docks, the noise and bustle of the sawmills at the lumberyards. Sawdust smelled sweet amidst the fetid odor of the salt and the tar. Stevedores unloading a ship shouted at one another and cursed the heat.

Butch threw a rock at a seagull resting on a piling and missed. The gull gave a raucous caw, flapped its wings, and flew away. "Shit. Seagulls make good eatin'."

"They're tough as an old woman's ass," Colin said, gnawing on the remnant of a potato he'd filched on the way.

"Yeah," Butch shot back, "your ma's."

It was Colin who finally broke the stare between them, saying, "Let's see if we can get some work on the docks."

Butch Kelly swung his stick. "Too hot to work." He pointed the stick into the lot. "Run out, Patsy."

Patsy made an ugly face.

"Run out."

Patsy Hearn shielded his eyes from the sun as he ran toward the heap of refuse near the back of the lot. Beyond it was some skimpy brush, and amid more garbage, a dying black walnut tree, its trunk slashed by lightning.

"Feckin' Butch Kelly with his feckin' games," Patsy muttered. Forever making Patsy the goat. When they played pitch-and-toss, Butch always cheated, stealing his feckin' penny. Just like now with the dago's coin. Butch would pocket the money and never share. And when they played tag or hide-and-go-seek, Patsy was always it. Now this cat-stick game. Here Patsy was in the hot sun, sweating buckets while Butch was swinging his stick, mostly hitting the air, sometimes hitting the pussy, and Tom Reilly and Colin Slattery was up close and catching it. And dumb shit-ass Patsy was out here in the stinking wilderness being cooked by the sun.

Butch hit the pussy and it flew high, way over Tom's and Colin's heads.

"Open your eyes, Patsy." Butch's laugh was nasty.

Patsy ran like a greyhound. If he caught the feckin' thing, maybe they could stop and get something to wet their throats. Nail some bloke toting the growler. Beer would taste good just about now. That's what he was thinking on when his wiry body slipped in the slimy runoff from the rotting waste. He took a header smack into the disintegrating trunk of the tree. Still, he reached up and damn if the feckin' pussy didn't drop right into his hand like it was meant to.

"Hey, boyos," Patsy yelled, brushing splinters from his hair, "I got it!"

He leaned against the scarred trunk sucking in short gasps of air full of soot and ashes. His eyes wandered to the pile of refuse on the other side of the tree, focused on something among the rubbish that caught the sunlight. Something shiny.

A silver dollar maybe!

Or maybe just a tin can.

He moved closer, then stepped back.

"Holy Mary." The boy crossed himself, but he was not afraid. He was barely ten and not even a year off the boat from Cork. It was not the first dead body he'd ever seen.

But it was the first *naked* dead woman he had ever seen. Curled up on her side she was, the ground a rusty black crust. What may have been her dress lay in rags all around her.

"Jesus," Colin said, peering over Patsy's shoulder as Patsy kicked the refuse away.

They milled around jittery, not able to pull their eyes from the sight until Tom nudged her with his shoe and she slid over on her back, totally exposed. The boys jumped. Her eyes stared blankly at them.

After a moment, Patsy said, "Don't she stink somethin' awful?" The four edged toward the body again.

"She's worm meat," Butch said. He gave Patsy a powerful push aside and reached down and grabbed the shiny object that had caught Patsy's attention in the first place.

"Hey, gimme that!" Patsy shouted. "I found it." He tackled Butch.

Tom and Colin jumped in and they were all trading punches and yelling and raising a huge volume of dust and dirt. Colin head-butted Butch, knocking the wind out of him, making him drop the treasure. Both boys dove for it, as did Patsy and Tom.

A whistle shrieked. "All right, all right, what's going on here?" A pudgy copper in blue came toward them swinging his stick.

The boys broke and ran.

Patrolman Mulroony grinned as the dust cleared. He made no move to go after the hooligans. He picked up the dusty stone the boys had been fighting over and wiped it on his sleeve. Well, well, well. He put it in his pocket. Hooking the strap of his stick on his badge, he lifted his hat and mopped the sweat from his head with the heavy sleeve of his uniform. Too hot. With August weather in June, the city was a stinking, rotting hell. Besides, they was just boys who had too much vinegar. Boys like that fought over nothing. He patted the object in his pocket.

Mulroony gave the lot a cursory look. Garbage every-where. Them sheenies think nothing of throwing their refuse right out the window. He shaded his eyes from the sun. What was that odd little flutter of white in all that refuse? He poked his stick into the pile, raising a most horrid stink.

"Mother of God!"

The girl, naked except for a blue hat with a sunflower, lay on her back, arms at her side, her long black hair tangled in the garbage. Her eyes were open, glassy. The hat, which made the forsaken soul look comical, was askew, magnifying the bathos.

Mulroony reckoned the rags on the bloody ground about and under her were what remained of a blue dress and a white shift. The white was what had caught his eye. Poor lass, exposed for all the world to see.

She'd been murdered horribly. Stabbed in the belly and then ripped up to the breast bone. The blood was dried black and the maggots were having their feast. Mulroony reached down, plucked the largest patch of blue cloth, and covered the girl's parts. Before he put his whistle to his lips, he straightened her hat too, so she wouldn't go to Jesus looking the clown.

The organ grinder lived in a room on the top floor of a tene-ment on Prince Street, around the corner from St. Patrick's. Not the big fancy church they built for the rich on Fifth Avenue, but Old St. Patrick's on the corner of Prince and Mott.

St. Patrick was an Irish saint, and this was an Irish church. They hated Italians here, making them go to the basement for a separate Mass. Church was for old ladies in black, not for Tony Cerasani. He hadn't been to confession

since he was twelve. He was thirty now. A man can collect a
great many sins on his soul in eighteen years.

His room was small, which was good. He could see everything he owned: the hand organ against the wall, his nice suit
hanging under his coat on the back of the door. At this
moment, his hat shared the table with his shaving gear.

Tony opened the straight razor. It was the only thing left
to him by his father. The face he saw in the small standing
mirror was his father's. He trimmed around his magnificent
mustache without benefit of lather. Tony had no use for King
Gillette's safety razor or fancy soaps. When he was finished,
he honed the razor on the stone and strap till it regained its
perfect edge.

Madonna, he had no use for anything in this terrible
country. Once he saved enough money he'd go home a
wealthy man and do nothing but drink and eat, have plenty
of women, and bask in Ciminna's nurturing sun.

After filling his cup with Chianti, he plucked a straw
from the bottle's woven covering and picked his teeth.
Immediately came a sharp twinge of pain. He opened his
mouth wide and held up the mirror. Christo, he'd lost one of
his gold teeth. The one in the back on the left. How could
this have happened?

He would retrace his steps to try to find it, or if by
calamity someone had already found it, get it back.

For now, he needed something stronger than wine to ease
the pain and warm his bones. Winter, summer, what did it
matter here? He was always cold in this country.

Grappa was comfort to Tony's belly; it calmed his pain,
restrained his anger. He sat in a dark corner of Giuseppe's
saloon for hours chewing his cigar. Drinking, thinking.

It was very late when he started home. In front of St.

Patrick's, he paused. The rectory door opened. A Sister of Mercy spied Tony, crossed herself, and retreated inside. Tony spat at the door and the Irish bitch behind it. How long he stood there, he didn't know. He finally decided to go into the church.

In the rear, to the left of the last row of benches, were the two confessionals. No parishioners waited on the benches. He ran his fingers over the lattice-work screen of the nearest priest door, his nails making a clicking noise.

He was startled when someone, clearly a mick, obviously awakened from sleep, said, "Yes? Do you wish to make your confession?"

"No." The organ grinder did not even try to keep the sneer from his voice. "Go back to your dreams of plump little boys."

On his walk home he saw himself as a boy at confession, a wrathful crucifix poised above him. The organ grinder shook his head and the memory disappeared. He had stopped drinking too soon. Instead of going home he returned to Giuseppe's.

The church was a jail. Worse, a rope around his neck. Damn the church. There was money to be made. Religion was for the rich. Or the old and the helpless. He was none of these.

"A few cents so I may sup, kind sir?" The hoary man's voice was frail as the old codger himself.

Dutch Tonneman, a detective with the Metropolitan Police, dropped several pennies into the unkempt fellow's outstretched hat. He walked into the saloon at 20th and Sixth and sat at the last table in the back. Noisy ceiling fans moved the hot air around, but the heat didn't budge. Flies hovered over the free eats: the hard boileds and the onions on the bar.

He had met Joe Petrosino once before. Stubby, dark, marked with pox, the Italian cop would be easy to recognize. But he almost never looked so, for his reputation was as a master of many disguises.

Detective Petrosino had a good reputation. The Black Hand's chief adversary in New York, in all of America, worked out of the Elizabeth Street station in one of the city's toughest neighborhoods, Mulberry Bend. For years he'd been trying to destroy the notorious Italian crime organization.

"Sir." The old man, dilapidated hat now plunked on his head, had followed Dutch into the saloon.

Dutch sighed. "Twice in five minutes is greedy, Grandpa."

"I agree."

The vitality in the voice made Dutch look again. On closer inspection, Dutch realized that the old man wasn't so old and that the rags he wore covered a rugged physique.

Dutch grinned. "All right, Petrosino, I'm impressed. But why the playacting? You don't need a disguise to talk to me."

Petrosino looked around. "You never know. The Black Hand is everywhere. Little Italy. Up in the woods past 100th Street, on the East Side. Why not right on the Ladies Mile with the rich Episcopalians?"

"What?" the squat man behind the bar called to them.

"Two beers," Dutch replied.

"Grappa," Petrosino said.

"One beer, one grappa," Dutch said.

"No grappa, this ain't no wop house. What I got is a jug of dago red."

Petrosino nodded, Dutch said, "Okay."

"I'm not showing off with this getup," Petrosino said. "I just came from the Hudson River docks on 23rd Street watching them unload a ship. The Black Hand is stealing some of those shipping companies blind, but I haven't been able to catch them at it. What can I tell you?"

Dutch drank his beer. "Do you hear about unusual knifings?"

Petrosino didn't react. "When I pose a question like that to a suspect, it usually means I'm more interested than I want to let on."

"If you're that transparent," Tonneman said, "I would suggest you don't pose your questions like that."

"All right. You have your secrets, I have mine." He rotated the tumbler of wine on the table. "The Black Hand has those who take care of any who cross them. I hear one wields a fine stiletto."

"I must say, you Italians talk real pretty at times."

The two smiled goodnaturedly at each other.

"We must have more of these talks in the future," Petrosino said. "Who knows what one might know that could facilitate the other?"

The Sicilian sun was warm and good. The young girl had smooth olive skin and big tits. With moist fingers she peeled the grapes and fed them to him. He savored the tart flesh. Suddenly the grapes were stones. The pain drove him awake.

Marie was always with him, singing a sweet sad love song, promising her tender kiss.

Tony seized the bottle of grappa on the floor next to his bed and filled his mouth with the coarse brandy, then clutched his jaw in agony. He swallowed, took another drink, guiding it away from the left side of his mouth.

He poured tepid water from pitcher to basin and tried to shave. The only place he could stand the feel of the blade was under his chin. He would let his beard grow.

The nick on his throat didn't bother him, though it was most unlike him, for he was a perfectionist. He knew that only a little pressure and the artery would feel the blade. Death would come in minutes. And for his suicide, he would burn in hell.

He laughed. "What makes you think you won't burn anyway?" he asked the image of his father in the mirror.

Dressed, he brushed his suit with the damp cloth and reached for the hand organ near the wall. He hesitated. No. Not today. Today he needed to move fast, unencumbered.

One final swallow of grappa. He was going among the micks. That meant he'd have to subsist on watery beer or tasteless whiskey. He would have to be wary because he didn't look like them and he didn't talk like them. They would consider him the enemy.

The Harp on Bleecker Street was the fifth mick bar he'd been to. This hole in the wall was near the precinct, where he knew the cops came for the free lunch served with the drinks. He stood at the end of the bar listening.

Next to him was a mick with breath as foul as the dead goat beard on his ugly face. He was running at the mouth about his friend Mulroony and the windfall he'd found in a vacant lot, a nugget of gold. A gold tooth, no less.

Everyone clustered round the goat, some actually drooling.

The goat pushed through the group to relieve himself out back, then returned and lurched along the bar drinking the dregs from glasses. He bumped against Tony, who did not move away. The goat gave him a bleary, pale-blue stare. "Tim Noonan's the name. You can call me Wingy."

"Tell me about Mulroony and I'll buy you a beer."

A shrewd glint came into Wingy's clouded eyes. "I'm fair thirsty. A thirst only whiskey can quench."

"Beer."

Wingy sighed. "Beer 'tis, then."

Tony raised a hand.

Jimmy Callahan took Tony's measure. Not many Eytalian's found their way into The Harp. This one's skin was a funny red, though he was dressed clean and neat. But why wasn't he with his own kind? What did he want?

Tony didn't like the scrutiny. "Beer for him, whiskey for me."

"Now is that fair?" Wingy whined. "I ask you, Jimmy, is that fair?"

The drinks served and paid for, Jimmy Callahan stood off to the side watching as he rolled himself a Bull Durham. Jimmy didn't trust dagos. He'd never met one worth a fiddler's fart.

Wingy slurped beer, Tony sipped whiskey. "If you tell me slow," Tony said, "I'll finish my whiskey. If you tell me fast, I'll leave it for you."

"What you want to know?" Wingy spoke quickly, but biting each word.

"Mulroony."

"Mulroony the priest, or Mulroony the cop?"

"The cop."

"Lost his ma recently. Very tragic." Wingy crossed himself. "Hail Mary, Mother of God—"

"The longer I wait, the less you get." Tony took a hearty sip of the whiskey.

Wingy's face screwed up as if to blubber. "You don't want to do that, mister. My friend Aloysius Rafferty, the famous bricklayer and stevedore—he seen Mulroony tearing after a bunch of young punks right before he found that dead whore in the empty lot a couple of weeks ago."

"Where can I find Mulroony?"

Wingy nodded many times. "Him and his wife live with his ma, God rest her soul. She ran a rooming house somewhere on the Bowery."

From the variety of signs on walls and in windows along the Bowery, there were far too many rooming houses. He would have to sweat to find Mulroony.

The saloons beckoned. Which one didn't matter. He opened a door and stepped inside to shouting and laughter. An Irish place, by their lumpy potato heads and the stink of cabbage and pig feet.

Irishmen loved to drink and talk and talk and drink and drink. They were braggarts. He preferred to drink alone, left to his own thoughts.

It was dark and dank, the smell of beer and hard-boiled eggs potent. The men sitting around tables or standing at the bar stopped talking to stare at him.

He didn't waste his time by asking for grappa. "You have red wine?"

"This is McSorley's. Beer and ale." The tone was unpleasant. "We don't serve wine."

"Or dagos!" a customer yelled.

Then, as others repeated the phrase, a firehouse gong went off behind the bar.

The organ grinder flicked his thumbnail on the edge of his top front teeth, spat on the sawdust floor, and left to loud jeers.

He didn't want to deal with another mick saloon. He renewed his quest. Two blocks north his luck changed. On the wall, inviting him, was the sign: MRS. MULROONY—ROOMS.

He knocked and pushed open the ground-level front door. This put him in a tiny vestibule. To his left, a small parlor, to his right, another small room that held a long table and ten chairs. The table was set for dinner. A narrow, tilting staircase led up.

"Yes?" A full-figured woman with a rolling pin in her hand came from behind the staircase. Strands of red hair crept from under her kerchief and she had spots of flour on her florid face.

"I need a room."

She looked him over. "All full up."

"I hear your husband is a patrolman. Maybe I could speak to him."

"Ain't home."

He tipped his hat. "Sorry to bother."

Tony walked into the alley to the right of the house. The abrupt scratching shuffle of claws told him he'd disturbed a pack of rats. At the back, keeping a cautious eye peeled, he found an open window. An unoccupied bedroom, by the looks of it. Good, that's how he'd get in if he had to.

He left the alley and crossed the street to a cigar shop. The bastard Mulroony was probably sitting in a saloon drinking, showing off Tony's gold tooth instead of going home.

With one of his twisted cigars between his teeth, Tony stepped out onto the street again and fired it up as he crossed the road.

The organ grinder was a patient man. He would wait.

The Bowery was a busy place at night. Carousers and pick-pockets. He settled in, back against the bricks.

Every workman who staggered past him he gave the eye. Two men, sailors by the bags slung over their shoulders, stopped at the Mulroony house, peered at the sign, and went in. No one came out, so the woman had lied. She had rooms. But not for Italians.

The tap of a club on bricks was unmistakable. Now the whistling of some awful Irish tune located a policeman on his rounds just a block away.

Tony eased back into the alley. The rats again. This time he saw the bright eyes staring at him from not ten feet away. Glints of white teeth showed in the dim light. Five or six filthy rats, on their guard and enraged, screamed at him.

He found a broken cobblestone, but didn't throw it lest the cop hear. The minutes passed with Tony and the rats staring at each other. When he could no longer hear the tapping or the whistling, Tony let fly.

An angry screech. When the stunned rat fell, his mates immediately turned and fed on him. It was to be expected. Such was the world. Tony headed back to the Mulroony house.

A heavyset man had his hand on the door.

"Mr. Mulroony?"

"No, I'm O'Neil. What you want with Al?"

"He helped a friend of mine with a problem. I have some money for him."

"Why don't you come inside? Money is always welcome. I'm sure his missus will give you a taste for the news of it."

"No. If she asks for the money, I'll have to give it to her. Then Mulroony may never know my friend was grateful."

The man laughed. "Begorra, you've got Alice Mulroony down all right. Don't you worry, I won't tell her."

"Thank you."

Shortly after O'Neil went in, a pudgy policeman paused in front of the rooming house to straighten his uniform. Just the type to be a cop in this city. Tony could smell the dust and beer on him.

"Mr. Mulroony?"

"Who wants to know?"

"If you're the right Mulroony, I have money for you."

"I'm Mulroony of the Metropolitan Police." His greedy eyes glinted like the rats. "What money?" he demanded.

Tony walked into the alley surreptitiously, drawing Marie from her place on his thigh up through the hole in his pants pocket. Mulroony followed.

The organ grinder fit his gold tooth back in place. He spat at the dead Irish cop and caressed Marie before putting her to bed.

A long day, a bad day. Tonneman was late coming home to the house on Grand Street where he lived with his widowed mother, Meg. There was a light on in the kitchen. She always left a light on for him and food on the stove or in the ice box, fussing over whether he was getting enough to eat while he did the good work of the police.

He came in quietly so as not to wake her, but she was there waiting for him.

"You have a visitor, John Tonneman." She was the only one who called him John, his birth name. And her tone told him that she didn't like his visitor.

"Where is he, Ma?" There was no one in the kitchen. He looked in the parlor. No one there.

"I wouldn't put him in the parlor," she said, shocked.

"Then where is he?"

"Out back. And I don't like the look of him."

"What's wrong with him, Ma?" Tonneman splashed his face with cold water and used the cloth his mother handed to him.

"He's a dago," she said in a loud whisper. "I gave him a bit of bread and ham. He didn't want beer. You see to him, and be careful. I don't trust them."

Tonneman opened the back door. Sitting on the steps was a man in heavy trousers, a long coat, and a shabby brown hat. An enormous mustache hid his mouth, which was only visible because he was smoking an Italian stinker. The man was a stranger to him until their eyes met.

"Petrosino."

With a half-smile, Petrosino put aside the empty plate. "Your ma was kind to a poor old dago."

"You heard about Mulroony?"

"Yes. The story I'm hearing is he found a gold tooth near the body of the prostitute, Delia Swann."

"So I heard, too. Same sticker. Stiletto. Right up the middle. Killer made off with the gold tooth."

A small stream of smoke came from the twisted stub of a cigar. "Killer may have lost the tooth when he was gutting the girl." He puffed on the cigar. "Mulroony took the evidence, a lot of good it did for him."

"I heard that someone looking like you made the rounds of the Irish bars looking for Mulroony. Wasn't you, by any chance?"

"No."

Tonneman sat down on the steps next to the Italian cop. "Great disguise, Petrosino. If you can sing, you could have a second career as one of those—"

"Dago organ grinders? Yes."

* * *

The organ grinder was back on his corner, where Broome met Jefferson. *Marie was always with him, singing a sweet sad love song, promising her tender kiss. He loved Marie. She was no virgin; she had tasted blood many times.*

Music, full and mellow, poured from his instrument, and it seemed to the few who took a moment from their hard lives to listen that his voice was the voice of an angel.

WHY DO THEY HAVE TO HIT?

BY MARTIN MEYERS

Yorkville

Maureen Moran was beautiful.

I met Maureen through Ted Stagg. They threw great parties in their small, crowded one-bedroom on East 81st Street between Second and First Avenues.

Barely seconds after Ted introduced us, Maureen dragged me into the bedroom where she proudly showed off her collection of Barbie dolls with a tuxedoed Ken lording it over the girls. We shared a joint and had Speedy Gonzales sex.

Even though Maureen and Ted made out outrageously with others, I knew that first night that they were committed for the long haul.

Ted was a press agent, a great guy. But dumb. He had asthma and insisted on smoking. Ted didn't have a long haul in him. A year after I met Maureen, Ted had an attack and died.

After that, Maureen, who always liked her booze, revved her drinking up to Mach speed.

My name is Eddie Coe. I'm an actor. You never heard of me.

I make my living doing voice-overs on commercials and documentaries. I pursue what I laughingly call my *acting career* by doing bits on movies and TV shows. I'm usually the waiter or doorman or cab driver who has great lines like, "Where to?" or, "Will that be all, sir?"

I used to play leads off-Broadway. That dwindled to small parts on Broadway. The money was better doing the latter but I preferred the glory of the former. Lately, my theater work had melted to nothing.

It became a habit to get together with Maureen for drinks when my girl Louise was out of town touring in a musical. I don't do musicals.

The deal was, if Maureen met someone I would fade from the scene.

We were at the Bucking Bull on West 72nd Street.

A fervent "Oh!" erupted from Maureen when Vitorio strutted in. It was as if someone had punched her in the stomach.

The first time Maureen and I met Vitorio Valley was the week before. Vitorio Valley. How's that for a show-biz name? He was body-builder sleek and she was wearing a tight green sweater with her nipples pushing at the fabric. They looked at each other and it was instant lust. Vitorio was a wrong dude and I knew it. But I wasn't Maureen's lover, I was her friend, and it was her life.

Without being asked, Clive the bartender set her drink down, announcing in deep practiced tones, "Chivas Regal." Like Maureen and me, and Vitorio, Clive Paige was in show business.

"I'll have a Chivas, too," Vitorio said, exuding his sexiest smile for Maureen. I was surprised he didn't strip, ripple his muscles, and rotate his tits. He sipped the scotch slowly, keeping his eyes on her while he drank.

"Pit stop," Maureen announced when Vitorio set his glass down. She spun around, twirling her black skirt, before heading back to the washrooms. You have to know that Maureen

had a steel bladder; she never went to the bathroom in public places.

In a very short while Vitorio stood. "Must be catching."
He too hurried to the back.

I sat there pissed off, drinking my beer. Why was I so
pissed? Was I hoping Maureen and I would make it again for
old time's sake? Would I do that? Could I? I loved Louise. But
to be honest, I wasn't sure what I wanted.

I liked that I was committed to Louise. What I missed—
what I missed more and more—was my youth, and the thrills
that came with various relationships. Not just the sex. The
adventure. The thrill of the chase.

Vitorio returned to the bar first, smirking like the rutting
Cheshire Cat he was. Forming a circle with his lips, he made
a slurping noise, nodded at me man to man, bragging with his
mean eyes. I wanted to knock his fucking block off.

When Maureen reappeared she was glowing. Freshly
made-up, she flashed an enigmatic smile. Bar stool to bar
stool, torso to torso, she and Vitorio exchanged breathy whis-
pers and biting kisses.

Abruptly Vitorio left. Maureen's face fell and I thought
she was going to cry. I talked her out of another drink and
walked her to Broadway, where I watched her board the east-
bound bus. Was I hoping she would invite me home for a
drink? Would my answer have been yes or no?

She didn't ask. I grabbed a cab to my place on Central
Park West, ate a grilled ham and cheese, and watched a
movie on TV.

During the following week while I made acting rounds, I
asked some friends about Vitorio. Word was that he lifted
weights and fucked anything that moved. His other favorite

pastime was getting into barroom brawls. Enough outlet for anyone's testosterone. You'd think.

I ran into Vitorio when I stopped at Actor's Equity on 46th Street to relax in the lounge. Flashing that smirk, he bitched about Maureen calling him all the time. I was angry but I'm no tough guy, so I didn't confront him. I simply walked away as fast as I could.

Friday, Maureen called me again about having drinks at the Bull.

I could hear the wind blowing through the park. It was supposed to rain. I'd ordered Chinese takeout and there was good stuff on TV.

But Maureen sounded so desperate. And I enjoyed going out drinking with an attractive woman other than Louise. And something could happen. "Okay. See you there about 8:00."

"I went down on the son of a bitch!" she yelled before I could hang up. "And he walks out on me like that. What a jerk I am."

My mind buzzed with words like *dignity* and *self-esteem* and *self-respect*, but I didn't say any of them. I listened to more ranting until we finally said goodbye. I was sure she'd been going to bed sucking on a bottle every night.

The calendar said September. The wind told me December. No rain yet, but the night wasn't over.

So there we were. She was hoping for déjà vu to happen in the Bucking Bull—that some guy or the same guy would show up. It was a fair bet that she'd buried the degradation down deep.

The Bucking Bull is a steak house with a small bar. The decor is a cliché of snorting bulls and brave toreros in tight yellow outfits and funny black hats, at the ready with red capes in one hand and raised swords poised to strike in the other.

This night the bar was almost as cold as outdoors. I ordered black coffee and a double Courvoisier. On the music machine Wynton Marsalis was blowing the blues.

I had successfully quit smoking the year before. But since Maureen met Vitorio I'd started again. I lit up, chased my booze with coffee, and puffed my cigarette, trying to form smoke rings while Clive made faces at me. It was illegal to smoke in the bar. That was the routine while I waited. Smoking and drinking and breaking Clive's chops.

Finally, Maureen raced in. She was wearing a shiny low-cut dress. Blue. It looked good with her pale skin and red hair. "Hey, pal," she said, pressing her cheek against mine, dropping a blue sequined purse on the bar, and draping a small blue cape on the stool next to me. The cold didn't seem to bother her.

That's when I noticed her split lip. The kind you get when someone smacks you. Hard.

I thought about asking what had happened but didn't. In spite of her battle scars she was still gorgeous, acting as if the world was her oyster. She pushed a bunch of quarters into the machine and danced over to me before the Latin music even began.

"Working?"

She nodded. Her right hand mimed holding a tray. Like many Broadway gypsies, she kept body and soul together waiting tables. She showed Clive an index finger.

"One Chivas Regal," Clive said, pouring and delivering a double along with a bowl full of cashews.

Maureen tossed her drink down and rapped the bar with the heavy empty glass. Clive obliged with another double.

She had a long svelte body, and though she'd gotten too skinny for my taste, she was still a looker. She was also very screwed up.

One of my oddest memories is of waking up with most of those twenty or so Barbies in bed with us, and Ken, the master and daddy, clasped to Maureen's chest.

Now I was the pal she told her sad stories to.

With a ballet dancer's grace Maureen leaned forward, and without touching the glass, delicately sipped a taste of her drink. Smiling, she *undulated*—that's the only word that fits—to the music, doing that hands-down-her-breasts move and continuing clear to her thighs.

The door to the Bucking Bull opened, bringing in the dark, cold night air, and the real bucking bull Maureen had been dreaming of. Vitorio.

I had a cigarette in my mouth, but I didn't light it.

Maureen stopped dancing. Her body tense, she stared at Vitorio. It wasn't all lust. There was dread there, too. Maybe that added to the sexuality. What did I know?

Vitorio glided over to Maureen, pulled her to him, kissed her, then flung her, Apache-style, across the room. Very Rudolph Valentino. Corny but it worked. They danced, looking great together.

After a big finish they settled in at the bar. Vitorio chugged Maureen's drink and ordered another round. What the hell. She would pay for them. Maureen talked to me a couple of times to support the fiction that she and I were there together.

Pretty soon I was the invisible man. That was fine for me. But I worried about Maureen. With each new round Vitorio got meaner and louder. He started manhandling her, grabbing her bare arms and leaving welts.

"Take it easy, friend."

"Fuck you where you breathe. You aren't my friend and I'll take it any way I want to."

I stood. Not to fight, to get out of there. To give me time to think, I grabbed a handful of cashews and popped them in my mouth. "Maureen . . ." I chewed and swallowed. "I'm working the new Redford film tomorrow. Have to get up early. You want a ride home?"

This was a sham. I lived on Central Park West and Maureen was across town near Second Avenue.

"No, I'll be fine." She leaned close and whispered in my ear, "He's okay. He's just hot for my body."

Yeah, I thought.

It must have been 3 in the morning when the phone rang. "Hello?"

I could hear her sobbing. "I'm downstairs. Outside the park. I need you."

"Maureen! What's wrong?"

"Come and get me. Please, Eddie."

I threw my clothes on and hurried out through the side door on 83rd Street.

The night was misty, colder than September had any right to be. Foggy, too. Murky clouds raced overhead, alternately hiding and revealing the moon.

Across the street the large, imposing black boulders in Central Park, looking like monster sentinels, cast great shadows on the street.

The wind wailed across the park, shaking the trees. Me, too. I wanted to rush back to the sanctuary of my apartment.

For a strange instant all was blackness and silence. Next I spotted a glint, then a shadow lurking just beyond the glow of the streetlamp. I ran across to the park side. Maureen stepped out of the shadows, her face highlighted by a macabre halo of lamp light.

Her blue dress, sans cape, was torn and bloody. Clutched against her chest, her sequined purse, a cell phone, and an elegant Barbie doll in a sparkling white wedding gown also specked with blood.

A yellow cab pulled up. "Taxi, folks?"

Maureen was in such a rush to get the door open she dropped her cell.

"Wait a minute," I said, peering at the shadowy ground.

"Forget about it!" Maureen shrieked. "Hurry."

The driver headed downtown to come around.

"No!" Maureen cried. "East. We've got to go across the park."

I patted her hand. "He knows."

She pulled her hand away. "Nobody knows."

After a few turns we entered the park at 86th and traveled the empty road east, past angry stone walls, moonlit hundred-year-old shuddering trees, and through their ground-bound silhouettes.

Above, clouds were scudding across angry sky while Maureen mumbled variations of, "Look for him by moonlight, watch for him by moonlight, he'll come for you by moonlight, fear for him by moonlight, fear him by moonlight . . ."

As we stopped on Second Avenue, thunder crashed. Then came the deluge.

Maureen paid no attention to the rain pelting down. She jumped out at Second Avenue and ran to 81st Street. Her building was on the left, perhaps a hundred feet away, next door to a book shop.

I shoved some bills at the driver and chased after her. By

the time I reached her building I was drenched. Maureen was nowhere in sight but I could hear her running up the stairs reciting her crazed mantra. "Seek the man by moonlight, snatch the man by moonlight, catch the man by moonlight, he'll come for you by moonlight, beware of him by moonlight, despair for him by moonlight. Despair for me by moonlight."

I raced up to the fourth landing two steps at a time and found Maureen in her apartment, soaked from the rain, sitting on the floor like a child. Her collection of Barbie dolls was piled in her lap and scattered around her. Within reach was a large, heavy frying pan and Ken in a dinner jacket, his head snapped off. Surrealistically, a bit of blood spotted his headless neck.

Trails of crimson led to the frying pan and to the open door of the bathroom and to Vitorio, his head bashed in.

"Why do they have to hit?" Maureen asked of her elegant Barbie. "Why do they have to hit?"

BUILDING

BY S.J. ROZAN

Harlem

Wouldn't none of it have happened, hadn't the Landry boy took to calling him "sir."

His mama named him Rex and he was still resentful. Might have been okay for some boy with a handsome face, but that wasn't him, and in school all it got him was, "Hey, lookee, here come that ugly Tie-RAN-o-sore!" Later, when he did his stretch in Greenhaven, when someone said his name, he only heard "wrecks" because that's what he'd made of his life.

It was a hard life, and nobody gave him nothing, not that that was some kind of excuse and he didn't pretend it was. His daddy could've been any of three different men and his mama never cared to find out. They stood around pointing their fingers at each other, and at her too, and so he didn't want none of them for a daddy even if they'd wanted the job. It meant he raised himself, pretty much, and he had to say, he done a lousy job of it.

But he wasn't making excuses, how he ended up at Greenhaven. Berniece rolled on him, but hell, girl was probably scared shitless. He wouldn't never hurt her, but how she supposed to know? What she see, he blown away her side man and was likely coming after her. Fact was, Chico'd porked the gun out, Rex just going there to talk to the brother, see about the rumors he was hearing down at the

Lenox Lounge. *Seen Chico with Berniece*, Bighead the bartender raised eyebrows at him, *what's up with that?* So Rex just wanted to talk to Chico, and he even laughed, so funny seeing little skinny Chico with that big .45. Then he looked in Chico's eyes, heard his voice, not the words but the sound just piling on. Chico never did know enough to shut up. Rex stood there as long as he could, looking at Chico, hearing his noise, and then a pressure started building inside him, building, building, and he threw himself on Chico and pulled the gun from Chico's hand.

Next thing he knows, NYPD Blue is breaking down the door. Door was wrecked, and Rex was wrecked, and Chico sure as hell was wrecked. And he heard his own named different after that.

In Greenhaven, anyhow, they called you whatever damn thing they wanted, whatever they thought would get your goat. Most times he let it roll off, like when it was the C.O.'s jawing. But sometimes he could feel it happening, that building. And the next asshole gave him a hard time would find his teeth in the back of his throat. That right there accounted for Rex not making parole until his third hearing.

But he'd made it, and now he was out. And since he got out, no more fighting. No more brawling, nothing, not even with that crew of hip-hop assholes hung on the corner. They pissed him the hell off, bopping like they do, like they own the world. They didn't never try nothing with him, though. They showed him some respect, behind his ten years at Greenhaven. Still, time to time he think they could use a little pounding.

But he ain't gonna be the one. He was on parole, next eight motherfucking years. No way in hell he was going back inside, that was one thing for certain. He reminded himself that every time he felt the building, felt his temper start to go, found himself about to get physical with half-a-dozen boys could've been his children. Might have been his children hanging there, too, if Berniece hadn't gone messing around with Chico, if she'd married him like he wanted, way back then.

Anyway, that was way back then. Berniece was packed and gone by the time he came out, and good riddance. He didn't want no more to do with her, to do with nobody. He had a steady job, hard enough to come by. All he wanted was to come home, watch TV, drink some beer, and go to bed. Less people you talk to, less trouble you could get in.

So he never did say nothing to the Landry boy.

That boy, seem like no one never gave him nothing, same as Rex. Raggedy clothes and no-name sneakers, tough way to make it on the street. But his mama raised him right. Kid wasn't no sissy. He put on that hard face Rex knew, face he used to wear himself. But he'd move out the way when the ladies come home from church, and he called Rex "sir."

Time to time, Rex wanted to tell him watch out. Wanted to say, *That crew you hanging with, they gonna drag you under.* He seen the kid's face, seen how it light up when one of them older boys hand him a paper-bagged Bud; the kid way too young to drink. *You fixing to turn out like me,* Rex thought to tell him. *You think these your homies, you think you tight with 'em. Next thing you know, one of 'em's gonna be facing some serious time. That happen, he gonna sell the cops everyone's ass, yours included.*

But he kept his head down. Kid wasn't his problem, and he never did say nothing.

Didn't keep him from noticing, though. Noticing the kid on his way to school every day, take his books, try to keep his raggedy self clean. Didn't cut school like the rest of them no-accounts. Rex wished he'd thought more about that himself, wished he'd kept up his schooling. Well, too late now. No, no one gave that Landry boy nothing but he kept trying. That's what Rex noticed.

The night the trouble all started, he noticed another thing. Noticed wasn't none of that crew on the corner when he come home. Seeing as the only way they could spend more time in that spot would be to drag their mattresses out and sleep there, it was damned unusual to see the streetlight and the mailbox standing by themselves.

Next thing he noticed, he was nearly at the stoop when the Landry boy burst out from the door. He looked wildly both ways, his eyes hitting Rex's. They had a look, asking for something, begging even.

"You okay?" Rex asked. First time he spoke to the kid.

The kid shook his head. He wetted his lips, like they was too dry for him to talk. Seemed to try to make words, but nothing come out.

"Chill, son," said Rex. "Something wrong? Tell me."

The kid moved his lips some more, but still there wasn't no sound. He shook his head again and charged down the stairs. He raced away, sneakers slapping concrete. Rex stared after.

Thing Rex noticed next, someone was pounding on his door.

First, he was confused. He was back inside, he thought. It was early on, and some damn C.O. was thumping his cell door, telling him if he didn't come out now he wasn't gonna get no dinner, fuck if he ain't hungry, see how hungry he be by morning.

But the pounding kept coming and Rex woke up. He

blinked around his room, small and with roaches all over but he could come and go and eat any damn time he wanted. Grateful for a minute for the noise waking him from that nightmare.

Then some yelling, "Police! Open up!"

Shit, he thought.

He yelled back, "Yeah!" He fought past the sheets, tight around him like they was tying him to the bed. "Okay, okay!" He slid the chain and threw the bolt.

"Rex Jones?" One white guy, one black, both in suits, saying his name like a question but it wasn't. They introduced themselves as Detectives Something and Something Else. They pushed in without asking, Something talking to distract him while Something Else looked around.

They couldn't touch nothing without a warrant. Anyone grew up in Harlem learned that with their mother's milk. They had a warrant, they'd have waved it in his face right away. And plus, if they turned his place upside down there was still nothing to find. That was a fact, but he felt the sweat on his lip just the same.

"A few questions," Something Else said, while Something smiled. The one talking was the black one, he had shiny white teeth. When the white one smiled he showed stained brown teeth. Like they was negatives of each other, Rex thought, and missed the question, didn't even know they'd asked one until the room got quiet. Hell, he thought, and he said, "Say again?"

"Come on, Rex, it's not hard. What did Tick Landry say to you this afternoon?"

"The Landry boy? He ain't said nothing."

"When you came in, he was going out. Running out, like he was doing something bad. He was, Rex. He ditched a gun that killed an old lady who wouldn't give up her handbag. Where's the gun, Rex?"

"How the hell I'm supposed to know?"

"Isn't that what he told you?"

"Ain't told me nothing. Just stood a minute, then went on down the steps. You telling me he killed a old lady?"

"We sure are."

"No way he done that. He all right, that kid. Gotta have been one of his boys."

"Well, you could be right, Rex. Have to say this, though: Doesn't matter much to us. That whole crew's garbage and we're gonna sweep 'em up. Might be another one who shot the old lady, but Landry's the one who was running scared that night. That's what we call 'suspicious behavior' in our line of work. All we have to do now is connect him up with that gun. Only we don't have the gun."

"I sure as hell ain't got it either."

"But he told you where it was."

"Fuck he did. Why would he do that?"

"Those boys, they look up to you. You did a dime at Greenhaven, Rex; that makes you someone on this block. Maybe you're even running with them, in a fatherly way."

"Me? Nuh-uh, man. I'm clean since I got out." The sweat started on his lip again, and his back, too.

"Are you? You'd better be. Let me tell you something." The cop stopped smiling. "I was new in this precinct when you went in. I've seen a lot of garbage like you go in and come out over the years, and I'm getting goddamn tired of it. In and out, in and out. I'm telling you: If you're running with these boys, Rex, my man, you are fucked."

That was the first day. The second day was pretty much the

same. He found the pair of them waiting on the stoop when he got home from work.

"Where's the gun, Rex?" This time it was Something, the white one, doing the talking. Rex preferred the black one, if they was gonna smile. All them brown teeth, shee-it.

"I don't know."

"Three people across the street swear you and the kid had a talk when he ran out of here. What did you talk about? Not the gun, then what? The old lady, maybe, how it felt when he pulled the trigger?"

"Didn't talk about nothing. Kid just move his mouth around, like he got words in there ain't coming out. Then he go on down the stairs. Like I told you yesterday."

"Yeah, that's what you told us. We're just having trouble believing you, is all."

"Ain't my fault."

"Well, but see, what it is gonna be, it's gonna be your problem, if you don't start making sense soon. Like I told *you*, we have witnesses."

"Across the street? What the hell kind of witnesses is that?"

The detective put his arm around Rex, like they was old pals. Rex felt the pressure building. He made himself not move.

"See, Rex," the brown teeth said, "you're on parole. Any trouble you get in now—like, say, assaulting an officer who's just being friendly—that could be bad. What do you have, another eight left?" His free hand brushed dust from Rex's jacket. "Rex, we want that gun. You say you don't know where it is. We don't believe you, but it could be. You might consider making it your business to know."

"What the hell do that mean?"

The cop shrugged. "These boys. They look up to you. That's all I'm saying."

The third day they showed up at his job.

"Rex? You in trouble?" His boss came into the boiler room where Rex was laying down sawdust to soak up spilled oil.

"No," he said, and added, "sir."

Before he went in he was a carpenter. Used to build things, good solid things. Something real—something wouldn't be, wasn't for him. Coming out, world was different. Not easy for ex-cons to find work, and no chance of getting back in the union. But one of the contractors used to hire him from time to time, he had a cousin, super at a fancy East Side building. The cousin put Rex on the maintenance crew. Now he spread sawdust and hauled the garbage out.

"Because there's two cops here," his boss said. "They want to talk to you."

Shit, Rex thought, but he didn't say it, just went out to the service alley. "What you doing here?" he said into the two smiles.

"We want that gun, Rex."

"I told you, I don't know nothing about that gun."

His boss was watching from the doorway.

"You shouldn't of come here," Rex told the cops. "I need this job."

"And we need that gun. And funny, we find none of those boys seems interested in talking to us. Can you believe that? Good thing the Landry boy already talked to you."

"He didn't."

"Well, then." The white teeth smiled, the brown ones following like a shadow. "Then it's a good thing he's going to."

The two cops made a point to nod and wave to Rex's frowning boss as they left.

That night Rex dreamed he was back inside. Not in his cell, but in one of them crooked, leaky passageways they got all over Greenhaven, connecting someplace you don't want to be in to someplace you don't want to go. The passageway was filled with garbage and he was digging through it, his heart pounding, fit to burst, things getting scarier and scarier as he went looking for something, he didn't even know what. He could feel the pressure building, building. And before he got even close to finding anything, a bright white shape and its dark shadow came and swept all the garbage up, and him too, buried him in it.

He woke up all tangled in sweaty sheets. Shit, he thought. Shit, and shit.

That day he didn't get as far as work, not even as far as the corner, before Something and Something Else come swooping, one from the front and one from the back, surrounding him all by their two selves.

"Let's take a ride downtown," Something said through them damn brown teeth.

"What the hell for?"

"You're a material witness, Rex. Maybe you remembered some details that might help us."

"I ain't remembered nothing because ain't nothing for me to remember! The Landry boy never said nothing to me!"

"Not even lately?"

"I ain't spoke to him lately."

"Why not? I thought we agreed you would."

"Didn't agree about nothing! I ain't spoke to the kid. Look, I can't go downtown with you. I got to get to work."

"That's okay, Rex. We'll call your boss. We'll explain where you are."

Rex looked at them, a matched set in different colors. Looked a couple of times. "Okay," he said.

"Okay, what?"

"Okay, I tell you where the gun is."

Because Rex had an idea, a great one, fucking genius.

Tell them a lie.

Why not? Say he seen someone, not the Landry boy and he wasn't sure who, but someone, seen him drop a .45 in the basement. Make him up: tall kid, with one droopy eye. Not one of them rapper assholes from the corner. Someone he ain't never seen before or since. Say, when he run into the Landry boy he'd been out to get some chips and beer, but when he come home from work earlier, he seen this tall kid then. Yeah. Yeah, that would work. Then he take them to the boiler room. They ain't gonna find nothing, and he'd say, *Well, shit, there's where I seen him drop it.* They'd be pissed, bust his balls that he ain't told them before, but who gives a shit? After that, they'd go away, leave him alone.

"Okay," he said.

He told them the story, listened to some bullshit about *How come you ain't told us before?* He said, because he's trying to stay out the whole thing, do they want to see the place or not? Of course they do. He took them into the basement.

"Here," he said, and pointed to the darkest, dirtiest place, the shadows behind the furnace. Above the white teeth and the brown teeth a black nose and a white nose wrinkled all up, like don't either of them want to go back there. "Shit," he said, "right here," and reached like he was gonna find something, moved his hand around. And thought, shit.

Shit if he don't feel something hard and cold.

He wrapped two fingers around it and pulled it out.

Both cops jumped back, so funny, like Chico. "What the fuck!" one of them yelled, he didn't see which. Then they both had guns pointing at him, standing legs spread, two hands like in the movies.

"Hey!" Rex told them, his heart thumping his chest like it want to get out and run away. "Chill! Y'all don't want to get your hands dirty, I'm just taking it out for you." He held up his hands, the .45 dangling.

Something Else took out a handkerchief, took the .45 with it, while Something kept his gun pointed at Rex. Whole thing over, they looked at it and looked at him. Finally they both smiled, all them teeth gleaming in the dark. "Thanks, Rex," they told him.

Cops so grateful, they gave Rex a ride to work, so he ain't late. He tell them drop him a block away, don't want his boss seeing them.

"You think you're a pretty smart son of a bitch, don't you?"

"Yeah, I do." And he did, finding them a fucking gun in a place he didn't even know no gun was. And he did all day, till he come home just in time to see them two motherfuckers hauling the Landry boy out in handcuffs. The boy's eyes looked right into Rex's again, like before, and this time they looked even more scared.

More like Chico's.

"What the fuck? What up with this?"

The white cop shrugged. "His gun, Rex."

"It ain't mine!" the boy shouted.

"Street says it's your brother's. Same thing."

"How's it the same thing?" Rex stood in their way.

"His brother's in North Carolina, has been for a month. So it wasn't him used it on the old lady."

"Wasn't me neither!"

"He just a kid," Rex said.

"Old enough to be tried as an adult if the charge is serious. We're talking about murder here, Rex. Hey, by the way, thanks." The cop smiled his teeth at Rex. "We appreciate that you gave up the gun. I'd suggest you get out of the way now, though. Unless you want to come with us?"

The kid's eyes widened when the cop said the part about the gun. He looked like Rex just took away all his candy, and he looked young enough to care.

That night Rex couldn't sleep for dreaming.

He dreamed the Landry boy's mama ask him to give the boy a Hershey's bar but he can't find him. He started to eat the chocolate himself but when he looked at it, it wasn't no candy, it was old smelly garbage.

He dreamed Chico was walking down the street and he wouldn't turn around when Rex called his name.

He dreamed he was standing in the middle of his apartment, pressure building inside him. The door and windows had bars on them, and he was stuck in there with the roaches.

At work his boss asked him, "How long did you work for my cousin, Rex?"

"Three years," Rex said. "On and off."

Rex could see him doing the math, see him thinking, *How much do I owe this guy?* Rex figured one more visit from them two detectives, he have his answer. Then where was Rex gonna get rent money from, even for that dump? And how was he gonna explain to his parole officer how come he can't keep a job shoveling shit?

That night, same as the one before. This time when he woke up, Rex couldn't remember what he dreamed, except all three of his mama's men pointing and laughing at him, him being so little and them real big. Make him so mad, make all that pressure begin building, but nothing he can do.

Next day on the way to work he saw the Landry boy's mama dressed in her church hat, getting on the subway. From the look in her eyes you might've thought someone punched her in the stomach. Long ride down to Rikers, Rex thought.

And more dreams the next night. This time he woke up at 4, sat staring out the window until the sky got gray.

When morning finally came, he called in sick. He spent the rest of the day getting let into Rikers to see the Landry boy. Shit, he thought, check out this shit, busting my hump to get *into* Rikers. Finally, they put him in a room and brought the kid in to sit across the table.

When he saw Rex, the boy put on that hard face. "What you doing here?"

"Got some questions."

"Who give a shit?"

"You just answer me."

"Why you tell them where my brother's gun at?"

"Didn't mean to."

"What the fuck do that mean?"

"Thought I was giving them a story. Trying to do the

right thing." He shook his head, to leave that be. "Must be me and your brother just think alike. How come he put it there?"

The boy stared. Seemed like the air went out of him. His shoulders slumped, the hard face sagged. "My moms don't let no gun in the house."

"Did you know where it was at?"

"No."

"Did your boys?"

The kid moved his shoulders, didn't say nothing.

"Suppose they drop the charges, let you outta here. What you gonna do?"

"'Bout what?"

"You tell me."

"Don't know what you mean."

"You going back to school?"

The kid blinked. "Sure."

"Why?"

"Why *what*?"

"Why you going back? You got plans?"

For a minute, the kid didn't answer. Then he nodded, real slow.

"What plans you got?"

"Gonna be a engineer."

"Why?"

"So I could build stuff. Bridges and shit. Buildings where there ain't nothing now."

Rex looked at the kid, watched him sit there, watched how young he was.

"That take college. You got a chance?"

"Grades, you mean?"

"Uh-huh."

"Got a A in math, A minus in physics. B's, everything else."

"You got a sheet?"

The boy looked around the scuffed room. "Till this, I ain't never been arrested."

"If you get outta here," Rex said, "I ain't gonna tell you stop hanging with your boys. They your boys, you ain't gonna turn your back. But you got choices. They got some shit going down, you stay out of it. You following me?"

The boy shrugged. "Don't see how it matter. Cops got my ass. I ain't getting out."

"Are you following me?!"

The boy jumped in his chair, to hear Rex shout like that. The guard in the corner turned to look.

Rex asked one more time, quietly, "Are you?"

The kid gave him a wide-eyed nod. "Yes, sir."

"Okay," said Rex. "Now you tell me one more thing. You kill that old lady?"

Right into Rex's eyes, the Landry boy shook his head. "No, sir."

Something and Something Else was both surprised to see Rex walk into the precinct squad room. "Hey, look who's here," the white one said, but Rex sat in the chair at the black cop's desk. Might as well give him the collar.

"Came to confess."

The cop's eyes opened wide, got white all around them. Matched his damn teeth.

"Confess? To what?"

"Was me shot that old lady. That gun I give you, it belong to me."

"Jesus, Rex, what kind of bullshit is this?"

"That kid ain't done nothing."

"Neither did you."

"You got a witness seen him?"

"We'll find someone."

"You won't, 'cause he ain't done it. You got his prints on the gun?"

"No, but—"

"You got mine?"

"Yeah, but I saw you pick it up!"

"Can you prove that's when them prints come from? Nah, forget it, I know you can't. I shot the old lady and I give you the gun, with my prints from when I done it."

"Rex," the white cop said from his beat-up desk, "you did this, tell us why."

"He was robbing her," said the black cop. "Wanted her pocketbook." Way he said it, it was clear to Rex he wasn't buying that.

"Uh-uh," Rex said. "Not that. 'Cause she look like Berniece, that's the reason right there."

"Who's Berniece?"

"Skinny-ass bitch that sent me up."

Something looked over at Something Else and Rex knew he had them.

"Fuck," Rex said. "Why you think I been jerking you ass-holes around? Do that kid a favor? Why I'm gonna do that? Do I owe him something?

"Then why'd you change your mind and give us the gun?"

"You was gonna take me in! I thought I could give you some bullshit story, put my hands on the gun so you'd think my prints come from then, and you'd be dumb enough to buy it."

The white one flushed. "And why're you having a change of heart now?"

Rex shrugged. "Didn't expect you to be *so* dumb to where you gonna go pick up that kid. He all right, that boy. Ain't done nothing."

"So you're just gonna give it all up? You're gonna go back inside, just like that?"

"Shit," Rex said. He thought about the room with the roaches, the job with the sawdust. He thought about the Landry boy's eyes.

He thought about things that wasn't there before someone made them, and he thought about the pressure building, building.

"I was going back in, sooner or later," he said. "I got tired of it, is all."

"Well, damn," the cop said. "What the hell, garbage is garbage, I guess. If we can't get one of those kids, I suppose we'll take you." He looked over to Something's desk and waited for the brown teeth to smile. "All right," the white teeth said, "if that's what you want, I'll book you. That it, Rex?"

"Yes," said Rex, and added, not to neither of these fools, but to himself, definitely to himself, "sir."

THE MOST BEAUTIFUL APARTMENT IN NEW YORK

BY JUSTIN SCOTT

Chelsea

I will cut her heart out," Tommy King announced in a loud, clear voice, placing near equal emphasis on each word.

I said, "You shouldn't be saying that."

"Who you going to tell?"

"See the blondes at the bar? How do you know one of them's not a cop? Or a cop's sister looking to get him promoted?"

Tommy King lowered the decibels to a vodka mutter. "Whoa. Almost blew it. Thanks, Joe."

We were seated at a four top in the back of Morans, an expensive Irish joint on Tenth in Chelsea around the corner from what I was already thinking of as "my apartment." Which was premature, considering how negotiations had gotten jammed up. Tommy King was the real estate agent who had steered me to it after a six-month search. The table was roomy because he always reserved for three and gave his name as "Dr." King.

"I don't want to give the cops any ideas. Shouldn't even tell you." He was finishing off his second martini, not drunk enough to ignore. I was used to his harping on his ex-wife, but suddenly he was vicious, gripping my arm and pulling me close to whisper, "I'm going to buy a surgeon's scalpel. What she did to me. I just have to figure out how not to get caught— What's the matter? You've never been mad enough to kill anybody?"

Hoping to shift the subject from ex-wife killing back to business, I said, "Right this minute I could kill the owner of that apartment."

"No, no, no. Jesus H., don't even say such a thing." He ducked lower. "You don't want to do that. Kill him and you'll end up negotiating with his heirs. I'm telling you, heirs are the worst. Soon as they inherit free money, it's not enough."

"It's the most beautiful apartment in New York."

"I used to say that about my wife. *The most beautiful woman in New York*. She still is, I'll give her that. Opens up that big smile of hers, she lights the whole street."

"I didn't realize you were still seeing her."

"From a distance. You have to get right in her face to see the evil."

Tommy waved his glass for a third drink.

I stood up. I'd heard enough evil-ex for one night. *From a distance* almost sounded like he was stalking her. "I'm out of here. We'll go up again tomorrow, right?"

"Seven p.m."

"Why so late?"

"He wants you to see the sun changing colors on the Empire State Building."

"He's enjoying jerking me around."

Tommy put down his glass and said, seriously, "Two things you want to keep in mind, Joe. He can only jerk you around if you show him he's getting to you. And, he knows what he's got."

"What's that?"

"What you just said, man. The most beautiful apartment in New York."

It was a walk-up. And the kitchen was a bad joke.

It ran the full length and breadth of the parlor floor of a Greek Revival town house built in 1840. It had two fireplaces and nine-foot ceilings. Listed as a one-bedroom, it had the extra nooks and crannies you find in an old house. One would hold a desk. Another, the upright piano I'd had in storage since I came to New York. It had a view in the back of narrow gardens and a view out front, across the street, of a gigantic plane tree in a green field beside a gothic stone seminary whose church, gardens, and dormitories occupied the entire block from Ninth to Tenth Avenues.

The plane tree spread its branches in a hundred-foot circle that screened the only ugly thing in view, the seminary's 1960s-modern three-story office complex that had all the charm of a suburban elementary school. When I asked how the church had skated it past the Landmark Commission— which maintained strict architectural control of historic blocks like this one—Tommy had answered, "This city was built on loopholes." The tree blocked most of it. Above the tree the Empire State Building sailed into the sky like a vertical ocean liner.

"Hard to believe you're in the city," said Richard, the owner. Richard had renovated the building forty years ago when—he told me every time I went back for another look— brave pioneers could buy crumbling property on a dangerous street for what today would buy a time-share in a parking garage. He had knocked down rooming house partitions and opened it up into floor-throughs, occupying the ground floor himself and renting the rest. Now, old and Florida-bound in a booming market, he had emptied the rentals by the simple expedient of jacking the rent to Park Avenue penthouse rates and had sold the third, fourth, and attic floors. "Mine" was the last and most expensive, since, Richard assured me, it was the best.

His negotiating strategy was effective, and downright intimidating. I had instructed Tommy to offer forty thousand less than his exorbitant asking price, then Richard raised his asking price by forty, making it insanely exorbitant. I should have walked away. Instead, I walked in at 7 o'clock, agreed that it was hard to believe we were in the city, and admired the light on the Empire State Building shift color from a metallic tan to red to blue-gray as the sun crept past the city.

It took a while, but Richard was in no rush. He was a non-stop talker who loved a captive audience. He told me that the reason the staircase sagged was some idiot had cut a main beam in the basement while running a new sewer line when they converted the original town house into a rooming house for the dockworkers back in World War II. He told me he put a new roof on the building. He told me that a disused air shaft could be converted to a kitchen exhaust fan in "your apartment."

He told me a bunch of gossip about people on the block who fell into two categories: amusing eccentrics who owned buildings and apartments, and gypsy peasants who rented. He cackled that the house of a neighbor he was feuding with was haunted. "Really is. You could buy an apartment in his building for half what it's worth."

I had checked that out already. It was going cheap all right. I didn't see any ghosts. But it was completely ordinary and the only view was of a housing project on 18th.

"Having the seminary across the street is like having a

country house outside your window. Except you don't have to drive there and mow the grass. You want to get outdoors, you walk two minutes to the river."

Then he made my blood run cold by telling me that a couple had looked at the apartment this afternoon and seemed to like it a lot. Money was no problem. The guy's parents were rich. And if they wouldn't help, the Swiss bank that employed the woman would front the down payment. He watched me react and seemed to like what he saw.

"You really should live here," Richard said. "You'll never find another place like this. Chelsea Piers, best gym in New York, is right down the street. I'm selling paradise."

I turned my face to the window. The Empire State Building had almost disappeared in the dark. Just then, they switched on a thousand floodlights, painting it white as an iceberg.

"Look at that," Richard crowed. "I just have a feeling in my gut you belong here. I don't know if I ever told you, but this apartment has a track record when it comes to romance. Everyone who ever rented it met somebody and had a love affair. Right here in these rooms."

I should not have told Tommy King that I wanted the kind of home that a woman would like to share.

"You're asking a killer price," I said.

"It will only get more valuable," he countered. "Nothing will bring it down. It didn't go when the Towers went down. I was watching on CNN thinking, *Oh, God, the Empire State Building's next, I'll never get my price without the view.* Then I realized the terrorists don't know from shit about the Empire State Building. You gotta be a New Yorker to love the Empire State Building—sure enough, they went for the Pentagon."

He was right. It would not be the most beautiful apartment in New York without that spire changing colors by the hour.

Richard said, "Nothing but a haunting will ever bring it down, Joe. And don't get any ideas, because this building is not haunted and never has been. No scary ghosts, no evil spirits. It's a great investment. Turn around and sell it in a flash. For profit."

"I'm looking for a home, not a stepping stone."

"Everyone wants to move up."

"Not me. This is up." Another mistake I realized as soon as I said it. I had told him exactly how much I wanted it and he didn't bother to conceal a smile.

Tommy King stepped in, too late to repair the damage, saying, "Listen, Richard, thanks. We gotta split. We'll come back tomorrow. Seven o'clock?"

Richard touched my arm, exuding fatherly concern. "You might want to think about if you really belong in New York."

"Beg pardon?"

"A lot of people your age who can't afford New York are buying in Brooklyn. Manhattan may not be your town."

On the street Tommy said, "I thought you were going to slug him."

I turned on him. "Next time you see a class of high school tourists from the boonies? Look for the straggler staring at the skyscrapers. That's the kid who's coming back. Manhattan's been my 'town' since I came here on my senior trip. I don't care who's moving to fucking Brooklyn, I'm not."

"Whoa. I believe you, man. You turned red as brake lights. First time I've seen fire in your eyes."

"I've settled for second best too many times." I couldn't believe I had just admitted that out loud, but I was so upset

I dropped every defense and proceeded to spill my guts to Tommy King. "I didn't hold out for an Ivy League college. I didn't fight to get into a first-rank law school. I didn't hold out for the job that really would have gone someplace."

"You're general counsel of the biggest printing company in the city."

"I sign off on contracts. If a problem gets interesting, I'm told to hire outside counsel. I married a woman mainly because I didn't know how to say no when she asked. And I didn't fight for a fair divorce. I'm through settling. I'm through letting things happen to me. *I want that apartment.*"

"I believe you, man. You look like I feel about my ex."

"I really blew it with Richard, didn't I?"

Tommy said, "I bought it today."

"What? Bought what?"

"Scalpel."

"What?" I said again, though I knew what he meant.

"It's just a skinny little handle with a bunch of blades. Like razors. Cops'll figure some kid got her with a box cutter."

I figured it was time to get a new real estate guy. Tommy King was nuts—creepy nuts—telling me all this because in his twisted heart he really believed that he was right and she was evil. It didn't matter that he was the listing broker. Richard would sell to whatever fool paid his ridiculous price.

On the way home I got a call from another broker at Tommy's agency, a partner named Marcy Stern, a woman with a shrill, demanding manner that matched her pointy face and darting eyes. "Listen, Joe, you're out of there tomorrow morning."

I was living rent free, baby-sitting an apartment for sale. Tommy had gotten me the gig and I figured I was safe until I found a place of my own because the plain white box in an ugly white box building was listed for an insane price. Wrong about that. "How can you close in one day?"

"All cash deal. The client wants to dump his stuff before he hops his flight to Singapore. Get your junk out by 8."

"Didn't I sign something that said I'd get a couple of days notice?"

"Not if you want help getting another free place. Call Tommy King." Tommy had a similar live-in security guard arrangement, sleeping in a succession of apartments on the market since he lost his home to the ex-wife he hated so much he wanted to cut her heart out.

I called Tommy.

"Don't worry about it, I'll get you another one soon as I can. Bunk with me till then."

I thanked him for his generosity and he repeated what he had said when he first offered me the apartment-sitting deal. "Why watch your down payment get smaller? Bad enough watching prices go higher."

At a quarter to 8 the next morning, Marcy unlocked the door with the agency key and looked surprised that I was still stuffing clothes into bags. "What are you doing here?"

"I'll be right out of your way." I picked up a garment bag, a laptop backpack, and a suitcase—everything else was in storage. The suitcase, which had been damaged by an airline, broke open. My laundry fell on the floor.

Marcy and the new owner, a Chinese guy in a blue suit, along with a huge guy who appeared to be his bodyguard, watched me crawl around picking up my underwear, and shut the door firmly behind me as I shuffled down the long, dreary hall to the elevator.

Tommy was on the phone when I got uptown to his latest temporary place—a glass and mirrored palace in the sky with views of the park and both rivers. He pointed me toward one of the halls and mouthed, "Third bedroom on the left." Then he continued loudly on the phone. "Hey, by the way, my ex is looking in Chelsea. She's got a new boyfriend wants a pied-à-terre. No, leave me out of it. If she hears I'm involved she'll run the other way. I might have something you can show her. I'll give you a heads-up."

As soon as I bundled my stuff into the bedroom, which had hardwood floors, a marble bathroom, and no bed, Tommy wandered in saying, "You gotta raise some more cash for a bigger down payment so the bank'll cut you a mortgage to meet Richard's price. So the question is, where do you get the cash?"

"I wish I knew."

"Most clients' parents chip in."

"My folks don't have that kind of money."

"Can't they take a home equity on their house?"

I explained that a bank appraiser would not bother getting out of his car for their tiny ranch with a shallowly pitched roof on a quarter-acre lot. "If every neighbor on their block chipped in with a home equity loan, they might raise enough to send a crippled kid to Disneyland. No, Tommy, not everybody is rich. It just seems that way."

"I gotta tell you, Richard is not lowering it. There are no minuses in that apartment. Once you accept the stairs and the kitchen—which you already did—there's nothing wrong to make him lower his price."

"Yeah, I guess not."

"Think about Brooklyn."

"No!" I felt my face burn red again.

"Man, you're looking obsessed."

I repeated what I had said yesterday: "I won't settle for

second best." Then I changed the subject to get him off my back. "I heard you on the phone. Sounds like you got un-obsessed with your ex."

"What do you mean?"

"Helping her look for her boyfriend's apartment."

"Is that what it sounded like?"

"Sounded like you got over her."

His face hardened up. "After what she did to me?"

"What *did* she do to you?"

His eyes widened. "Are you kidding? *What* did she do to me?"

"You keep saying it, but I don't know what it was."

"I told you. *She got the apartment.*"

"My ex got our apartment. But I'm not going to kill her for it. Much less cut her heart out."

Tommy got really mad and started hacking away at me. "She got your apartment? What kind of apartment? Tell me about it. View? Big? Classy building? High ceilings? Skylights? Granite and nickle bathrooms?"

"No. No. No. And no. It was just a nice apartment. Nice layout."

"Nice layout means small."

"It was small. It was a New York apartment."

"Yeah, well I wouldn't cut my ex's heart out for a piece of shit like that, either. But my apartment was fantastic. First of all, it was the best deal in New York. I bought it right out from under my firm—previous firm. Went to check it out. Found this old guy, just got widowed, starts weeping while he's showing me. It was gorgeous. He had no idea what it was worth. He just wanted out. I made an offer on the spot. Condo, so I didn't have to go through board shit. Gave my banker oral sex to get a bridge loan to close the deal— Hey!

Lose the I-just-got-here-from-Topeka expression. She wasn't that bad."

Maybe she wasn't, but Tommy had no smile for the memory.

"I thought I was made," he raged. "Fucking brass ring at last. It had it all. Views, high ceilings, kitchen to die for, class building. She turned around and flipped it for *ten times* what I paid five years ago. She is fucking rich and I'm sleeping in a sleeping bag. Which is why—"

"I know, I know. You're going to cut her heart out."

That afternoon he called me at work. Richard had canceled our 7 o'clock meeting. I felt a cold lump in the pit of my stomach. It sounded like he had gotten the higher offer he'd been waiting for. "Any idea why?" I asked.

"No idea," said Tommy.

"Can you reschedule?"

"I'll talk to him next week."

I had an awful feeling Tommy was trying to blow me off. In fact, I had an awful feeling that he himself had found the client who had made the higher offer. Hating myself, I did a terrible thing, telephoned my folks in Missouri and asked to borrow the fifty thousand dollars they'd been saving, buck by buck, so they could move south when my father finally retired from teaching.

The damnedest thing was how they didn't even hesitate. I promised I would pay it back as soon as possible, thinking maybe I could in five years, and right after work hurried down to Chelsea prepared to meet Richard's insane price with an extra ten thousand to beat the offer I just knew he must have gotten.

Richard was sitting on his front step, leaning against a

pillar that was topped with a welcoming wrought-iron pineapple he'd had recreated by Spanish craftsmen to match one stolen. The front door closed behind him and I could hear somebody creaking up the steps.

I said, "I got the money. I can meet your price."

"Too late. A woman's buying it right now."

"I can top it by ten thousand."

"Top what by ten thousand?"

"The extra forty you wanted."

Richard laughed. "She's already topped that. I've got seven hundred thousand on the table."

"*Seven hundred thousand?* Sight unseen?"

"She saw it this afternoon. Woman looking for a pied-à-terre for her boyfriend."

"*Seven hundred thousand?*"

"This woman is so in love she'd have paid a million." Richard shook his head. Even he seemed awed and it made him seem more human as he asked, "You know how when somebody is really happy after being unhappy for a long time? How they glow? This woman is glowing like Venus on a dark night."

"How'd she find out about it?"

"Your friend Tommy showed it to her broker. Tommy was so excited he was red in the face. He really is a greedy prick."

"Is Tommy up there?"

"No, he and the broker were here earlier."

"Did you actually see Tommy King leave?"

"No."

I thought to myself, Tommy wouldn't kill her up there. Richard knew he had set it up with her broker. He'd get caught. Except he didn't care about getting caught. He thought he was right.

I hesitated for longer than I should have. I knew exactly what would happen, and when it did, the price of that apartment was going to plummet. A bloody murder would knock the price lower than a ghost. All I had to do was walk away from a crime about to happen. Or better yet, just stand innocently chatting with Richard who, as usual, was talking up a storm. All I had to do was listen and wait.

"Hey, Richard," a woman called down from the front window of the apartment. "Where is that air shaft for the kitchen exhaust?"

She was not the most beautiful woman I had ever seen in New York, but she came close—a perfectly lovely blonde, slim, not boney, sky-blue eyes set wide in a heart-shaped face, and a mouth that wanted to smile. Quite a few years older than Tommy, I thought. I wasn't surprised they had gotten divorced; what I couldn't figure out was how they had hooked up in the first place. She just seemed better than Tommy, who while handsome enough to squire a beauty like her around town, had an empty mind and soul even when he wasn't threatening bloody murder.

She looked down at me gaping up at her, and her smile erased every line that hinted at age. As Richard had said, she glowed. "Hi. I'm Samantha King. Do you live in the building too?"

Before I could answer, she disappeared—like a reverse jack-in-the-box—and the window slammed shut. I ran up the front stoop. The door had swung closed and locked. "Open it," I yelled. "Unlock the door!"

Richard located the key on the crowded ring on his belt, inserted it, and unlocked the door. I pounded up the stairs. Halfway up the flight I heard her scream. When I reached the landing something heavy slammed against a wall. The old house had thin paneled wood doors and I ran full tilt into the nearest, splintering it open with my shoulder.

Tommy had chased her into a corner, bent her backwards over a radiator, and was hacking at her chest with his scalpel. He looked up at me crashing into the room. His face was covered in her blood.

"Stop!" I shouted, too late to do any good.

Tommy let the poor woman go and her body slipped off the radiator onto the floor. "I can't get it out," he said. "Should've brought a fucking saw." He reached down and tried to close her staring eyes, but the lids popped open again and all he did was leave bloody prints on her cheeks. He gave up trying, pressed the scalpel to the left side of his neck, and gouged deep.

I got what I deserved.

The *Post* and the *Daily News* exaggerated the blood, of course. *Times* and *Sun* readers learned that Tommy did not cut his ex-wife's heart completely out, but had given up halfway and ripped the scalpel across his own throat in what the *Sun* writer had termed "a spasmodic *mea culpa.*" Still, there was blood enough.

Marcy Stern, speaking for the real estate brokerage, swore that Tommy King had been "terminated for cause" before the attack. Asked what effect the crime would have on property values in Chelsea, West 20th Street, and Richard's 1840 town house in particular, she fired back, "Don't even think of lowballing us."

Unfortunately for her and Richard—and fortunately for me—no one thought of making any offers at all, lowball or otherwise. I got the apartment for the original asking price and didn't have to tap my parents' little nest egg. Richard, shaken, agreed to all my terms, especially a floor-to-ceiling cleaning by professionals before I moved in and a repainting of the room where most of the attack had occurred. I moved in the afternoon of the closing to a home smelling of fresh paint and floor wax.

Samantha was waiting in the window, her heart-shaped face super-imposed on the Empire State Building. Her ghost? Or just my guilty imagination reflected in the glass? Didn't matter which, I saw her clear as I saw the sunlit spire by day and the white iceberg at night. I tried moving around the room, shifting perspective. At angles, the nineteenth-century glass distorted the light, but she kept moving with me. Wispy hair, blue eyes, paler than in life, and a small, sad smile that grew sadder every day as the lines around her mouth deepened. "Why didn't you stop him?" she asked one morning. And that night, "You knew he wanted to hurt me."

After a couple of weeks of her, I called in a broker for a hint of what I could get for the place. He liked it, at first. I didn't have much furniture yet, but my piano made it look lived in and there were the fireplaces and the killer view from the front windows. All of a sudden he shivered.

"Weird feeling in this place. Like something's here? You ever notice? Hey, is this where that woman got killed?"

He didn't wait for my answer.

Samantha was waiting in the window. She said, "The thing that makes me saddest is that I had finally found a great guy. My friends were asking me, does he have a brother?"

I said, "I can't sell this apartment. I can't move. I can't change what I did to you. So I guess I'll have to get used to you. With a view like this I'll get used to anything. If I have to live with you, I will. If you can stand it, I can too."

I awoke the next morning to a mind-shattering screaming roar echoing in the street, looked out the window, and saw a bunch of guys with chainsaws and a crane lopping branches off the plane tree.

I raced downstairs in pants and socks. Across the street sawdust was flying from the main trunk. Marcy Stern was on the sidewalk, taking people's business cards and handing out pictures of model apartments slated for a new twenty-story residential tower. Each had a wonderful view of the Empire State Building.

"You can't build here!" I and several panicked neighbors screamed. "The seminary is landmarked."

"Not this part."

"The whole block."

"Not the new part."

"But—"

"We found the same loophole they did when they built the new part."

Steel rises quickly in New York. The last Samantha and I saw of my view was a hard-hatted iron worker silhouetted against the Empire State Building like King Kong.

THE LAST ROUND

BY C.J. SULLIVAN

Inwood

D anny Stone woke up angry. He sat up in his lumpy double bed and felt a rage tearing through him. His fists were clenched and he was breathing hard. He knew it was the dream. It was always the dream.

He shook his head and tried to erase the images of his long night. He knew he threw punches in his sleep and that is why he slept alone. Since he lost his wife, every woman he went to bed with woke him yelling that he was hitting them while he was dreaming. Sleep boxing, he told them, he suffered from sleep boxing. He said it as a joke but none of the women found it funny. Or slept with him again. In his waking life he had never struck a woman, and even in his dreams it wasn't a woman he was trying to hit.

He got out of his bed and stretched his tight body. The cold linoleum felt good on his bare feet as he walked over and looked out his bedroom window down to Sherman Avenue. A cold blast of wind blew brown leaves around a fire pump. Danny watched an elderly man carrying a plastic black bag and rummaging through a garbage can looking for beer and soda cans for the nickel reward.

Danny turned away from the window. He felt a lump in his throat. He blocked that out with another long stretch. His muscles and bones popped and then he dropped to the floor to do one hundred sit-ups followed with fifty push-ups.

Some men woke up to coffee, some to brushing their teeth. Danny Stone woke up and worked out. He did this every morning since he could remember. As a young boy he wanted to be a boxer and that is where it began. It took him through his fighting career and it would now take him into retirement.

"Too old, boy . . . you too old."

He tensed up on his last ten push-ups as he heard those words in his mind. His trainer, Victor Garcia, had said that to him at Obert's Gym yesterday when Danny floated the idea of one more fight.

Too old? How is thirty-five too old? he thought. Thirty-five is the prime of life for most men. But for a boxer? He knew the dirty secret of his profession. You didn't slowly lose your skills in the ring. They deserted you in seconds, and a contender for the middleweight crown—which is how Danny thought of himself, although *Ring Magazine* had never ranked him higher than number ten—could go from youthful potential to a washed-up bum in under three minutes. That is all it took. One bad round. You cannot hide in a boxing ring and all your weaknesses are eventually exposed. In his last fight, one of the best middleweights of all time, Roy Jones Jr., looked old at thirty-five, and Danny knew he was no Roy Jones Jr.

"You too old."

Those words.

Cutting and cruel.

He knew there was something to them. Age for a boxer is deadly. It is like a door you pass through, and when it closes behind you there is no going back. A part of Danny Stone knew that was true, but like most boxers he thought he could go one more time. He figured he could get a $50,000 pay date as an under card at the Garden. Good enough for a stake. Start a business. Maybe use it as a down payment for a condo. Take on some rising young kid and drop him on his cocky ass with his still-powerful left hook.

He could see it as he laced up his running shoes. The bright lights. The blood. The crowd yelling. The punch as Danny stood over the kid with his gloves raised. Danny smiled as he threw on his gray Champion sweat suit and burst out of his third floor apartment and ran down the stairs.

"Hey, Champ, what are you doing? Lock your door!" Mr. Ruiz, the super, yelled at him as he swept the floor.

"Nothing to steal," Danny called back with a laugh.

He ran out of the lobby and his legs tightened up as they pounded on the cement. The cold air hit his lungs like he had inhaled pipe tobacco. He put his head down and ran along the street toward Inwood Hill Park. The first ten minutes of every run was a killer for him. Even when he was young he hated the start of the run. But after ten minutes, even now, when he found his rhythm and groove, it got good. Real good. Running and boxing are what kept him sane all these years and he wasn't ready to let go of them. If no one else believed in him, Danny thought, at least he did.

At least he did. Those words comforted him as he ran up Dyckman Street. He passed the Alibi Inn and a white-haired man waved to him from the window. Danny smiled and waved back. Everyone in Inwood knew him as "Champ." He thought not many knew anything about him other than he was a boxer. The furies that drove him. He passed Sherman Avenue and made a right to avoid Pitt Place.

Danny knew that was where the ghosts lived. 209 Pitt Place. The last time he had seen his wife and baby daughter alive was in their tidy two-bedroom apartment there. He was deep in training out in the Poconos when the house was hit by a crew of home invaders. They came for the money they knew he had hidden in the closet. He had made some offhanded comment to a *New York Post* boxing writer about not trusting banks, and it cost his family their lives.

That the men were arrested, tried, and convicted with life sentences never gave him peace. That he won the fight was no solace. The only time he felt good was when his fists were pounding another man.

He shook his head to chase that ten-year-old memory away. He turned into the park and picked up his pace as he ran up the first hill. A mother pushing a baby carriage smiled at him when he huffed by. He kept going deeper into the park, deeper into his run. Away from the cruelty of life in New York City. Where the streets can snatch your whole life from you for a few thousand dollars. He went faster. His body felt good. He threw a few punches and let out a grunt.

He turned onto a path through the old woods and now ran on the dirt. As he came to the top of the hill, he saw a man standing in a thicket of bushes. The man looked up and Danny knew it was the guy he called the Mad Russian.

The Mad Russian was a local character who once told Danny his name was Yuri and he was once a Soviet botanist, now reduced to manual labor by the cruel capitalistic system of America. He said he came to the park to study the flora and the fauna. Danny waved to the Russian, but the guy looked through Danny like he wasn't even there.

Just another New York psycho, Danny thought. The city was full of them, and if he kept it up, Danny Stone would join them. Lonely displaced people haunted by their past. The ghosts of your horrors were always chasing you.

He came out of the park and leaned against a stone wall

to stretch his legs. It was a good run. Five miles. Good pace. Good wind. He was still in shape.

Danny walked down 207th Street and grabbed a newspaper and went into the Loco Diner. There, the waitress, Rosa, smiled at him and motioned him to a front table. She yelled to the cook to make an egg white omelet.

"How was the run, Danny Boy?" Rosa said as she put a cup of coffee down in front of him.

"Good. Five miles in twenty-eight minutes."

"Damn! You can run."

"You should come out with me sometime."

Rosa smacked her wide hips. "Not built for running, and I do enough running around here. Now, if you took me to dinner . . ."

Danny blushed as Rosa smiled at him. They had been doing this for the last year. Two thirty-five-year-old people acting like school kids. Rosa was pretty enough. A little heavy, but she carried it with a Latin charm.

Danny knew he needed something to change in his life. He was tired of being alone. He was ready. For anything. So he asked.

"Hey, Rosa, so why not?"

"Why not what?"

"Why don't me and you go out. Tonight. Benny's Steak House on 194th is good. You want to come with me?"

"You asking me out?"

"I think so."

"Well, it's about time."

"I work slow."

"I'll say."

"So we'll go. I'll meet you, like, 7."

"Yes, Danny, I would like that. I would like that very

much. Seven. Now here . . ." She put his omelet down in front of him. "You better eat this. You might need your strength. You ever been with a Latin woman?"

"Not one as pretty as you."

Nice line, Danny thought. Rosa smiled and went over to a couple at a booth to take their order. Danny sipped on his coffee and picked at the eggs as he read the lead story: "Inwood Jogger Missing."

A twenty-year-old college student had been last seen running through Inwood Park and she never got home. A runaway, Danny thought, as he turned the page and read about a elderly jeweler stabbed on Sixth Avenue. Crime is down in New York, but there's still enough mayhem to go around.

Danny finished his eggs and gave Rosa a wave as he threw ten dollars down on the table.

"Seven, Champ, I'll be here," she called after him.

Danny walked down to Obert's Gym and said hello to the regulars. He walked past Victor Garcia without saying a word. He put on some light gloves and worked the speed bag. He loved it when he got the *rat-a-tat-tat* sound as the bag hit the wood and then his glove with blinding speed.

He walked over to a heavy bag and motioned Khalif Little to hold it. He slammed the bag for three minutes, then held it while Little pounded it. Kid is strong, Danny thought.

The day dragged on. Danny trained a couple of local kids in the ring. He did foot work and shadowboxing with them. Good kids, but no real boxing talent. They were in the gym because they couldn't play baseball or basketball. Boxing was their last shot out of Inwood, and it was a cancelled check they were holding.

As Danny moved around the ring his mind kept going

back to Rosa. That warm smile. Those big hips. He needed a woman and he needed a fresh start. Maybe she could be the one. That is, if he didn't knock her out of bed.

Danny decided to skip some rope. Victor Garcia leaned on the ropes and watched him.

"You know, Danny, I was thinking about what you said. Maybe you're right. You can still fight. I'll look into it. We could both use a payday, and who knows."

"You know me, Victor. I never back down from a fight. You get it and I'll give it my all."

"You always did, kid. You always did."

Danny jumped out of the ring and said his goodbyes. He left the gym feeling pretty good. He walked home singing a song from the 1970s. Johnny Nash. *I can see clearly now the rain is gone.*

In his apartment he watched the evening news. A local TV reporter did a story on the missing jogger of Inwood Park. He heard her name. Sara Miller. Twenty. Blond. Pretty. Full of life. Honor student. All the things Danny never was.

The news went on with the weather report and he got ready for his date with Rosa. He took a hot shower, and as he dried off he threw talcum powder on his body. He went to the closet and put on a crisp, white button-down shirt and new black jeans. He thought about a tie and knew that wasn't him. He looked in the mirror. Not bad, he thought. Slim. Face not too banged up. Maybe Rosa saw something in him.

He threw on a black leather jacket and walked out the door. He stopped at the corner florist and bought a rose. A Rose for Rosa, he said to himself and smiled. He walked with an easy stride and felt good in his body. Then he turned the corner on 207th Street and felt his gut tighten as he saw the Loco Diner.

No time for doubt, he thought, and walked inside with a goofy smile. Rosa was standing there in a flower print dress with her black hair up.

"God. You're beautiful," Danny said, handing her the rose.

"A rose. How sweet. Shall we?"

Danny helped her with her coat and then they walked out of the diner. On the street she put her arm in his and matched his stride down Broadway. Danny felt good and kept taking sideway glances at her and smiling.

"We should have done this a long time ago. This . . ." he said, patting her arm with his hand, "feels good. Feels right."

"You asked when you did. Who knows? Maybe I wouldn't have went if you asked in the past. It all happens when it is supposed to."

They walked down Broadway chatting about their days. They entered Benny's and Rosa smiled as he led her to the bar.

"They'll get us a table in like fifteen minutes. The *Times* did a review last month. A good one. All the Manhattan people are coming up now."

"Danny, we are Manhattan people."

"Rosa, geographically Inwood might be in Manhattan, but it is more like the Bronx. We are Inwood people, not Manhattan people."

Rosa laughed at that. He ordered a red wine for her and water for him. Danny learned years ago that alcohol and staying in shape did not mix. As they finished their drinks a waiter took them to a back booth for privacy. Danny had called in a favor with Benny and they were treating him like the Champ he always wanted to be. He hoped Rosa was impressed.

They each ordered a steak and it came fast, hot, and rare. They were both hungry and ate their food with passion.

"Man, that was some good steak."

"I'll say. We ate like we've never been out before," Rosa laughed.

Over coffee Danny started to talk about his past. He felt like he had to. Like she had to hear what made him the way he was. And if she didn't run away screaming . . . then *maybe* . . .

When he got to the part of his family's murder, Rosa held his hand.

"I know, Danny. I am sorry."

"You know about what happened?"

"Well, yes, it was horrible. The whole neighborhood felt for you."

A tear fell down Danny's face. He never talked about that night. He only dreamt of it. As he talked of the hurt, he felt something leave his body. Something bad and bitter. He just rambled about his broken heart and his eyes never left Rosa's face. She sat in silence, just watching him with soft, brown eyes. Eyes like a healing light, he thought. She has a face like a saint on a church mural.

Danny ordered Rosa another glass of wine while he had a coffee, black.

"I just want to thank you for listening, Rosa. It was like taking bad air out of me. God, it felt good telling you all that."

"I'll listen anytime, Danny."

He asked about her life and Rosa told him the sadness of a divorce and the ruined dreams of her youth. She was going to be a lawyer but a child and an angry husband made her put that on the back burner. Where it stayed simmering into a bitter stew.

They left Benny's, and on the corner Danny stopped and held Rosa's face in his hands. He lightly kissed her lips and she caressed his neck.

They walked up Seaman Avenue and Rosa pointed to a "*Missing*" poster on the light pole. "That's the jogger in Inwood Park that went missing."

"Yeah. That is weird. You know, I run every day through that park and never saw her. I see that psycho Yuri but not Sara Miller."

As they walked, Danny told Rosa how the Mad Russian looked right through him earlier that day in the park.

"He creeps me out, that Yuri," said Rosa. "About two months ago I saw him running down 207th Street after some young college girl, cursing at her. The girl got away but Yuri had this sick look in his eyes like if he had caught her he would have done something bad."

"Really? You think . . ."

Rosa exhaled. "I don't know, but I got a feeling about him. Show me where you saw him."

"Rosa. It's dark out. That park is dangerous at night."

"Oh, come on. I go out with a boxer and he's afraid of the dark. Here . . ." She reached into her purse and pulled out a small flashlight. "Come on, it will be romantic."

They walked up the street and followed Danny's running route. As they entered the park, Danny's body tightened. He looked everywhere and anywhere.

The woods were empty and dark and Danny needed the flashlight to find the trail he took. He held Rosa's hand as they headed up the hill.

"There. He was standing right there."

Rosa walked into the thicket carefully and shined the light on the ground.

"What are you looking for?" Danny asked as he looked around. Who knows what's in here at night.

"I don't know. Anything."

Rosa took another step and hissed, "Oh my God."

Danny went over to her side and saw a body under a bush. Then he heard a low moan. Rosa shined the light into the bush and Danny reached in. He felt an arm and gently pulled it toward him.

"That's the jogger. That's her. Sara Miller," Rosa said, as they looked down on the young girl. She lay on the ground unconscious and barely breathing, but it was her. Her blond hair was a dirty mess and her face had cuts and bruises.

"We got to get her to a hospital," Danny said, as he bent down and picked her up by the torso and put her over his back.

"Careful, Danny."

Rosa lit the way as he tried to gently carry Sara Miller. He could feel her body moving on his back like she was trying to get away. They got back on the path and Danny picked up his pace.

"Memorial is like ten blocks. Call an ambulance. Have them meet us by the park entrance on 207th Street."

Rosa took out her cell phone and tried to keep pace with Danny's long strides. As Danny walked down the path, he sensed something coming at him from his left side. He turned and saw Yuri charging out of the trees with a huge limb.

"That is mine!" Yuri screamed, and swung the branch at Danny's leg. Danny's knees fell from under him. He was in a kneeling position and was able to lay Sara Miller down, when the branch hit his back, knocking him to the ground. His mouth tasted dirt. He saw Rosa swinging her purse at Yuri.

"Get off him, you friggin' psycho!"

Yuri grabbed Rosa's purse and punched her. She fell onto a park bench. Danny was on his feet now. Woozy. Unsteady. But ready for a round.

"Hey. Fight me. Fight a man."

Yuri turned and came at Danny. Jesus, Danny thought, this guy is big and moves like a boxer. A heavyweight. He hit Danny a glancing blow, and Danny came up inside of him and landed a body shot. Yuri gasped and punched Danny's ribs.

The punch hurt. Worse than anything he had felt in years. Like something went inside of him. Then he saw the knife in Yuri's hand. Yuri lunged at Danny and missed. Danny pivoted, and with everything he had, he hit Yuri with a left hook to the temple. It was a career punch. Maybe the best one he ever threw.

The Russian fell to the ground. Out. Danny jumped on top of him, beating Yuri's face. He punched until his hands were a bloody mess and he felt Rosa tugging on his shoulders.

"Danny, come on. Stop. He's done. You're hurt."

She helped Danny to his feet and he limped over to the bench. He put his hand on his ribs and felt the thick blood. It was like something was leaking out of him. Hate. Strength. Sadness. He felt like he could float away.

Rosa wept as she looked at his white shirt stained with blood.

"Just hold on, Danny. Just hold on."

"I'm cold, Rosa."

She embraced him, and in the distance an ambulance siren wailed. He leaned into her neck and smelled her. Then he kissed her neck and moaned.

"You're bleeding, Rosa. He hit you. Your lip," Danny whispered.

Rosa licked the blood off. "I'm okay. Just a fat lip. You just hold on, Danny. Hold on! That ambulance is for you and Sara. You saved her, baby. You saved her."

Danny looked up and smiled at Rosa. He felt lighter than he had ever been. All the weight he carried for years was leaving.

"I won, Rosa. I knocked him out."

"You did, Champ. You did."

Danny's eyes shut as Rosa held him and cried.

CRYING WITH AUDREY HEPBURN

BY Xu Xi

Times Square

for William Warren

Yeah, the ring's for real. Why would I pretend about that? So what is it you want to know, kid? That I wouldn't be "dancing" if not for Ron? That things might be different if he hadn't pulled his vanishing act? Ron never introduced me to his family. Said they didn't give two shits about him after his mom remarried, so why stay in touch? Guess I can't blame him.

Of course, I'm hardly one to talk.

Still, though. Might have been nice to have some American in-laws, even if they'd never come to Manhattan.

Okay, kid, write this down.

Mother cried over Audrey Hepburn movies . . .

"She's so elegant," she sniffed, "and helpless. No wonder men look after her."

On television, *Sabrina* was approaching its illogical conclusion. It was Saturday, February 29, 1964, the night of my father's fifty-ninth birthday. I was fourteen. A-Ba was at a dinner hosted by my three older brothers. We didn't go because of Audrey, but also because Mother said fifty-nine wasn't a big deal, and that my brothers and their wives were wasting time sucking up to A-Ba, hoping to get his money.

"I don't know what you're crying about," I said. "It's just a movie. It isn't real."

My mother dried her eyes with a silk handkerchief. "It wouldn't hurt you to soften up a bit and be a little more elegant."

Mother was Eurasian, but if you looked at her face front, she passed for Chinese. Exotic perhaps, but Chinese. Her mother was an American missionary's daughter who married a wealthy Cantonese trader against her parents' wishes. My father was a Cantonese businessman who made and sold soy sauce—"Yangtze Soy"—when he wasn't boozing. Whenever his commercial aired, the one where sauce cascades down cleavage to the opening of Grieg's piano concerto, Mother switched off the television in disgust.

"Here," she said, handing me her crochet work. "Put this away, please."

I complied and escaped to my bedroom, grateful to surface above the vale of tears.

Elegance. Facing the mirror in third position, I studied my feet. Six and a half and still growing; already, it was hard finding shoes my size. Mother would die if she knew I danced all the boys' parts. "Ballet will help you be more graceful," she insisted when she started me up nine years earlier. "It's important for young ladies to be graceful because gentlemen like that." Mother's graceful. She had jet-black hair, large eyes, high cheekbones, and a figure like Audrey's. I could imagine her in Humphrey Bogart's arms, dancing to "Isn't It Romantic." Mother loved to dance, but A-Ba couldn't fox-trot to save his life.

Sabrina is such a silly story. Bogart and Holden are these unlikely brothers of a wealthy Long Island family. Audrey's the chauffeur's daughter who has a crush on Holden. She disappears off to cooking school in Paris, returns grown up and sophisticated, which is when he finally notices her. But the family doesn't want her marrying Holden, so Bogart turns on the charm, intending to pay Audrey off. Instead, Bogart falls for her, and they end up getting married. The End.

My hair's limp and a faded mousy brown. I have Mother's height and A-Ba's frazzled eyebrows, beady eyes, and ugly mouth. I look *pathetically* Eurasian. My brothers inherited the best of my parents; they pass for Chinese and all made it over 5'8", a real asset among Hong Kong men. Leftover blood coursed through me, the accident, seventeen years after the last boy. Good thing I was a girl. That way, Mother fussed over me in her old age and didn't even mind the way I looked.

In the living room, Bogart and Audrey were sailing off to their Parisian honeymoon in black-and-white. Personally, I couldn't see what she saw in him. I would have taken Holden any day, philanderer though he was. After all, there was no guarantee what Bogart would be like after Paris.

But kid, I'm getting too old for this.

What? You think Ron happened yesterday? Audrey Hepburn died, that's what happened yesterday. Papers said cancer. Too bad Ron's not here. We'd have honored her passing together.

So you want to hear the rest of this story or not?

On her way home from lunch with friends the next afternoon, my mother was killed by a hit-and-run driver.

"She was running across the street again," my father shouted. "Always running!"

He had seldom been as angry. A-Ba's an ugly man who was once better looking. Smashed his face against a cracked toilet bowl when he was drunk one night, and emergency did a lousy job on his jowl. In his fury, his gnarled, contorted face resembled a lion's head in the dance—a shiny red and gold mask with fierce eyes.

"It was an accident," I said. "The police said so. Besides, the driver should have stopped."

"Always running," he muttered.

Can't recall much about the funeral. My three brothers did the adult things and said very little to me. We were virtually strangers, since they were gone by the time I was born. I wanted to scream at everyone to shut up and stop crying. I didn't cry. My thoughts zigzagged from the driver who left my mother on the road to die, to my father who never spent time with her, to Audrey, dancing in the moonlight in the arms of Bogart, the ugly industrialist, the man who would look after her for the rest of her life as Sabrina. Only in celluloid, not in Hong Kong.

Hey kid, I'm on. We do five shows Friday night. You're going to wait? Suit yourself. Back in fifteen, max.

How *did* he get me started? Asked about the ring, that's how. This one's different. Got a little class. Been in a few times, always buys me a drink. *Looks* at me when he speaks. Most guys can't. All they see is . . . well, you know.

Ron couldn't even watch me dance, never mind this act. But if it weren't for my little specialty, I couldn't keep this job, not now. Occasionally, he'd wait outside, even in the snow, before things got bad. "Times Square's no place for a girl after dark," he'd say, whenever he walked me home. Afterwards, we'd watch movies together till sunrise.

I miss that.

* * *

Vegetables? Funny? I suppose they are. There was the cigar, until some joker lit it. Scorched thighs hurt. Like the boss says, every act needs to change. Cucumbers taste better anyway.

Oh, so now you want to know what happened next? You're the funny one, kid.

Six months later, A-Ba sent me away to an all-girls boarding school in Connecticut.

"You've been begging to go to the States," he said over my protests. "I've made all the arrangements. Besides, I can't look after you."

He hadn't touched any of Mother's stuff since the funeral. I wanted to find a keepsake among her silks and jewelry, but didn't dare without his permission. Being the only girl, it was my right to have the first go. Once I was gone, my sisters-in-law would ransack all her beautiful things and there'd be nothing left for me.

I sulked my way to Connecticut.

Didn't like the school. We weren't allowed late-night TV. Despite the rules, we sneaked out after dark to meet boys. My classmates were in competition to lose their virginity. I won on my sixteenth birthday, easy. You don't have to be either graceful or beautiful in the backseat of a car. Being the only foreigner added to the freak factor. Anyway, it's not like those boys would bring me home.

I wrote home, dutifully, once a month. My brothers I never heard from. A-Ba only wrote brief notes with money, once each semester.

Mother would have written me long, gossipy letters, full of movies and news of society friends. If she'd seen an Audrey, her words might have flown. Mother survived on sentiment. She used to say, "One day, I'm taking you to New York where we'll do 'breakfast' at Tiffany's. We'll buy the diamonds for your wedding there." When it all got too much, I'd shout, "Mother, don't be silly! Who'd marry *me?*" And she would hold me tight, tears rolling down her cheeks, promising, "Trust me, my darling, someone will. Someone will."

I never wasted time crying.

Fantasy home. That's what this club is. Guys come in for escape or relief because they can't make it. A-Ba wasn't like them. He had Mother because he was successful. Problem was, she needed someone classier. Wasn't his fault. Other than his temper, he wasn't all bad. It's just that you can't manufacture class the way you can soy sauce.

Maybe I came along too late and caught a dismal closing act. They must have had a better life once.

I didn't talk about family to anyone.

Summer after graduation, I finally was allowed home. In Connecticut, it was possible not to think about her or her miserable life with A-Ba. But home, without Mother, was worse than being kept away at school.

In late August, *Wait Until Dark* made it to Hong Kong's cinemas. It was petrifying, watching a blind Audrey stumble around, stalked and terrorized like prey. I'm glad Mother didn't have to watch. Fear isn't romantic.

Listen, kid, you want to tell this story? I'm getting to the Ron part. Didn't you learn in your writing school that stories need history, plot, suspense? Character flaws? Otherwise the beginning muddles to the middle and you thank god it's The End.

Southern Connecticut State was a bore, but it was better than high school.

* * *

The boys were less frantic. I majored in something. All I cared about was dance. My feet, though! They felt way too big, having ballooned to a seven and a half.

Fall of sophomore year, Ron Andrews danced into my life.

His troupe was performing "Dance Nostalgia." Astaire routines. Porter, Kern, Gershwin. Ron did this solo soft-shoe number. The grand finale was him leaping onto a straight-back chair, tipping it over, and sliding toward the apron's edge on his knees. I jumped up, shouted, "Bravo," not caring what anyone thought. Maybe I started something, or maybe he was just that good, because the whole audience rose in a swell, cheering.

Later, backstage, Ron stood there, a towel round his neck. In his T-shirt and tights, one leg cocked on a stool, he looked like a blond William Holden. People congratulated; voices rose in a frenzy. He wasn't very tall, but there in the center of all that adulation, he was a giant.

When we were introduced, I couldn't help gushing, "You were incredible. Absolutely, amazingly marvelous!" He smiled, nodded in acknowledgement, and that was that.

Back at the dorm that night, I cried myself silly. It was such a weird sensation. I mean, I didn't know the guy to save my life, and crying wasn't my thing.

The next day, I went along to audition for their troupe's summer stock.

I was a good, but not brilliant, dancer. The point was, it didn't matter a whole lot whether or not I performed. Other students had rehearsed for weeks, desperate to make the cut. My friend Sara co-opted me as her "male" partner. I'd agreed, but that was before Ron. Of course, I couldn't very well back out now, not when the show had to go on.

"Smile, will you?" Sara hissed, just before we made our entrance. "Don't be such a dog face. Think Astaire."

We did "Dancing in the Dark." Sara was this tiny brunette, graceful as sin. In her white ball gown, fitted to her gorgeous figure, she was stunning. I was in tux tails, my hair pinned tightly in a net, a mustache pasted on for effect, feeling absurd. Sara was a strong dancer, but she hammed things up too much. Every dip swooped a bit too low, every turn was overdone. Friends applauded, but I knew we weren't much above passable.

Later, while removing makeup, I looked up in the mirror and saw him. He wasn't as young as he appeared onstage. He pressed both hands down on my shoulders and studied my face. "Do you ever dance the lady's part?" His voice resonated. Baritone.

Nodding and shaking my head simultaneously, I stammered, "Sometimes."

"Come on, then." Taking my hand, he led me onstage. In my tux shirt and tights, I looked ridiculous, but Ron didn't seem to care as we stood side by side, arms outstretched, my hand in his. I was the taller, and nervous.

"Dancing in the Dark" came on.

"Follow me," he commanded.

My feet flowed. It was better than magic, because all of me danced, guided by heaven and his lead. When the music faded, it segued to "In the Mood." His hands gripped my waist and he swung me in the air. A perfect partner, confident without being bossy, leading without stifling my movements. When we finished, the applause went on for a long, long time.

Onstage, I smiled at him, exhilarated, my heart pounding from exhaustion. Ron had barely broken a sweat. He pulled me toward him in a final twirl. "What's your name?" he asked. His eyes were a deep blue-green, as deep as the ocean, only deeper.

I quit school and followed him to New York. He was thirty, the senior member in the troupe.

"A dancer?!" my father screamed over intercontinental telephone wires. "You're living with a *baahk gwai* dancer? What are you, crazy?"

"But you married one. Or at least, a half–*baahk gwai*. I just wanted you to know."

"You'll get no more money from me."

"I don't need your money. I can work."

"Doing what? Shining his shoes? What do you expect to make without a college degree?"

I hung up. Ron never got to speak to him.

That was the last time I communicated with my family. What do you suppose Mother would have said?

I remind you of your sister? Another funny face, huh? Everything comes back to family, kid. We all start there, even if we end up someplace remote. Like Ron. Despite his step-dad, who beat him up and hadn't a clue, calling him a fag and all, he still thought about his mom. Oh, he'd never admit it, but I knew. Every Mother's Day, he used to cry in his sleep, like clockwork.

Ron and I got married six months later.

Life was great. He scored tickets to Broadway shows because he knew people in the business. Ron had tons of friends. He was like this solar system, burning bright, in whose orbit everyone sparkled and spun. He found places to perform, way off-Broadway, all across the country, even in Alaska, while other dancers waited tables or collected welfare. "I've got to dance," he said. "Doesn't matter how or where."

We did dance contests and exhibitions for money whenever he was between real gigs. Other than that, we didn't work together much. His act, the dance of his heart, was solo. Money was tight, but that never mattered because I loved him and we were rent-controlled. He used to work a lot then, going to every audition, trying for the big break. Such energy! "Disco won't last," he predicted. "It'll bore itself to death. You wait and see."

We talked. I told him all about my mother, about my Tiffany's "wedding," about her crying with Audrey Hepburn. Sometimes, talking made me weepy. He'd hold me until I calmed. Blood talk, he called it. Healing that scabs the pain.

After two years in New York, I took a job as a typist and filing clerk. It was way more lucrative than dancing and had health insurance. Ron didn't want me to do it. "What about your career? You're a good dancer when you try."

"You dance," I replied. "I'll feed us. Anyway, we'll still do the contests."

He picked me up, effortlessly. "Lazybones. Always wanting the easy way."

Up in the air, I laughed. "Life doesn't have to be tough all the time."

"Then what would you say if I tossed you out the window?" He swung me horizontal and held me there.

"Don't you dare."

He gave up when he saw I wouldn't budge. That was Ron: never made me do anything against my will. As long as he was our star, I was happy.

Besides, I liked shining his tap shoes. His feet were small and elegant, as if they'd been bound and sculpted to dance from the womb.

* * *

This rock? It's fake. You think I'd be dancing if it wasn't?

After I heard about Audrey yesterday, I hauled myself up to Tiffany's. Some things you just do. Colorless things, diamonds. Don't know what Mother saw in them. At least she loved me in her own silly way. Ron was right about that. He was right about a lot, especially love. He said deep down, my father loved me because I was his flesh and blood. His own father had been a dancer, but died when Ron was eight. So he knew all about what he called the "empty spaces of the heart."

But Ron was wrong about A-Ba. All these years and he's never once tried to find me, I don't think.

When Audrey Hepburn made her comeback in '76, it was all Ron and I talked about.

We'd missed her. I'd seen every one of her movies, in memory of Mother, but Ron liked her too. She looked pretty good for her age. You know, if you look at her face front, she could almost pass for Eurasian.

That year, I dyed my hair and eyebrows coal-black, and cut a young-Audrey bob. Ron said it made me look exotic. All the guys at work noticed. That was also when I started wearing makeup every day.

Funny stuff, makeup. One reason I never took performing too seriously was because I didn't like all that stage goo. Ron was tireless and careful about his; he needed to hide the lines. Mother wore makeup like it wasn't there, long before the natural look. Her foundation and powder blended into the skin tones of her neck, unlike women who didn't match their complexion properly and looked as if they'd severed and reattached their heads. She painted on eyeliner with a brush, rapidly, expertly, like an artist, but never used eye shadow.

"Women with blue lids," she declared disdainfully, "look frostbitten."

Letting Ron pluck my eyebrows was a revelation. "You see, you do have eyes," he said. "They were hidden by all that bushy fuzz." With a little eye liner, my eyes became wider, brighter, more open.

I smiled at people now, instead of looking down all the time. I even admitted my feet were *not* too big. As Ron said, seven and a half is an average size in America. I began wearing stylishly nostalgic dresses from secondhand stores. Ron loved my quirky new look. "Lady fair," he declaimed, "you put the stars and models to shame!"

That was the happiest time of my entire life. I felt elegant, even graceful.

Trust me, I don't talk to just anyone. It's not like I tell every writer who asks. What, you didn't think you were the first, did you?

I started dancing here because welfare ran out. After getting laid off, it was great not working for a while. Like vacation. I loved playing housewife and not having to answer to anyone. Ron said not to worry about getting another job, something would turn up. He even suggested auditioning. But at twenty-eight, I felt silly competing with the kids. Wouldn't say that to him, though. Why hurt his feelings?

In the beginning, I just used to dance. I tried a striptease, but it wasn't a success. As the boss says, you have to have tits for that, and I wasn't about to go silicon. So I stuck to the cage, or pole, because gams I've got. I'd come up with costumes for variety, like a see-through cheongsam with the waist-high slit, the Suzie Wong look? Oh well, I guess you are too young. Anyway, that was a big favorite. The act didn't come about till much later.

I don't remember exactly when Ron and I stopped dancing together.

What is it you want to know, kid?

Shortly after Audrey's comeback, things started going badly for Ron.

He didn't let on at first, laughing off problems and carrying on as if he were eternally onstage. First year, his agent was slow about returning calls. He talked about getting another. Then, even friends in the business stopped returning calls, and his agent only had truly awful gigs, like the commercial where he had to wear a cow costume and tap dance around these giant milk bottles. I told him it was just the times, that the economy sucked and things were bound to get better. There were still occasional road shows in Alabama or someplace. We'd saved a little money, which was enough to live on, because I was a careful housekeeper, although Ron teased, calling me stingy.

Then I lost my job, it was tough finding another, and yadda, yadda, you know the rest. But back then on 42nd Street, they always needed fresh girls.

By daylight, Times Square was seedy, but not terrible. Reminded me of Wanchai back home. When I was thirteen, I used to hang out on Lockhart Road after school. The *mama-sans* would stand around posing, fat old broads with painted masks and too-tight *cheongsams*. They'd catcall passing American sailors, pointing at the curtained doorways. It was like watching a show, somewhere very far off-Broadway, right at the edge of the grid. I gawked and giggled with my friends until they shooed us away.

Don't know where I found the guts to walk into the biggest joint that day. Looking good helped, and I could still dance. They hired me right off. I was nervous the first night. It was a Tuesday. Place was dead except for a bunch of geezers in the corner. "Pretend you're in a movie," one of the girls told me. "That way, you're not flesh."

Ron was mad, but kept quiet because we needed the cash. After the first three months or so, he relaxed when he saw I always came straight home. "Just a job, I guess," he'd say. I never expected him to dance, never breathed even the slightest hint, though he would have been terrific. He was way too fine for all this.

If only he'd kept going.

The kid. He looks a little like Ron.

You're leaving town tomorrow? Getting married?
    Ron went away, oh, ages ago.

Before he left home that winter afternoon, he claimed he was tired of the whole damned thing, said I would have been better off with Bogart. I didn't get what he meant because I was running late for work.

In the morning, they found his tap shoes on the Brooklyn Bridge, his wallet and wedding band inside them. All I remember is, it was the day before he turned forty.

See you, kid. Good luck with the writing and all. Hey, what's your name? I'll look for your book someday.

So that's the end. No one listens after the story's over.

I cried myself to sleep for months afterwards. Ron kept me going, gave me hope, made me feel I was as good as any star despite my life. "Audrey Hepburn doesn't hold a candle to you," he'd say. He filled up my heart with so much love I thought it would burst. What more could a girl want?

Crying over Ron made me remember Mother. They would have adored each other. There were days I thought about going to join them both. Every night, I'd get up onstage and dance to whistles and catcalls, or the dead space of labored breathing, and I'd be okay. But away from here, alone in daylight, the space in my heart became immensely empty and bare. Tears cascaded from some mysterious source, against my will, until the day ended and night returned again.

And then one day, I'm not sure when or why, I just stopped crying.

Dancing's been a kind of life. You get used to it. It's better than hammering away at a noisy electric typewriter, mucking with carbons, hoping the cartridge won't run out halfway. Plus no office politics. Girls who dance, they'll be friends or leave you alone, whatever you want. Independent types. I like that.

The boss was good about things. Kept me on after Ron died, mostly because he felt bad for me. But business is business, and let's face it, I was over thirty and this place *is* about fresh girls. So I came up with the cigar. He was skeptical, but gave it a whirl. I was a big draw. After the lighting incident, we moved on to vegetables. These were fine except for daikons, because those taste bad raw. But the boss was right. Variety *is* spice, so out I strutted on spikes, hiked up the skirt, sucked in, spat out, and caught each tubular from between the legs, shoved each one between the lips, and crunched, hard, the pale, peeled daikon being the finale. Like juggling, with dance.

When I turned forty a few years back, the boss and girls gave me this big party. I look pretty good for my age. You can't see the lines unless you look close. Makeup works. The girls come and go while I hang on. You have to keep going.

The act keeps me going. These days, we need to be careful. There's less you can get away with. Mood of the times; a conservative feel's in the air. That'll blow over, like disco. Besides, it's time to think about retiring. Economy's improving. Ballroom's hot again and there are gigs at shopping malls and the Y. I could do those. You don't need to be either young or brilliant to foxtrot or jitterbug. All you need is a partner.

It was a silly way for Ron to exit. I would have supported us forever. He was all the home I wanted, even on those days when he couldn't get out of bed. If only he hadn't given up. He would always have been my star.

Show time. Feet hurt.

Funny Face is on later. That's *my* favorite. Yes, it is just an earlier *Fair Lady*, except she does the actual singing. Astaire's supposed to be this famous fashion photographer who turns plain-jane bookworm Audrey into a top model. Naturally, they fall in love, and their wedding day is the grand finale.

Astaire dances delightfully, and Audrey wears the most delicious dresses. Story's hilarious. I love it where she's all in black, among the Parisian pseudo-intellectuals, dancing past their stony faces. And the corny ending makes me laugh. Fred's way too old for her, of course, and the plot's quite impossible. But in the movies none of this matters, because it's always a perfect match, made only the way those can be, in heaven, and never on earth.

ABOUT THE CONTRIBUTORS:

CHARLES ARDAI, a lifelong New Yorker, spent his first thirty years living either at 51st and Second or 52nd and First, before packing the Conestoga and lighting out for the wilds of 10021. His first novel, *Little Girl Lost* (written under the pen name Richard Aleas), was nominated for both the Edgar and Shamus awards. Ardai is also the cofounder and editor of the award-winning pulp-revival imprint Hard Case Crime.

CAROL LEA BENJAMIN, once an undercover agent for the William J. Burns Detective Agency, a teacher, and a dog trainer, is the author of the Shamus Award–winning Rachel Alexander mystery series, as well as eight acclaimed books on dog training and behavior. Recently elected to the International Association of Canine Professionals Hall of Fame, she lives in Greenwich Village with her husband and three swell dogs.

LAWRENCE BLOCK has won most of the major mystery awards, and has been called the quintessential New York writer, although he insists the city's far too big to have a quintessential writer. His series characters—Matthew Scudder, Bernie Rhodenbarr, Evan Tanner, Chip Harrison, and Keller—all live in Manhattan; like their creator, they wouldn't really be happy anywhere else.

THOMAS H. COOK is the author of twenty novels and two works of nonfiction. He has been nominated for the Edgar Allan Poe Award five times in four separate categories. His novel *The Chatham School Affair* won the Edgar for Best Novel in 1996. He splits his time between Manhattan and Cape Cod.

JEFFERY DEAVER, the author of *The Bone Collector* and a number of other international bestsellers, was born outside of Chicago but lived in downtown Manhattan for nearly twenty years. He was an attorney on Wall Street before turning to writing thrillers full-time. One of his first novels was titled *Manhattan Is My Beat,* an Edgar Award–nominee about a crime involving a (fictional) film noire.

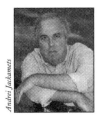

JIM FUSILLI is the author of the award-winning Terry Orr series, which includes *Hard, Hard City*, winner of the Gumshoe Award for Best Novel of 2004, as well as *Closing Time, A Well-Known Secret,* and *Tribeca Blues*. He also writes for the *Wall Street Journal* and is a contributor to National Public Radio's *All Things Considered.*

Andrei Jackamets

ROBERT KNIGHTLY was an NYPD patrol sergeant in the 1980s and worked at one time or another in every precinct in Manhattan South (below 96th Street, East and West). In the '90s, he turned to the Dark Side as a Legal Aid Society lawyer in the criminal courts at 100 Centre Street.

Rose Knightly

JOHN LUTZ has long enjoyed setting suspense novels in his favorite city, New York, one of which was made into the film *Single White Female*. His latest book is *Fear the Night,* set in . . . New York.

Jennifer Lutz

LIZ MARTÍNEZ is an editor and columnist for police and security publications. Her short fiction has appeared in *Combat,* OrchardPressMysteries.com, *Police Officer's Quarterly,* and *Cop Tales 2000*. She was born in New York City and is on the faculty at Interboro Institute, a two-year college in Manhattan. For the record, unlike Freddie Prinze, she is Mexican-American.

Jeff Robles

MAAN MEYERS (Annette and Martin Meyers) have written six books and multiple short stories in the Dutchman series of historical mysteries set in New York in the seventeenth, eighteenth, and ninteenth centuries.

Mariana Cook

MARTIN MEYERS grew up on Madison Street, a couple of blocks from the East River where the Manhattan Bridge hovers—the *Lower East Side* then, *Chinatown* now. He currently lives on the Upper West Side with his wife, author Annette Meyers. In 1975, when he was still an actor, he wrote the first book in his Patrick Hardy P.I. series, *Kiss and Kill.*

Marion Ettlinger

S.J. ROZAN, author of *Absent Friends* and the Edgar Award–winning Lydia Chin/Bill Smith mystery series, grew up in the Bronx. Having misspent her youth in lower Manhattan, she always wanted to live there, and now she does.

Henrietta Parker

JUSTIN SCOTT was born on West 76th Street between Riverside and West End, grew up in a small town, and came back to Manhattan to write mysteries, thrillers, and the occasional short story in Midtown, the Upper West Side, the Village, and Chelsea. Twice nominated for Edgar Awards, his New York stories include *Many Happy Returns, Treasure for Treasure, Normandie Triangle,* and *Rampage.*

Steve Goodman

C.J. SULLIVAN grew up in the Bronx and is currently a reporter for the *New York Post.* Along with writing, the loves of his life are his two children, Luisa Marie and Olivia Kathleen Sullivan.

Fellow Mui

XU XI is the author of six books, including the novel *The Unwalled City* and *Overleaf Hong Kong* (stories and essays), and has edited two anthologies of Hong Kong literature. She teaches at Vermont College's MFA program, and lives and writes primarily between Manhattan, upstate New York, Hong Kong, and the South Island of New Zealand. For more information, visit www.xuxiwriter.com.

Also available from the Akashic Books Noir Series

D.C. NOIR
edited by George Pelecanos
304 pages, a trade paperback original, $14.95

Brand new stories by: George Pelecanos, Laura Lippman, James Grady, Kenji Jasper, Jim Beane, Ruben Castaneda, Robert Wisdom, James Patton, Norman Kelley, Jennifer Howard, Jim Fusilli, Richard Currey, Lester Irby, Quintin Peterson, Robert Andrews, and David Slater.

GEORGE PELECANOS is a screenwriter, independent-film producer, award-winning journalist, and the author of the bestselling series of Derek Strange novels set in and around Washington, D.C., where he lives with his wife and children.

BROOKLYN NOIR
edited by Tim McLoughlin
350 pages, a trade paperback original, $15.95
*Winner of SHAMUS AWARD, ANTHONY AWARD, ROBERT L. FISH MEMORIAL AWARD; Finalist for EDGAR AWARD, PUSHCART PRIZE

Twenty brand new crime stories from New York's punchiest borough. Contributors include: Pete Hamill, Arthur Nersesian, Maggie Estep, Nelson George, Neal Pollack, Sidney Offit, Ken Bruen, and others.

"*Brooklyn Noir* is such a stunningly perfect combination that you can't believe you haven't read an anthology like this before. But trust me—you haven't. Story after story is a revelation, filled with the requisite sense of place, but also the perfect twists that crime stories demand. The writing is flat-out superb, filled with lines that will sing in your head for a long time to come."
—Laura Lippman, winner of the Edgar, Agatha, and Shamus awards

DUBLIN NOIR: *The Celtic Tiger vs. The Ugly American*
edited by Ken Bruen
228 pages, trade paperback, $14.95

Brand new stories by: Ken Bruen, Eoin Colfer, Jason Starr, Laura Lippman, Olen Steinhauer, Peter Spiegelman, Kevin Wignall, Jim Fusilli, John Rickards, Patrick J. Lambe, Charlie Stella, Ray Banks, James O. Born, Sarah Weinman, Pat Mullan, Reed Farrel Coleman, Gary Phillips, Duane Swierczynski, and Craig McDonald.

BALTIMORE NOIR
edited by Laura Lippman
252 pages, a trade paperback original, $14.95

Brand new stories by: David Simon, Laura Lippman, Tim Cockey, Rob Hiaasen, Robert Ward, Sujata Massey, Jack Bludis, Rafael Alvarez, Marcia Talley, Joseph Wallace, Lisa Respers France, Charlie Stella, Sarah Weinman, Dan Fesperman, Jim Fusilli, and Ben Neihart.

LAURA LIPPMAN has lived in Baltimore most of her life and she would have spent even more time there if the editors of the *Sun* had agreed to hire her earlier. She attended public schools and has lived in several of the city's distinctive neighborhoods, including Dickeyville, Tuscany-Canterbury, Evergreen, and South Federal Hill.

SAN FRANCISCO NOIR
edited by Peter Maravelis
292 pages, a trade paperback original, $14.95

Brand new stories by: Domenic Stansberry, Barry Gifford, Eddie Muller, Robert Mailer Anderson, Michelle Tea, Peter Plate, Kate Braverman, David Corbett, Alejandro Murguía, Sin Soracco, Alvin Lu, Jon Longhi, Will Christopher Baer, Jim Nesbit, and David Henry Sterry.

CHICAGO NOIR
edited by Neal Pollack
252 pages, a trade paperback original, $14.95

Brand new stories by: Neal Pollack, Achy Obejas, Alexai Galaviz-Budziszewski, Adam Langer, Joe Meno, Peter Orner, Kevin Guilfoile, Bayo Ojikutu, Jeff Allen, Luciano Guerriero, Claire Zulkey, Andrew Ervin, M.K. Meyers, Todd Dills, C.J. Sullivan, Daniel Buckman, Amy Sayre-Roberts, and Jim Arndorfer.